Frederic Henry Balfour

Waifs and Strays from the Far East

Being a Series of Disconnected Essays on Matters Relating to China

Frederic Henry Balfour

Waifs and Strays from the Far East
Being a Series of Disconnected Essays on Matters Relating to China

ISBN/EAN: 9783337277239

Printed in Europe, USA, Canada, Australia, Japan

Cover: Foto ©Andreas Hilbeck / pixelio.de

More available books at **www.hansebooks.com**

WAIFS AND STRAYS

FROM

THE FAR EAST;

Being a Series of Disconnected Essays on Matters

relating to China.

BY

FREDERIC HENRY BALFOUR,

HONORARY MEMBER OF THE INTERNATIONAL CONGRESS OF ORIENTALISTS.

LONDON:

TRUBNER & CO., LUDGATE HILL.

SHANGHAI: KELLY & WALSH.

1876.

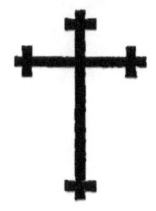

IN

AMICI MEMORIAM

DILECTISSIMI

𝕽. 𝕰. 𝕾.

CONTENTS.

PREFACE.

THE following chapters are intended for English readers whose knowledge of Chinese matters bears an inverse ratio to the interest they take in the subject. No claim is made to originality or profound research. But at a time when all questions relating to China have, or should have, some attraction for those who have never visited that country, it may be permitted to an obscure writer to add his quota, however humble, to the stock of general information; and the present volume will, it is hoped, shed some additional light upon certain points which have not, hitherto, been brought prominently before the reading public. In such a work, there cannot but be many shortcomings; but its aim is, as far as possible, to combine an unavoidable superficiality with lucidity and distinctness, and its best apology is to be found in the Chinese motto upon the cover,— "There is no book from which *something* may not be learnt."

F. H. B.

Kiukiang Road, Shanghai.

November, 1876.

CHAPTER I.

Different Views of the Chinese.

IF the great Lavater had ever come to China, it is more than possible that many vexed questions of the present day would long ago have been set at rest. By virtue of the simple though perfect and beautiful science which he discovered, he would have been able to read, almost at a glance, the real character which underlies the hard square faces, the small noses, the oblique and elongated eyes and stolid expression of these Eastern folk, and would probably have arrived at a surer and swifter estimate of their character than the most accomplished sinologue of our time. And in all seriousness we cannot help believing that the verdict of such an authority upon this disputed point would have helped to simplify many matters which have arisen in the history of our relations with the Middle Kingdom, and which are even now a source of strife and mystification to hundreds. What is the true attitude of the Chinese towards Western nations? is a question that appears to us to be still becoming daily more perplexing, on account of the wide divergence of opinion which exists upon the point. The true reply, we firmly believe, can only be found in determining the true character of those with whom we have to deal; and this will prove the key to all the contradictory assertions and representations of those who, from their diplomatic position, or by virtue of their linguistic accomplishments, have spoken with authority upon the subject.

It will suffice for our present purpose to adduce what may be termed the two extreme views of China, politically considered, and to place each in striking contrast to the other. The two parties who hold these sharply antagonistic opinions may be called for convenience' sake the Sinomaniacs and the Sinophobists; and we have only to give the slightest possible sketch of their respective creeds to convince our readers that, in comparison with such contradictions as we here discover, the Mohammetan may be regarded as the co-religionist of the Christian, and the lion expected to eat straw like the ox. To begin then, with our Sinophobist friends: China, as represented by them, is unknown in such a capacity to the Chinese Government. What we understand by China is, to the Imperial authorities, simply the Central State of all the states under Heaven, over which the Potentate commonly called the Emperor of China, rules and reigns supreme. But as a country among countries, there is no such place as China. The Exalted Monarch acknowledges no dominion smaller than the entire world—the P'u T'ien Hsia—the 'All Under Heaven.' He is the High-Priest of Humanity. Any attempt, therefore, to place Western Sovereigns upon an equality with him, is simply sacrilege. He is the Universal Lord—they are the rulers, more or less loyal, of certain outlying Tributary states, all of which are as much subject to his sway as the Central State which is divided into Eighteen Provinces, and called 'China' by the barbarians who know no better. Consequently—(we are still sketching the doctrine attributed to the Chinese Government by its Sinophobist detractors)—war with China is looked upon by the Emperor and represented to the people as rebellion; peace, as a return of the rebellious State—Eng, Fah, or whichever else it may be—to submission. The independent existence of such a 'state,' apart from the Great Ching Empire, is not recognised. Every Treaty, therefore, every Letter of Credence, every diplomatic despatch, written in the sacred character, teems with insults, hidden indeed from the dull eyes of our representatives, but easily discovered by the keener glance of the amateur champions of our rights. The very title stipulated for by our Ministers and accorded by the Chinese Government, means, to them, the exact reverse of what it seems to. 'K'ing-ch'ai Ta-chên'—

Great Imperial Minister—surely, is not that an adequate acknowledgment of a Foreign Minister's rank, and of the equality of
his Sovereign with the Emperor? On the contrary, replies our critic, with astounding logic: there being only one Emperor in the
World, according to the Chinese idea, the 'Imperial' refers to
him, not to the Western monarch; so that the Foreign representative is here really described as a servant of the Emperor of China.
Nothing satisfies men of this school. They see treachery and covert insults, systematic evasions, premeditated assassinations even,
lurking everywhere; and the aim of the Chinese Government, according to them, is to be hoodwink, circumvent and grossly insult
the 'public messengers' of these troublesome tributary states as
long as they are pestered with their presence in Peking, and eventually, if necessary, to rid themselves of the entire body of barbarians in every open port, by a general and discriminate massacre.

Turning, however, to the no less rabid and probably far more
mischievous party of the Sinomaniacs, what a marvellously different picture do we behold! A great, admirable, almost reverend
nation, a prey to the selfishness and savage onslaughts of a few
Western traders. A Government of almost perfect organisation—
lavish of concessions, moderate in its responsive demands, courteous and just in its dealings with the rapacious foreigner, preserv-
ing a firm and dignified position when forced at the cannon's
mouth to permit the importation of a poisonous drug, and pursuing a simple, straight-forward policy and unswerving course of
friendly, cordial co-operation, gradually uprooting the grievances
and grudges of the past and sternly insisting that no more seeds of
mischief be sown! Such is China's portrait as painted by the glow-
ing fancy of certain writers, and such apparently is the appearance she presents to the remarkably oblique vision of the distant
doctrinaires; for mark you, most of the men who imagine they see
this imposing picture never came to China, but content themselves
with admiring her afar off. We need not dwell upon either view
for long. Like all extreme opinions, they are uncontestibly both
erroneous. The Sinomaniac, blinded by sophistries and utterly

devoid of all practical experience, shows his ignorance by the most glaring blunders when he treats of things in detail; formulates a theory, twisting every occurrence into violently distorted shapes to suit it; and rapidly acquires the malignancy which is inseparable from the bigot and the man of one idea, in supporting his pet conviction. The Sinophobist, on the other hand, attaches exaggerated importance to metaphorical expressions which have their origin in Oriental conceit and ignorance of geography, and tortures a high-flown and somewhat meaningless figure of speech into the declaration or assumption of a specific political right. The Tartar Monarchs of China have not shown themselves so utterly devoid of common sense in other matters as they are represented as doing in the particular instance before us; and we deny that there is any more significance attached to the Imperial titles so strongly reprobated than there is to the imaginary claim of the Emperor to the Brotherhood of the Sun and Moon. The Hwang-ti of China no more believes himself to be Emperor of the Earth than a long succession of English monarchs considered themselves Kings of France, in spite of that title being appended to their names for a period of no less than four hundred and thirty years.

The truth, therefore, lies between the two extremes. And reverting to the physiognomical solution of the difficulty to which we have before alluded, we fancy that in the Chinese we should find a strong development of obstinacy tempered with a quick perception of self-interest, an intelligent appreciation of Western accomplishments in spite of their ingrained conservatism and conceit, and sufficient energy of purpose and strength of will to carry out all the reforms which, as time wears on, and brings experience with it, are shown to be requisite to the future welfare of the Empire and the prosperity of the Chinese people.

CHAPTER II.

The Ta Tsing Dynasty.

It is perhaps a moot question whether the Chinese are or are not what we Westerns understand by the term 'loyal.' That they are full of national pride, and overflow with extravagant ideas respecting the importance of their country, is of course undeniable. The old tradition which represent China as being the Middle Kingdom of the world, surrounded by insignificant and distant states which are far inferior to her, whether they pay actual tribute or not, is doubtless firmly ingrained in the uneducated mass of the population, just as much as ever it was. But even this form of patriotism is shallow in the extreme; while as for pure loyalty, it seems absolutely inconsistent with the fundamental principles of the Chinese character. And yet the Chinese, in common with all other Oriental nations, attribute titles to the Emperor which allowing even free scope for the range of Eastern metaphor, would seem at first sight to imply a very hearty and earnest devotion both to his person and to the dynasty he represents. In every act of State policy, he figures as the Autocrat of Universal Benevolence. He is the Son of Heaven, reigning by Divine grace and in virtue of his own inherent perfection, not by the will of the people. When Hung Siu-ts'euen, the T'ien Wang, was in the early bloom of his short prosperity, and aspired to play the rival to the Ta Tsing monarch, he fully recognised the fact that what loyalty there was to be found in the breasts of the people sprang in no small measure from hereditary belief in the semi-divine character of the ruling prince; and it was to this, as much as to other and more apparent

motives, that we trace his assumption of the religious titles which
he claimed.   The Son of Heaven could have no other rival than
the Elder Brother, or the Heavenly Prince ; that element of greatness, at least, must be preserved if he wished to appear in the eyes
of his compatriots in any way worthy to contest the sovereignty of
the Empire with Tao-kuang.   But in this extreme reverence for
the Imperial office we do not recognise what can be defined with
scrupulous exactitude as loyalty, pure and simple.   It is a superstitious tradition ; it is not that personal devotion which would induce
a man to lay down his life with cheerfulness and pride for a
cherished lord.   Towards the person of the Emperor, indeed, it is
impossible for an ordinary Chinaman to harbour feelings of loyalty.
He is to him simply a dim abstraction, enshrined in the mystic
retirement of the Forbidden City, whose name is too sacred to be
written, and who wields unchallenged and universal power.   The
peasant knows little or nothing of his Sovereign's private life or
family, and certainly never saw his face.   The only character in
which the Emperor is ever placed before his mind, in any way
calculated to win his attachment, is that of the People's Father ;
and there is no doubt that upon many of the peasantry of China
the effect of this is, so far, good. A public deed of charity or beneficence, which in Western countries appears, truly enough, as a
Parliamentary measure, an act emanating from the Government,
in China is referred exclusively to the Emperor's grace.   It is the
Emperor who provides grain for the starving population of a flooded
province, it is the Emperor who showers honours upon sons and
widows whose virtues call for Celestial recognition, it is the Emperor whose gifts of money and coloured silks reward particular
instances of bravery or merit, it is the Emperor who weeps tears
of blood for the sufferings of the people whose father and mother
he is. This agreeable fiction no doubt has its good results; but we
should hesitate to say whether the superficial sentiment which
springs from it among the rank and file have made his Throne one
whit the firmer.   The Son of Heaven is to them any ruler under
whom they are able to earn their living, eat their rice, and pass

their days in as little molestation as may be; and it matters far
less to them whether the Occupant of the Dragon Throne be a
wise or foolish prince, than whether the mandarins to whom they
are immediately subject are lenient or tyrannical.

Turning therefore to the mandarins themselves, it is hardly to
be expected that they can possess any very great attachment to a
foreign autocracy under which certain of the more important posts
in the Empire are reserved for the Imperial clan. A large number of these officers are practically beyond the power of the Crown,
and having virtually no greater responsibility than to supply it
with a certain tribute yearly for the Imperial expenditure, prey
upon the province or district in their charge and keep the surplus
of their depredations for themselves. Receiving a nominal sa-
lary, barely sufficient to pay their servants—if they *did* pay them,
which they very often don't—it is only natural that they should
live upon the resources which their position places at their disposal, and respecting which no questions are asked so long as the
tribute is transmitted regularly to Peking. This is a system which
is no doubt very congenial to a vast number of officials; but the
basis upon which it rests is insecure in the extreme. Who shall
say what disruption might ensue from the pressure brought to bear
upon the Government by two European Powers? The country
with which we may some day be engaged in conflict is a divided
one. The Chinese have a theory,—whence derived we cannot say
—that the natural life of a dynasty is, or should be, limited to a
couple of hundred years; a term which the Ta Tsing has already
exceeded. Are they beginning to chafe under the Tartar yoke?
Would a Chinese monarchy be more popular than the present
rule? Would the country hail the appearance of a second Warren
Hastings to oust the Manchus, establish military law, and place a
native on the Throne? Would a Chinese Emperor, chosen and
protected by European arms, introduce a better system of Government, exercise a purifying influence on official corruption, smoothe
the way for foreign intercourse, and inaugurate a more hopeful future for the Chinese people, where the Manchus have failed? We

must remember what it was that led the people to implore the interference and protection of the Tartar General, when King Stork replaced King Log. What were the circumstances to which the present Tartar dynasty owes its establishment upon the throne of China ? Wearied out with the maladministration of the Mings, and torn with intestine distractions in consequence of their continued misdirection of affairs, the country at last collapsed, and a rebellion of more than ordinary magnitude broke out about the year 1636 of our own era under the leadership of a bold adventurer named Li Tsze-ching, who, after a struggle of eight years' duration, succeeded in reducing a third of the empire to his sway. The reigning Emperor, finding himself alone and unsupported, committed suicide in his palace ; while an Imperial General, as a last resource, implored the assistance of the Manchus against the rebel chief, who by this time had obtained possession of the capital. The request was acceded to without hesitation ; the Manchus lost no time in coming to the rescue, but, as might have been expected, availed themselves of the golden opportunity to seize the reins of Government.   This, after a Seven Years' war, involving terrible bloodshed, they eventually accomplished; obtained possession of the Imperial throne, and have kept it ever since. Such, at least, is the orthodox and popular belief, and we have certainly no legal proof that the account is not authentic in this last particular; but there is a secret though deeply-rooted idea among the Chinese that *the line of descent has not been preserved intact.*   The Sovereigns of the present dynasty have been nine in number ; *viz.,* (to adopt the designations of their respective reigns) Shun-chi, who gained the throne as above related, in 1644 :— Kang-hi, of happy memory,—Yung-ching, Kien-lung, who reigned from 1736 to 1796 and received the Embassy of Lord Macartney in 1790—Kia-king—Tao-kuang, with whom Sir Henry Pottinger had to do—Hien-fêng, familiar to us during the mission of Lord Elgin—Tung-chi, who died in January 1875, and Kuang-hsü, the present Emperor. Now the impression we refer to takes its rise, we believe, from the partial disclosure of some Court intrigue which is said to have occurred during the reign of Yung-ching, and although the story has no political significance, even supposing it to be true, it is at least interesting enough to excuse us for narrating it. The Empress had long hoped, in vain, for the blessing of a son; but the entire family born to her consisted of a Princess. When this daughter was a child in arms, the wife of a certain Minister of state, Kien-chai by name, a native of Chekiang, gave birth to a son, who was forthwith carried to the Palace to be presented to the Emperor. A brilliant idea now struck the Empress. Childless herself—from a Chinese point of view—she determined on retaining the son of the noble and sending back her own daughter in his place. That both the Emperor and the Minister were parties to the arrangement cannot, of course, be doubted. The adopted youth grew up as the Emperor's son, and according to every known law of romance ought to have received the hand of the exiled Princess in marriage. A different fate, however, was in store for both. The Princess was married to a literary grandee of Soochow, with whom she lived for many years, being regarded by the people of the city as a special favourite or *protégée* of the Empress. This belief was fostered by a present from the Palace of two handsome barges, for the use of the Princess, which bore her name and were always exempted from duty by Imperial decree. The youth meanwhile was married to a mandarin's daughter of pure Tartar blood; and shortly afterwards, upon the death of the old Emperor, assumed undisputed possession of the throne under the title of Kien-lung. This is the legend firmly believed by multitudes of Chinese who, however, dare not of course discuss it openly or circulate it in print; and they argue that considerable colour is lent to it by the very frequent visits of this Emperor to the city of Hangchow, to the tomb of his (alleged) father. It is a singular fact, too, that the wife of the succeeding monarch, Kia-king, made strenuous efforts to revive the ancient costume of the Mings; but the Emperor feared the change might be impolitic. The story is graceful and romantic, though we know so little of the intrigues and mysteries of Eastern

Courts that it is difficult to offer an opinion upon its merits. That the youthful Emperor Kuang-hsü is to all intents and purposes a Tartar, cannot for a moment be doubted; indeed, even according to the above theory, he is descended from a Tartar ancestress; but if there is any truth in it at all, he has at least a very strong dash of Chinese blood in his veins. It is however impossible that China will ever recognise him as in any way the representative of a Chinese stock; and more than doubtful whether the country would be at all better off (to suppose a possible contingency) by the restoration of such a dynasty as the Ming than she is at present. Whatever changes may eventually take place, the immediate predecessors of the now reigning family will never again be represented on the Dragon Throne. The only Chinese, to-day, who has made any special mark, is Li Hung-chang, a man immeasurably inferior to the late Tseng Kuo-fan both in ability and patriotism. But events are marching steadily onwards, and we believe a crisis is looming in the distance. China is destined to be the scene of a great drama, in which the tragic element will inevitably have a place; but what the plot will be, or who are cast by fate for the most prominent characters in the play, we none of us can tell before the curtain lifts. One thing however may be affirmed without presumption; that whatever changes may occur in the political administration of the Empire, neither a Chinese nor a Tartar dynasty will ever prove a useful or trustworthy ally of ours without constant watchfulness and care. Chinese or Tartar, what matters it to us? Unless one may be more pliable than the other. But we shall look in vain for perfect frankness and good faith from either, while duplicity is a characteristic of Oriental nations, and China rules the East.

CHAPTER III.

The Previous Dynasties of China.

WE hazarded a belief in the last chapter that the question of a possible restoration of a Chinese Dynasty to the throne of China was comparatively unimportant to ourselves as foreigners. But there is another view of the matter which demands our notice, and that is, the interest of the Chinese themselves in the contingency. There is probably no country in the world which has been subject to so many conquests, revolutions and dynastic changes as the Empire of China; and it may therefore be not wholly unprofitable to take a bird's-eye view of its chequered past career, and strive to form some notion, however crude, of the influences for good or ill which have been thereby brought to bear upon it. Of course we do not propose to summarise the history of China. Life is too short for us to even contemplate so colossal and so practically useless a task. But there are a few salient points which present themselves to every student, however superficial, of the intellectual peculiarities as well as the political fortunes of this people, and from a careful observation of these phenomena we may possibly arrive at a conclusion which, even though imperfect, will nevertheless be a step towards a clearer apprehension of many problems which are yet unsolved.

The early history of the Middle Kingdom is, we need hardly say, a sealed book. A Chinaman will expatiate to you, with almost pathetic pride, upon the glories of its ancient Emperors, the immortal Yao and Shun, whose reigns constitute, in the minds of the Chinese generally, their country's Golden Age; when the

principles of virtue were the mainspring of its political and social
life, and the wise precepts of the sages were no dead letter, but a
living force. Such is the theory taught by the Confucian writers,
and such is the orthodox belief. There is a school of modern criticism, it is true, which sees nothing more in the history of these
old heroes than a Chinese version of the cosmogonical allegories
common to all nations of the East. Yao is said to be identical
with Ouranos, and Shun with Vishnu, while Yü, the third Emperor of the great hierarchy, was simply the Greek Minos, the Manu
of the Hindoos and the supposed progenitor of the whole Aryan
race. Fu-hi, the earliest philosopher, whose works form the
groundwork of most later systems, was an impersonation of *Fêng*,
the wind : the Sacred Yih-king are a palpable forgery of the earlier Han. It is however only fair to state that these extreme
views, so consistent with the destructive spirit of the age, are held
by a very scant proportion of sinologues having a claim to eminence. But it cannot be denied that the theory is plausible, while
there seems, as far at least as we have been able to discover, but
little collateral evidence in favour of the more flattering hypothesis. One thing is certain: native historians are almost entirely
silent upon the subject, or at best throw very meagre light upon
its present obscurity ; while no assistance is rendered by any of
those ancient monuments which, in the case of other countries,
have been of such value to the antiquarian in filling up the gaps
in their imperfect records, and elucidating the riddles of the past.
We know nothing of the date when the colonisation of China took
place, and but little more of the tribes who first settled on its
boundless plains. Nor has any satisfactory solution been offered
of the identity of the ancient worthies whose names are so reve-
renced by their descendants after a lapse of well-nigh fifty centuries. There have been certain philologists, principally we believe
among the early Catholic missionaries, who, inspired by a fine
enthusiasm for the nation in which they saw so grand a field for
evangelistic enterprise, and led astray by the ideographical nature
of the written character, attempted to trace a connection between

their names and those of Adam, Abraham, Abel, Enoch and Noah;
but such speculations are as vain as they are, at first sight, cap-
tivating, while the reckless theorising of later and less cultured
writers amount to a mere exegetical impertinence.* One of the
more moderate, though not perhaps least prejudiced, of Western
commentators places the commencement of the historic period in
the reign of Huàn-ti, an Emperor said to have flourished 2697 before the Christian era, three hundred years before the time of
Yao, and two hundred years after the existence of Fu-hi. Huàn-
ti is called the first legislator of China. It was one of his Ministers who invented the celebrated cycle of sixty years; to other
statesmen of his reign is attributed the construction of the astronomical, musical and ceremonial systems; while the Empress busied
herself with the cultivation of the silkworm. But this hypothesis
is doubtful in the extreme, nor is the contemplation of times so
manifestly obscure, not to say fabulous, in any way connected
with the object we have now in view. It will suffice for our purpose to confine our observations to the twenty-two acknowledged
dynasties that have reigned successively in China; the first of
which, known to posterity as the 'Hia Ch'ao, belongs still to the
semi-historic period. Even here we feel that we may be assuming
too much. The history of the first four dynasties—the 'Hia, the
Shang, the Chow and the 'Tsin—is somewhat vague; and while
the very act of formulating the meagre details at one's command
imparts an air of tangibility to them which they do not in themselves possess, that is all the greater reason for excessive guarded-
ness. Still there can be no doubt that even by this time China
was growing in power, and that the neighbouring tribes were
beginning to regard her with something of respect. Latterly, as
we know, the changes of Government were perpetual, and the

---

* For instance. A missionary lately attempted to prove the identity of P'an
Ku-shih, the 'Adam' of the Chinese, with Cush, the father of Nimrod; and this
is how he did it. In the name Cush we recognise the Hebrew *cus*, a cup—his symbol being a golden goblet; P'an is the Chinese for basin, and Ku-shih the nearest
approach a Chinaman can make to the pronunciation of Cush; consequently, the
two men are evidently identical! 'The force of bathos can no further go.'

Chinese people passed many times beneath a foreign yoke. Out of the twenty-two dynasties which at various times held sway, a comparatively fair proportion were 'barbarian;' for it is a curious fact that in moralising upon these vicissitudes the Chinese contemptuously stigmatise their early conquerors as '*hu-jin*, or savages, complacently oblivious that their present rulers belong to the same nomadic stock.

Prejudices apart, however, it is for us now to see how far the fortunes of China have been affected by the successive conquests she has undergone at the hands at these outer tribes ; and common fairness compels us, in the face of facts, to conclude that her gain has been by no means inconsiderable. The infusion of the Tartar element into her body politic has had the strengthening, hardening influence of alloy in combination with a softer and more precious metal. Of themselves the Chinese appear to be intrinsically weak. It was when China was under the bold sway and subject to the severer discipline of some detested foreign yoke that she was, as a nation, most respected, because most self-contained. Then it was that the more elegant pursuits of social life were forced back into their proper place, and the arts of warfare, government and political economy brought into greater prominence. Native dynasties fostered those humaner and more attractive accomplishments which have done so much to earn for the Chinese their reputation as a cultured people, and have so nearly proved their ruin. The two greatest of the native dynasties were incontrovertibly the Tang and the Sung, and the history of both exemplifies most cogently the justice of our remark. To the latter, the period of whose power may be looked upon as the Augustan era of the Middle Kingdom, is universally ascribed the prëeminence ; but the Tang claims and will always hold the supreme honour of having given birth to the oldest and most celebrated University in the world. The Han-lin Yuen was founded by Heuen-tsung, the ninth monarch of this dynasty, A.D. 725. Its first title was the Tsi-sëen Tien, or Palace of the Heavenly Immortals, which was afterwards changed to Tsi-lien Tien, or Palace of the Sages ; then it was called, for diplomatic reasons, the Tsi-hien Wên, under which name it commenced its flourishing career. This inaugurated the golden age of Chinese literature. Essayists, historians, and writers on ethics and morality multiplied exceedingly, headed by Li T'ai-pih, the greatest poet China has produced. This eminent man enjoyed the special favour and protection of the Emperor, who was himself a *dilettante*. Every possible encouragement was now given to letters; the highest honours were awarded to the most accomplished penmen, and the power of rhyming elegantly was a sure password to distinction. In fact the age was essentially luxurious; a refined and cultured taste degenerated into epicureanism, and sensuous pleasure into sensuality. The country had no backbone; it was absorbed in literary dalliance, and suffered the inevitable penalty. Serious internal trouble soon arose. The Emperor, who cared for nothing but women, letters and wine, had a lovely concubine who exercised unlimited influence over his heart and head alike. He eventually raised her to the rank of Empress, and spent all his time in her society and that of his numerous minions, leaving the affairs of state to go on as best they might. At length it so fell out that the Empress cast wanton glances at a fascinating foreigner or *Hu-jin* called Ngan Lu-shang, and, publicly adopting him as a son of the Imperial family, in reality became his mistress. The inevitable *dénouement* followed, and a formidable insurrection was the result, which nearly cost the Emperor his throne. It was only with the utmost difficulty that the rebel and his followers were repulsed; but after a severe tussle order was re-established, and the Emperor presented his faithless consort with a silken cord. But the lesson was thrown away. The country relapsed into its former state of lettered indolence; poetry flourished, but more important matters sank into comparative oblivion. At last the Tang Dynasty was overthrown, about the year 908; and for half a century the Empire was in disorder. Still the Imperial College continued to increase in reputation and prosperity until the accession of the Sungs, under whose auspices a second period of protection was inaugurated for the literati. Then it was that the College received its present name of Han-lin Yuen, and the annals of Chinese literature were enriched with the name of Chu Fu-tsze, one of the greatest commentators whom this land of letters has produced. It would be almost impossible to give our readers any adequate idea of the works issued from the Imperial College, of which a complete catalogue now lies before us. Suffice it to say that there are entire libraries each devoted to a separate subject, including archæology, numismatics, moral philosophy, philology, chronology, and iconography; histories of caligraphy and painting, of the ancient Imperial palaces, as well as official records of the various dynasties; annals of the Coreans and all states tributary to China, dictionaries in abundance—Manchu, Mongolian and Chinese—geography, bibliography, systems of religion and ethics, legislature and jurisprudence, poetry of all ages, and last, though far from least, encyclopædias the dimensions of which are vast beyond belief. A fellowship of the Han-lin is to-day a position of the highest consideration, of which a Chinese may well be proud; for the institution is in every way most venerable. Above all, it was founded by a Chinese monarch and fostered by successive Chinese dynasties; and it is one of the noblest monuments that a monarch ever left behind him. Therefore we consider ourselves justified in saying that China owes her intellectual superiority to herself; while it is equally true that she owes her political power to her conquerors. Her lack of strength became at once her ruin and her salvation. The native dynasties were ousted, and a foreigner ruled instead; but with the change came civil and military reforms, radical and searching in their nature, but how much needed the people knew full well. The Yuen Ch'ao inaugurated its term of power by the commencement of works which form bulwarks in the history of China. Endorsing with admirable policy the high position awarded to literary talent, Che-tsou, the first Emperor of his line, encouraged the profession of arms by fitting out an expedition to Japan, and gained for himself a worthy immortality by that unique and splendid work, the Grand Canal; which, stretching its magnificent length nearly seven hundred miles across the country, is now justly acknow-

lodged as one of the greatest blessings ever given to a people, and
the second wonder of the world.   The succeeding Emperors of this
dynasty were alike remarkable for the attention paid to military
affairs; but as years wore on, signs of restiveness became apparent.
The administration of Chuen-ti, the last of the Yuen Ch'ao monarchs,
was signalised by great severity, and the pursuit of practices into-
lerable to one and all.   Among other tyrannies an enactment was
framed and put in force, by virtue of which every Chinese family
was compelled to adopt and bring up a Tartar, who was entitled to
the lion's share of everything.   No privacy was sacred from this
absurd and preposterous infliction: and in many instances the
unwelcome guest is said to have claimed, and generally secured,
the privilege which history ascribes to the feudal lord in the Middle Ages on the occasion of a marriage among his serfs.   But at
last the reaction came.   The secret societies, of whom more anon,
had laid their plots with inconceivable perfection; and on a certain
night, without one man whispering it to his neighbour, without the
faintest hint or sign being given, these Tartar incubi were all
murdered by common understanding, from one end of the Empire
to the other.   This was the signal for a general revolt; the Emperor was driven from his throne and died in banishment; and the
Ming Dynasty appeared upon the scene.

   We have thus attempted to give a rough idea of the varied
influences brought upon the Chinese people by their different
rulers; and we think that the conclusion at which we have
arrived is not altogether unsupported by facts.   The Manchus and
the Chinese are essentially distinct, both in physical and mental
calibre.   One need only compare the specimens of the two nations
as they are to be seen in China every day; an excellent opportunity of doing which fell to our lot a few months ago.   At a trial
at which we had occasion to be present, the presiding judges were
respectively a Manchu and a native of Hangchow—a city, be it
observed, famous for the beauty of its people.   Here were the two
types, as widely different as might be, perfectly represented.   The
Manchu has a dark complexion and a roughish skin; he is a large-

boned man; his face is long and lantern-jawed; he has a wide
mouth, and firm, decided nose. The expression of his eyes is
shrewd, and under the gloss of etiquette you can detect the natural
fierceness of the nomad. The Chinese is the exact reverse. His
build is small and flexible; his face,—round, unctuous and fat,
unseared by the suspicion of a wrinkle,—is the colour of Devon-
shire cream. His movements are graceful and suave; they give
you the idea of liberally-oiled joints; his hands are delicate, slim,
and very plump; his expression is courtly; he has a winning smile
and bow for every one. His manners are irresistible; he orders
the application of some frightful torture to a criminal with the
persuasive air of a fashionable physician; he dresses in rich silks
and priceless furs; his white fingers are adorned with jade, and
his whole person is redolent of musk and ambergris. He is the
impersonation of luxury, good breeding, and good feeding; but his
veneer is hardly thick enough to hide the remorselessness and
cruelty which lie ready at a moment's call.* Good emperors are
not made of such material; and the Mings, courtly, false and
hopelessly unpractical as the Stuarts of our own country, having
wearied the people out by their misgovernment, came to an
ignominious end as detailed in the last chapter. Their descendants
will claim a passing remark in another place. The Tsings, who
have now reigned since 1644, are perhaps the best Tartar dynasty
that China has ever had. They levy no black-mail upon the ranks
of Chinese women; and, what seems to have gained them to no
small extent the respect and gratitude of their subjects, is their
admirable policy with regard to their predecessors. The presiding
deity of the greatest Chinese festival, Ch'ên Huang by name, was
a hero of the Ming dynasty, who is appointed by the present
Emperor to rule the spirits of the dead Mings in Hades. The
worshippers of this god, or P'u-sa, celebrate their solemnities in the

* The gentleman more especially referred to here is a very jovial person. Not
long ago he was present at a public reception at the house of a foreign official; and,
late in the evening, his heart being merry with wine, he performed an animated
pas seul in the drawing room, entreating another native gentleman, though unsuc-
cessfully, to join him in his capers. A more amusing Chinaman we never met.

Ming costume, and the festival is held under the especial sanction of the reigning sovereign. This appears to us a masterpiece of state-policy, tending most materially to bind both people and officials to the present dynasty. The Tsings have also left undesecrated the tombs of the old Ming emperors; and indeed, when one considers that a descendant of the Mings is keeper of the Ming tombs by the Emperor's permission, and that he has access even to the Court and Palace at Peking, it would be a curious study to investigate the arcana of the State Councils, and discover what kind of influence the Mings are still allowed to hold over the people. A peculiar festival, called the Birthday of the Sun, is also permitted by the Government, who wink at the well-known fact that this title is simply a convenient periphrasis for a political commemoration. Its true signification refers to the last Emperor of the Ming dynasty, and it is really the anniversary of his death. It may be said that by a poetical metaphor the Emperor and the Sun are sometimes almost synonymous. In short, the Tartar rule is far from perfect, but it might be greatly worse. The Tsing Emperors have done much that is good, and that will be always remembered with veneration. Kang-hi was in every sense a noble and enlightened sovereign, and his contributions to the literature of China are in themselves sufficient to immortalise his name; while the adoption of Western principles of engineering and naval architecture proves the good sense of his successors of to-day. We have already pointed out in the preceding chapter what appear to us some of the weaknesses of the present rule; but there is much to be said upon the other side. The Government is not without many elements of stability. It is true, of course, that there are germs of rebellion in various parts of the country, and that insurrections of a more or less disastrous nature are continually breaking out. The Mahometan propaganda is at this moment spreading fast and furiously. Hitherto, however, although these evidences of unsettled feeling have cost the country much trouble and no little blood, not to mention the expenditure of more money than it can afford, in so unproductive an undertaking,—it is undeniable that the *régime* at present holding sway

has received no very serious or violent shock. Outwardly at all
events the position of the reigning family is unassailed. Shrouded
in dignified obscurity at Peking, they have contented themselves
with issuing occasional Edicts informing the lieges in a grand and
off-hand manner that the rebels in such and such a locality have
sustained a severe defeat, and meanwhile authorising the Viceroys
in various parts of the country to contract fresh loans for the pro-
secution of a hopeless and unnecessary warfare in the West. The
bad economy of this is obvious enough. The principal question,
however, is this: in what does the present strength of the Government consist? What is the nature of that power which it exercises
over the Chinese people, and in virtue of which it has maintained
dominion over an alien and a vanquished race for the last 200
years? It is much the fashion to speak in a loose and somewhat
informal manner of the Tartar system of Government as a despotism,
pure and simple. It is not so. There are many links and rivets,
overlooked by superficial observers, welding together the two great
classes of society: the governed and their governors. It is true
that the autocratic system of political administration which exists
in China does not afford any authorised and acknowledged means
by which the people at large are able to take any part in the legislation which immediately concerns themselves, to modify in any
way their own taxation, or to exercise the slightest check upon the
tyranny of an unworthy Emperor or his subordinates. Such indeed
is the apathetic nature of the average Chinese husbandman or
merchant that he will submit to years of oppression and robbery
ere he will fash himself to resist the aggressions of the authorities;
although when the boundary-line of his extensive patience *has* been
overstepped, the rebound is generally terrible. This is the natural
result of a system which cannot fail to be abused. But although
the administration is undeniably most imperfect, and the fault to
which we have alluded, a radical and fatal one, there are other
features in the organisation which are an undoubted source of
strength to the Government, and go some way towards compensating
it for the weakness we have pointed out. The average middle-

class Chinaman, it is true, has no voice in the affairs of his country: and he is more or less at the mercy of the local mandarins. But he may rise to some of the highest positions in the State. There is no select circle of favoured ones who have a primary right to official honours. There is no hereditary legislation. Every China-man in the Empire—unless we except barbers and play-actors—has a perfectly fair chance of obtaining a place in the Government; mandarins are taken with strict impartiality from all classes, and consequently all classes may be said to be represented in the hier-archy of the Empire at large. The tyranny and corruptibility of many of these officers is undeniable : but they meet with their just recompense in the hatred of the people, and, in many instances, with the fearless and outspoken denunciations of the Censorate, and the consequent disgrace. Then, again, official honours are among the most coveted of earthly blessings to a Chinaman : so that personal distinction and posthumous fame are thus immediately associated with the existing Government. These links seem slight enough, but when we take into consideration the salient features of the Chinese character—the placidity, the love of learning, and the singular developments of their ambition—developments no less remarkable than the scope and aims of the passion itself: when we give full weight to these various reflections we shall see that the Ta-Tsing Dynasty does not owe its two centuries of sufferance entirely to despotic force. How much longer, however, the present balance of power will be kept up, is a difficult question. It is extremely hard to get at the true condition of affairs, and thereby form a sound judgment with respect to the amount of danger involved to the reigning family by the various disturbances to which we have refer-red. That there are vulnerable places in the body politic is undeniable. Hitherto the equilibrium has been wonderfully pre-served : but the dangerous leaven has been working all the while, the worms of disaffection have been gnawing at the very roots of the Empire itself. Yacoob Beg is looked upon by many as the Coming Man, and at the present moment he has a large number of sympathisers among the hundreds of thousands of Chinese Maho-

metans.   But it is also possible that ' China for the Chinese' may
some day become again the war-cry of the people, and a purely
Chinese Dynasty be once more established on the Dragon Throne.

CHAPTER IV.

Secret Societies and their Political Significance.

It is well-known fact that there are a large number of Secret Societies in China, which exert considerable influence upon all who are in any way connected with them, and are regarded with much suspicion and distrust by the Government. The fact of the T'ai-p'ing Rebellion having had its origin in a religious movement causes the authorities to be jealous of any sect or congregation of men professing doctrines at variance with the recognised creeds of China, known under the collective title of the Sêng, Tao, Ju; the existence of such schismatics is a source of perpetual though secret anxiety to the Government, and is considered, with just cause, dangerous to the general peace and welfare of the country. The subject is one about which much has been written at various times, and is far beyond the scope of a solitary chapter, embracing as it does an extensive literature of its own; but so much attention has been drawn to it during the last few months that we propose to embody the result of our researches in this direction in as concise a form as is compatible with so very significant an element in Chinese social life.

Now these Societies exist throughout the length and breadth of the Empire, and have so existed long prior to the amalgamation of the country under a single Crown. The secrecy of their operations, which of course forms the principal barrier to enquiry, is no less remarkable for the stringency of its observance than for the success which its inviolable nature ensures, whenever any widespread political movement has been brought about. Their name

is Legion; but whether they are all separate and independent
associations, or merely ramifications of one great body has, we
believe, never been accurately ascertained. By far the most
formidable and widespread of these confederacies is that known
indifferently as the T'ien-ti, or the San-ho, Hwuy, (the Heaven-
and-Earth, or Triad, Society), which may be said to rank with
the ancient craft of Freemasonry in the West, in point of power
and extensiveness; while there are so many features of similarity,
and such striking analogies between the two, as to afford strong
evidence in favour of the belief of certain writers, that the two
systems had a common origin. For not only is the highest antiquity claimed for the Triad Society by its members, but everything that is known about it goes to prove that its political and
revolutionary character is more or less of a recent and accidental
nature. The mystic doctrines which it embodies are cosmogonical
and moral; but these, if we understand the matter aright, have
undergone important modifications during the last two hundred
years, and been twisted into concrete forms foreign to their primary signification. It is scarcely to be expected that, in so limited
a scope as that now at our disposal, we should attempt to enter
upon an elaborate analysis of so obscure a subject; but there are a
few salient features about it which are sufficiently interesting to
deserve passing notice, both as regards the close relationship of
the occult doctrine with the principles of the Masonic craft, and
its subsequent developments in the direction of political conspiracy.

As we have remarked above, the Society bears two names. It
is sometimes known as the Sect of Heaven and Earth, and sometimes as 'San-ho' Hwuy; and it is in the second designation that
the greatest difficulty has been found. But here we have that
most ingenious of all puzzles, a Chinese pun. 'San-ho' is frequently written 三 河,* an ellipticism for 三 河 水,† which is simply the name of the place where the League is said to have
originated. But this is the League in its lesser and more popular

---

* *Ho*, river.   † *Shuy*, water.

sense, 小 會, the Petty League, as it is called; the Greater League, which is contained in the principle of Heaven, is written 三 和,* and refers to the Three-fold Harmony formed by Heaven, Earth and Man, from which the Sect derives its other designation. The more esoteric teachings of the faith are intimately allied with those of the earliest philosophers, both Indian and Chinese, and deal almost entirely with the generation of the Cosmos. The mystic union of the three great forms or principles of being is expressed by the masonic symbol △, which, on being analysed, may be reduced to the character 入 *juh*, to enter or penetrate, and — *yih*, one; the combination of the two in the perfect triangle meaning, therefore, Three blended into One. Such, at least, is the interpretation given in the *Shwoh-wên*, and, whatever may be the demerits of that work as an authority upon philological questions, it is undeniable that the idea here expressed is as beautiful as it is ingenious. The object of the cult was, primarily, the discovery of the Pure Light, (Ming) or Truth; and here again we are curiously reminded of Freemasonry. In details, however, the resemblance is still more striking: and we beg our readers' attention to the following catechism, regularly rehearsed at the opening of a Triad Lodge. It is a translation from one of the Society's books, quoted by Gustav Schlegel with a commentary:—

Q.—How high, brother, is the lodge?
A.—As high as one's eyes can reach.
Q.—How broad, brother?
A.—As broad as the two capitals and thirteen provinces—(the whole Empire—the world).
Q.—Whence do you come?
A.—I come from the East.
Q.—At what time did you come hither?
A.—I went at sunrise when the East was light.

The Lodge is square and perfectly oriented, as in masonry: while the East, as the Source of Light, is sacred. On entering the Lodge, the candidate is received at the point of a sword, directed against his uncovered breast, and is dressed in linen or cotton clothes of white. In or about the year 1730 the vigilance of the

---

* 和 *Ho*, harmony.

authorities compelled the members to exercise the utmost caution; they still retained, however, a most elaborate code, pages upon pages long, of secret signs whereby to recognise each other wherever they might meet. They continued to hold lodges by night, performing their peculiar ceremonies and initiating candidates under oaths and pledges of a most solemn character. These conclaves were held for some time in deserted places, and the approaches to the scene of action defended by artificial pitfalls cunningly concealed under light wickerwork covered with sod and leaves, so that any would-be intruders upon the solemnities could not avoid falling into the trap. The mysteries celebrated by this strange cabal are said to open with a rather riotous feast, accompanied by music; after which the brethren range themselves in front of an idol, the Master occupying a lofty chair, supported by eight men with naked swords. A large amount of paper seems to be burnt by way of a propitatory sacrifice in the course of the rites which ensue, in which the candidate for initiation bears an active part. Stripped to the skin, with the exception of a pair of trousers, he is then brought forward, and, kneeling with the eight naked swords resting on his neck, his examination is commenced. The first question is as to his identity and birthplace; the second, as to his parentage; while to the enquiry "Are your parents alive "or dead?" the answer is, under any circumstances, "Dead"—as all members of the Society are supposed to be free from every earthly tie. Various other test-questions are then put, the answers to which are sometimes flatly contradicted by the Master, who compels the candidate to confirm his statement by an oath. Finally the Vow of Secrecy is taken under the mystical emblem of drinking blood; but happily for the candidate, this most disagreeable part of the ceremony only consists in swallowing a cupful of arrac or wine into which a few drops of blood have been let from his own finger. The business of the evening is then brought to a close by the Master commanding the novice to apply on the morrow to the Secretary of the lodge, who will give him a book containing all the secret signs, pass-words, and marks of mutual recognition by dress and habits of eating, for which he will be charged the moderate sum of a dollar. Such are the ceremonies of initiation practised by one branch, at least, of the Triad Society, which seems to have grown rapidly both in numbers and power; and the pernicious influence it exercises has been ever viewed with jealousy and alarm by the metropolitan and provincial authorities. In 1817 no fewer than three thousand of its members were captured by the Governor of Canton alone; but hitherto no means have proved effectual to stamp it out.

As far as we can discover, it was about the year 1630 that the T'ien-ti Hwuy assumed a political character. There are many extraordinary stories current, all more or less fabulous, to account for the degradation of the cult. The watchword *Fang Tsing fuh Ming** is said to have had a miraculous origin, and it was with the establishment of the Tartar rule that the Society became professedly political. The formula 明 朝† —Reign of Light—which had hitherto expressed the pure object of the brethren's worship, became now materialised, and accepted as meaning simply the Dynasty of Ming. Under the *double-entendre* conveyed in the formula Ming Ch'ao, the members of the sect engaged in the most desperate endeavours to overthrow the power of the Emperor and to restore the family of Chu: and with this end in view, they joined their fortunes with those of Hung Siu-tseuen, and made common cause with the T'ai-p'ings. Indeed, if we may believe Schlegel, the T'ai-p'ing rebellion sprang originally from the Brethren of the Three-fold Bond, the leader himself being a member of the League. The ideas he thus imbibed were supplemented by still more daring speculations drawn from an imperfect view of Christianity; the very designation 'T'ai-p'ing,' so far from symbolising the spread of Gospel peace, was already in vogue among the Triad confederates in the sense of 'Equality,' and the lodges in which they met were called the T'ai-p'ing Ti, or land where all are equal. According to this

---

* Overthrow the Tsings, establish the Mings.

† *Ming Ch'ao*, convertibly used as meaning the 'Reign of Light,' or the 'Ming Dynasty.'

writer, who has done good service by translating several important secret Hand-books which came into his possession, the Wangs themselves were simply Grand Masters of the Order. This may be; but we cannot consider it proved, and there is but little sterling evidence in its favour. What is certain, however, is that the doctrines of the T'ien-ti Hwuy may be traced back to very ancient times: that the political character of the Sect is an entirely modern innovation; that, primarily, the points of resemblance between its ethics and those of masonry are so striking as to present much evidence of the two confederations being branches of the same root: and that, at the present moment, the Triad Society is as strong, as active, and as indestructible as ever.

The confederation which ranks next, perhaps, in power and malignity is that which has adopted as its badge the White Lily, or White Lotus-flower, under which designation it has achieved no small amount of notoriety. This fraternity is said to have arisen in the reign of Kien-lung; and during the sovereignty of his successor, Kia-king, there is no doubt that it assumed very formidable proportions. The rules of the Order were very strict. All the members lived on what is known as *su-tsai*, answering to the French expression *maigre*, as applied to diet, being rigid vegetarians; the Sect possessed a common fund of immense wealth, contributed to by all the members; and both men and women were admitted. At the period of which we write the Grand Master of the Order was a man of the name of Fang Yung-shên, whose wife, known as Ma-erh Ku-liang, was celebrated no less for her mental energy than for her enormous physical strength and stature. The headquarters of the conspirators was at Nanking, and it was during the leadership of this well-assorted couple that an extensive plot was hatched to blow up the Imperial Palace at Peking. The plans were laid with perfection. No suspicions were raised by any carelessness or laxity of speech or manner on the part of the initiated, numerous though they were. But at the very moment of their triumph, almost as the torch was to be applied,—darkness favouring their design—a violent storm of wind and rain suddenly came on, and disorganised all the arrangements. The alarm was given, and the Palace saved. This was the signal for a Crusade against the sect, and the Viceroy of Nanking was foremost in his exertions to crush the nuisance. Some sharp fighting ensued, and the Viceroy's forces eventually succeeded, though after a terrible struggle, in capturing Fang himself, together with a number of his associates. What became of the lady we do not know: but the treatment of the prisoners by the authorities was most remarkable. They were offered their lives and further mitigations of their penalty, if only they would consent to *eat meat*. This Fang, the leader, valiantly refused to do, and he was killed accordingly; others of the confederation acceded, but, it is said, suffered a far more horrible death at the hands of the Society, afterwards. But ever since these reverses the sect has been much less dangerous. The hot chase made after its members by officials has even induced them to renounce their designation, and to adopt the substitute-title of the 無 爲 敎 Wu-Wei Këaou or Do-nothing Sect; not, we may remark in passing, as it is sometimes erroneously written, 無 僞* or No Hypocrisy, religion. But the fraternity still exists, and, what is more, the Chinese dread its influence greatly. They believe the members to be in possession of magical powers, and the red-paper sprites which are said to have been instrumental in cutting off the queues of the good folk at Nanking, Soochow and Shanghai some months ago—of which more anon—are attributed to their incantations. Indeed we have been gravely assured by Chinamen of no small experience and culture that the initiated are able to cut birds out of paper, and then, in virtue of a certain charm, endue them with life and motion. But the most interesting speculation connected with this body is, what lies at the root of their mysteries? Is their object purely political, in pursuance whereof they practise upon the credulity of the masses by all this hocus-pocus, or is there some deep religious feeling at the bottom of it all? Both elements are visible. One of their most extravagant pranks, confined, however, to the leaders of the sect, consists of

---

* Also pronounced *Wu-Wei.*

holding the breath on special occasions long enough for a man to eat two meals of rice. They get black in the face, and perfectly rigid; meanwhile, the soul is supposed to leave the body and collect information of a more or less miscellaneous kind. When the trance is over it comes back; the breath returns, and the revelation is divulged. A man once failed to recall his errant soul, and died; a mishap which produced much disruption among the members. The stringency of their moral regimen is certainly in favour of their being genuine mystics, who prefer death to breaking their vows of abstinence; while the political character of the association is illustrated with equal cogency by the fact that its organisation is carried on in the strictest political form, the members assuming the rank and titles of regularly-appointed officials and being bound by a Code of Laws as rigidly enforced as that of any recognised community. During the spring of 1876, a perfect panic prevailed in the principal cities of Kiangsu and Chekiang, occasioned by the mysterious and sudden loss of people's queues, above referred to. When first the rumour spread, it was simply laughed at. But very soon the cry arose from Nanking, Soochow, Shanghai, Ningpo, Hangchow, and all the surrounding districts, and it proved to be no fable. Men and boys suddenly found themselves *minus* their cherished tails, and the strange occurrence admitted apparently of no explanation. Asleep, alone, in their own houses, out of doors—under all conceivable circumstances the mysterious influence reached them. Foreigners affirm that they have themselves seen a Chinaman's tail drop off suddenly, without any apparent agency. The victims were nearly beside themselves; and for weeks every man wore his appendage either over one shoulder, or twisted round his head, or tucked into the collar of his coat, for safety. Of course the phenomenon was regarded as supernatural, and was generally attributed to a paper sprite, cut in red paper, and magically endowed with diabolical powers by a sect of necromancers. A large business was done in paper charms, which were sold at all the shops, and carefully worn about the person to ward off the evil spirit. One talismanic sentence ran thus—*Wa nan tsa ch'ih hung*, which is the Chinese version of the Sanscrit *Vi namati sata hûm :* "He bows down "before the hundred *hûm.*" Another, written in a grotesque and clumsy cypher, was to the following effect :—" Ye who urge filthy "devils to spy out the people ! The Master's spirits are at hand "and will soon discover you. With this charm any one may tra- "vel by sunlight, moonlight, and starlight, over all the Earth." But, as may be imagined, the precaution proved inefficacious ; and for months the nuisance raged. It is hardly necessary to remark that the whole thing was nothing more than a piece of superlative legerdemain on the part of the agents of a Secret Society, which we believe to have been the Lotus-flower Sect. In the majority of instances the abscission of a queue is dexterously effected by means of a peculiar little instrument not unlike a pair of scissors, intensely sharp and small enough to be held in the palm of the operator's hand, where indeed it is entirely concealed from view by certain curious contrivances. There are always two, and sometimes three, persons concerned in the operation ; one, to attract the at- tention of the doomed man : another, generally, to sell him a charm —which of course he does not *yet* need—and a third to snip the tail off, or else to cut it so that it subsequently drops. This done, the principal operator disappears, leaving his victim to buy the talisman—too late ! This is not always the exact routine, but the difference in various instances is slight. Of course it is obvious that, the queue being essentially a Manchu appendage and there- fore a sign that the Chinese are a conquered race, its abscission is intended as a intimation that the power of the Manchu dynas- ty is doomed.

The next confederation which claims our notice is that of the Chinese Moslems. The existence of a complete and formida- ble Mohammedan organisation in China has been recently dis- covered by the authorities in Nanking, ramifications of which extend throughout the length and breadth of the country. The investigations of which this is the result have also established the fact, long suspected, that the Chinese Mohammedans look to the Ameer of Kashgar as their natural lord; and that communications between Yacoob Beg and his co-religionists in China are not only continual but systematic. The number of Moslems in the eighteen provinces is estimated by some officials at twenty to twenty-five millions; but we have no details. The ceremonies imposed on converts to this persuasion are three in number and very simple. The first requisition is the payment of a good round sum of money. This ordinance having been complied with, the candidate is presented for a further mark of favour, and thereupon receives a sound thrashing. But his lustration is not yet complete; the most painful ordeal has yet to be undergone. The unhappy victim is then condemned to drink a large quantity of soap-and-water, in order to cause the evacuation of any *pork* that he may previously have consumed. This accomplished,—and the measure never fails to produce very speedy and complete results—the neophyte is considered tolerably pure, and is admitted to the ranks of the *Hwuy-hwuy jin* accordingly.

Numerous and powerful, however, as the Moslem party unquestionably is, it would be a mistake to suppose that were the Ameer to reach Peking he would find a universal welcome, even from the enemies of the Ta-Tsing Dynasty, for there are other confederations as powerful as the Moslem sect, whose cry is for a Chinese Emperor. To them the invader from the West would be as odious as the Tartar; and in the event of such a change as we are now supposing, the two factions would most infallibly come into violent collision. Perhaps the most violently anti-foreign confederacy in the Empire is that known as the Ko-Lao Hwuy, or Sect of the Elder Brother. This is an organisation which may be almost likened to the Cave of Adullam, in that it consists to a great extent of malcontents, rowdies, persons hopelessly in debt, and desperate characters generally; but it is said that it numbers one Viceroy and two provincial Governors in its ranks, and is spreading rapidly. It was started originally in Tsêng Kuo-fan's army at Nanking, and there are not a few whisperers who say that Tsêng himself was the founder. All the Hunan, Honan and Ngan-hui braves belong to it, and it is in those provinces that it flourishes most strongly. Its primary object was avowedly for mutual assistance and protection; but it is in reality a seditious association of the men of Central China, binding them together against foreign usurpers, whether Chang-mao,* Cantonese, or, as is just now the case, the Manchus in Peking. Their watchword is 'China for China'—or, as they themselves express it, the Glories of the Tang Dynasty; and all foreigners, of whatsoever nationality or sect, be they Tartars, Southerners or Western Chinamen alike, are the objects of their hate. They represent the old exclusive pure-blood race of Han, and look upon the inhabitants of the more distant provinces with jealousy almost as fierce as that with which they regard the Tartar Dynasty itself. As the T'ai-p'ings emblazoned on their banners the legend 'Canton from Sea to Sea,' so the brethren of the Ko-Lao Hwuy contend for the Central Kingdom to the Borders of the Universe. The bulk of the confederacy consists of soldiers: indeed it is more strictly military than any other society of a like nature. Besides these there are a large number of disbanded braves, together with their families; and there is not the slightest doubt that if one of their old generals were to raise the standard of rebellion he might have a hundred thousand men around him in the time it takes to spread the news from Ngan-king to Hankow. The agents of the Society generally travel as itinerant doctors, professing to sell nostrums; really engaged, however, in conveying news from chief to chief, and keeping up the fire which, without fomentation, would, we fancy, be very likely to die out. There is an elaborate code of secret signals, as in the case of the T'ien Ti Hwuy; but we have been only able to discover a very few. For instance, two buttons of the coat undone, and the queue worn carelessly in a double loop over the shoulder in front, are two of the signs whereby the members of the sect are enabled to recognise each other. The fist clenched and the thumb elevated constitutes a third, but we sus-

---

* *Chang-mao, i.e.* 'long-hair' (men). The T'ai-p'ings; so called because they did not shave the head.

pect that the ritual varies in different places. The confederation is kept together by the central truth that, if the initiated would exist apart from the surrounding Chinese—if they would gratify the hope which the importance they achieved during the T'ai-p'ing times has led them to entertain—and if, again, they would become a dominant power in the country, they must preserve the strictest unity and adhesion. Some clever schemers of still sharper wit have seen that by inventing a mysterious ceremonial, full details of which were known only to the instructed few, they might gain the upper hand of their simpler brethren, and the latter were easily persuaded that the ritual was inseparably connected with the end in view. In short it was the history of the Church over again. Men wanted to get to heaven, and a priesthood professing to be in the possession of secrets specially revealed and powers specially conferred upon them obtained almost infinite power over the uncultured masses, whom they thus brought into more abject slavery than they were subject to before. The fact is, all secret societies are, in essentials, very much the same; a specific aim lost sight of in some ridiculous ritual, nominally constituted to enable the purposes of the institution to be carried out, but really invented to give some few clever and ambitious people an importance to which they have no right. The Ko-Lao Hwuy has given much trouble in times past, and some five years ago raised a serious disturbance in Hunan. In July of the succeeding year, the capture of one of the conspirators was reported in the *Customs Gazette*, arising, it was said, from the misdelivery of a secret letter in which a confederate detailed the plot of blowing up the powder-magazine at Hu-k'ow, and afterwards looting the town. The man was summarily beheaded, and subsequent events showed how very apprehensive the authorities had become of further plots, resulting from revenge. A more recent instance is one which occurred at Sarawak only a few months ago; for the system in question is by no means confined to the soil of the Flowery Land, but exists among Chinese wherever they are found. The name of this particular sect is not given, but it seems that for many years past the members of it have caused much annoyance and anxiety to the other portion of the Chinese community, in consequence of their threatening the lives of all who did not belong to their especial clique. In the year 1869 one unlucky victim was actually made away with, and the efforts of the police to discover the murderers were fruitless. The *Sarawak Gazette* then proceeds to inform us that the Government passed an enactment in 1870 making it a capital offence to be a member of a Hwuy; but the immediate object held in view by these agitators remains a mystery to all. They seem to be simply mischievous; and the authorities, determined to stamp the whole thing out, executed, the other day, the first man they caught, by way of salutary example. He was a danger-ous agitator, but hardly a desirable member of a close fraternity; for the night before his execution he scratched upon the wall of his cell a statement, naming three members of his sect, whom he said were the actual murderers of the victim whose fate had never been cleared up. The Chinese in Sarawak cordially support the Government, for your easy-going son of Han hates nothing so much as disquietude and trepidation.

So much, then, for the Sects which, as far as we have been able to discover, are most feared by the Chinese authorities. Many others of course exist, and we will now proceed to give a brief sketch of a few of these minor associations, which are of importance chiefly to themselves. To commence with: at Tientsin there flourishes a fraternity called by its members the Tsai-li Hwuy, a title that may be freely rendered the Fellowship of Reason. Its tenets appear to be obscure; but, as far as we can learn, the prac-tices observed consist principally in a rigorous abstention from alcoholic liquors, opium, and tobacco: in the worship of the Peh-yün Ta-ti, or Great God of the White Cloud: in the habitual wearing of white clothes (the usual symbol of mourning), even to their boots and hats: in the preaching of doctrines from a pulpit: in the severe rapping of their heads upon the ground during prayer: and in profound secrecy. To use the quaint expression of a native friend, a man may not reveal this creed to his father, his mother, or his wife; nor, even, to his elder or his younger sister. So far, however, the association seems a harmless one enough, in spite of the mystery in which it is enshrouded. But the members are closely watched, and, on the principle of *omne ignotum pro horribili*, the authorities have come to the conclusion that they are a very pestilent set of men. A change from their peculiar garb of white to the ordinary 'five colours'* of the middle class was consequently ordered some time ago by the Tsu-sze, or Chief Patriarch; but this was not sufficient to shield them from the jealousy of the Government. As far as one can form any idea of the Society in question, it would appear to be a Teetotallers' Association combined with a certain amount of the hocus-pocus and mysticism so dear to human nature; answering, in fact, in some respects to the Good Templars who have recently made their appearance in the West. The idea of the British Government gravely instituting an enquiry into the tenets of the Peculiar People, the Good Templars, or any other innocent and well-meaning eccentrics, is ludicrous enough; and the great difficulty would be to know where to stop. We can fancy Dr. Maurice Davies appointed President of a Committee of Investigation, and his works on Mystic, Heterodox, and Unorthodox London gravely appealed to as an authority on matters supposed to be endangering the welfare of the State. And yet, allowing for the narrow education of the Chinese, this excessive vigilance and suspiciousness is hardly to be wondered at. The shrewd but simple doctrines of the Superior Person are to them all that is necessary for perfection, and contain in themselves the highest wisdom of which they can conceive. Little or nothing has been allowed to transpire with regard to the secret doctrines of this Sect; but the authorities are possibly not far from the truth in hesitating to look upon the movement as purely religious, and nothing more. Religious vitality can scarcely be called the distinguishing characteristic of the Chinese as

---

* Green, red, yellow, black, and white. It is characteristic of the Chinese that blue, which is almost universally worn, is omitted from the formula.

a nation; and the satire conveyed in the scepticism of the Government, though unconscious, is acute.

Most of the other confederacies appear to be simply eccentric. For instance, there is one society which professes what it is pleased to call the Rice-Pudding religion—Tsze T'wan Këaou—a peculiar euphemism that calls for explanation. The ceremonies consist in the eating of small dumplings made of a particularly glutinous and adhesive kind of rice; a symbolical act, during which the initiated take oaths of secrecy and adhesiveness to one another and the doctrine they profess. But what that doctrine may be, we cannot say. The Tan-Pei Këaou, or religion of the Spread Cloth, also has many adherents; and these individuals appear to be very much detested by the authorities. Of course we are quite in the dark as to their creed; but to judge from their behaviour we should simply say that they were a lot of harmless lunatics. The rites are said to consist in the spreading of a large cloth or cotton drugget upon the ground, on which the members kneel and go through their devotions; these finished, at a given signal the four corners of the sheet are raised, and tied in a knot,—the unfortunate worshippers find themselves all huddled together in a great bag, and are then supposed to go to sleep. It is wonderful to think what an amount of personal discomfort people will undergo for the sake of gratifying some preposterous whim. Then there is another Society springing up in the South of China which can be best expressed by the designation of the Associated Blackguards. The Cantonese gambling-house keepers are at the head of it, and as blackguardism is in the ascendant in the South, any organisation uniting ruffians and cut-throats is more or less formidable. Hitherto however the members of this new and illustrious sect have not found either a ' cry ' or a name, and until they do there can be no cohesion among them. There are no particular grievances to be made capital of; the anti-foreign hullabaloo is played out, or at least has lost its novelty, and unless the mandarins give them cause for disaffection the entire alliance will soon crumble into dust. As it is, several instances have occurred in which the members have proved unfaithful to each other. We cannot help wishing that some more respectable body would take up the cry of Free Trade; this would give any confederation the strong backbone so greatly needed, and if 'Death to Illegal Taxes' were their watchword, foreign influence would at once be thrown into the scale.

One word in conclusion. The plots of secret societies in China, it must be remembered, are not directed exclusively against the powers that be. At least, so say the Chinese themselves. A certain influential official of Kweichow is generally credited with being a member of a confederacy the object of which is the extermination of Europeans. It is further said by the Chinese in that province that the project has the strong support of Prince Ch'un, the father of the reigning Emperor; and of others of equal influence. Such is, at any rate, the story believed among the gentry of Kwei-yang Fu, and indeed all over Kwei-chow; and as such, we think it worth a passing notice, even if no importance be attached to it.

CHAPTER V.

The Armaments of China.

THIS is a subject which just now and for some time past has occupied the anxious attention of the Chinese Government. The threatened war with Japan in 1873, the critical relations with England in 1875 and the perpetual outbreaks of rebellion in various parts of China itself have apparently combined to awaken the authorities to the fact that the military condition of the Empire is alarmingly defective, and at the present moment they are actively engaged in repairing the negligence of years. One of the strangest features of the whole subject, however, is the especial attention paid to naval matters at the expense of the troops on land. The infant navy of China is looked upon as a skilled service entitled to high reward, whereas the soldiery are miserably paid and composed mainly of the scum of the nation. One result of this preference has been the establishment of Arsenals, where ships-of-war are built, and, we must not forget to add, pieces of artillery cast; though the latter enterprise may be regarded as having hitherto proved of greater danger to the gunners than to their enemies. In a word, the Chinese army is in a most deplorable condition; nor is the reason difficult to find. "Any iron will do to "make a nail, and any man will serve to make a soldier." So says the Chinese proverb, and very few of the axioms of the Flowery Land are more generally acted upon. It is generally considered that the material necessary for the manufacture of a brave may be of the coarsest kind. We ourselves are addicted to the same notion. The expression 'food for powder' is a household word,

and we have recently read a passage penned by a high authority confirming the popular impression. Writing of the recruits of 1829, the Duke of Wellington said: "The man who enlists into 'the British army is in general the most drunken and probably "the worst man of the trade or profession to which he belongs, or "of the town or village in which he lives. There is not one in a "hundred of them who, when enlisted, ought not to be put in the "second or degraded class of any society or body into which he "may be introduced." This is very strong language, and proves that the classes from which Falstaff drew his notable ragged regiment were until quite recently regarded as the classes who were . to supply our national defenders. In spite of the changes in modern warfare and its new systems of enlistment we opine that such will ever be the case. The soldier of to-day may be better educated than the soldier who fought at Badajoz and Salamanca, because all Englishmen are better educated now than they were in the time of the Peninsular war; but he will never belong to any other class than that made up of the humblest and least instructed men. If this is so amongst a warlike and aggressive nation like ours, how can we expect it to be otherwise in a country like China, which values a man of thews and sinews at a far lower price than Western folk have ever done? Here, according to the classical phrase, arms yield to the gown, and laurels are of less account than lore. The Senior Wrangler is in China a greater man than the astute and valiant general. The Chinese soldier, too, with his smattering of modern tactics, and his superficial and half-forgotten reminiscences of European drill, is a less formidable opponent than the Chinese soldier who understood his old rude tactics and could manage with ease his own imperfect weapons. The drill that the Imperial army has received appears to have unfitted it for carrying out its old fashion of fighting and by no means rendered it efficient in the civilised methods. This is to be accounted for by the extreme stupidity of the mandarins in using their European instructors. All the foreign officers who have been in their employ testify that the men were never allowed to be long enough in camp to learn modern drill thoroughly. Directly the soldiers knew the A B C of their profession they were drafted off and sent where they would speedily forget their recent acquisitions, while a new levy was in turn taught the rudiments, only to share the fate of its predecessors. Frail bamboo spears, rude tridents that might have been used by the Roman *retiarius* in the arena, guns that will burst at the first discharge, and bayonets encased in rust, are the arms of the majority of the soldiers. The European instructors have been qualified men, but they have never been given a fair trial. Of course the Chinese troops are numerous, but the spell of Oriental multitudes has been broken long ago, and we need not be told that numbers are often an absolute hindrance when the discipline is slack, and the commissariat deficient. We are not prepared to deny that when well led the Imperial troops have ere now conducted themselves bravely before the enemy, but this was when they were convinced of the perfection of their own arms and tactics, and had not been rudely undeceived by finding themselves beaten by Western weapons and Western strategy. Now, everything has been broken down. The *prestige* of invincibility has been shaken. Like David they are asked to go out against a formidable Goliath, in armour they have "not proved;" and hence they would be uncertain in their movements, difficult to handle, and easily stricken with panic. Their fire-arms would in all probability play them false in the first engagement. Those troops who had their drill fresh in mind would be obedient and steady; but the men who had forgotten or imperfectly learnt would blunder, hesitate, and throw everything into confusion.

Again. It is utterly impossible to arrive at the numerical strength of the Chinese standing army: we can only say that the mandarins receive pay for the maintenance of about ten times the number of soldiers that actually exist. The Chinese soldier is not only dirty, ill-armed, lazy, and unpractical, but he has not the remotest notion of how to handle even such a rifle as is handed out to him— much less of keeping it clean; while the weapons provided for his use are infinitely more dangerous to himself than to the man he shoots

at, and are dear to the Government at seventy-five cents a piece.
In fact the Chinese Government is being universally 'stuck' in its
purchase of both fire-arms and gunboats, and as long as the soldiers
are provided with rifles which will explode, and with gunpowder
which won't, so long will the army be an utterly useless institution.
Then as to military discipline, properly so called, such a thing does
not exist.   Eighteen hundred men out of two thousand are mere
coolies; while as for native *drill!*   Picturesque it may be, but
grotesque is no adequate expression for it.   Some time ago a
'water-drill' took place among a contingent of the soldiery at
Ningpo; a performance which, albeit intended for the delectation
of His Excellency the Fu-t'ai, seems to have reached the Ultima
Thule of absurdity.   The manœuvres of the soldiers reminded one
more of the cow-like gambols of Miss Tilly Slowboy than of a
formal military review held in the presence of a provincial magnate.
They danced and capered about in a fashion as useless as it was
insane; they brandished their clumsy swords, and 'flashed' their
ponderous shields, and yelled like lunatics.   Then, encouraged by
the martial sounds of a lugubrious ram's-horn, they slipped gingerly
into the river, having first provided themselves with life-belts, and
then gravely paddled about.   Here they remained, marching in
line, describing circles, forming cross-lines in the shape of the letter
X, letting off crackers and burnstone, flourishing staves, and hooting
for all the world like owls distraught.   And is this farce Chinese
warfare ?   " Of what possible use," remarked a foreign gentleman
who witnessed this edifying performance, " they could be, save in
" duck-shooting, I know not, for they might make capital decoys;
" but in a fight, a duck-gun or a good strong fishing-net is all that
" would be required to effect their capture."

What, then, would be the ultimate fate of the helpless and undisciplined banditti whom the Chinese complacently look upon as
an army, in the event of any rupture with a Western Power?
The large-hearted philanthropist, according to whom all the sons
of Adam rank together, must regret that it should be in the power
of stubborn wrong-headed officials to compass the almost certain

destruction of a large section of their fellow-countrymen, while the pitiless utilitarian will probably be of opinion that it is a good thing for the country that so large an amount of worthless surplus population should be improved off the face of the land. Whatever may be the cause of it, it is certain that the Chinese have never thoroughly comprehended the vast disparity between their military power and that of even the weakest of European states. For them it is sufficient that a certain number of men exist and are paid for the protection of the empire, but it would be considered contrary to etiquette to ask questions (which might be inconvenient) of the mandarins as to the strength of the force actually doing duty in the ranks, and to compare it with that which is represented on paper. It seems surprising that a nation as keenly alive as the Chinese are to the advantages to be derived from foreign science, notably the electric wires and travelling by steam, should be so grossly apathetic in everything that relates to the organization of their armies, and so practically ignorant of the important part which that science now plays in the tragedy of modern war. When danger threatens they have rushed into the market and bought up the discarded fire-arms of other nations ; this done, they have placed them in the hands of undrilled coolies, and now fondly imagine that they are in a position to cope with European powers in the field of battle. The lesson of their inferiority they must learn from bitter experience, when lines of disciplined troops open fire on their helpless columns and their forts crumble away under the bombardment of foreign artillery. It may be urged that it would be impolitic to give the Peking authorities proof of this inferiority, but we are of opinion that when they rightly estimate their own military inefficiency, and the actual horrors of war are brought home to the people, outrages, such as the late murder of Margary, will be unknown. China has never known yet what it is to be at war, as we understand it. It will be the duty of any Government which has the interest of the mercantile community at heart to impose the burden of a future war not only on the Court, but on the country ; for hard as the lesson might be, it is only

by pursuing such a line of conduct that we may hope to open the
eyes of the people to the gross corruption and misgovernment
under which they are at present living. The reason, however, of
these military shortcomings we have already pointed out. From
time immemorial the profession of arms has been looked down
upon in China. *Cedunt arma togæ;* the civil mandarin takes the
'pas' of the military officer, and the latter except in rare cases
has little hope of advancement. The instruction that has been
afforded to the men by competent foreign officers has been of comparatively little value, owing to the utter indifference displayed
by those in command to the acquirement and practical knowledge of their profession, and the inability of subordinate officers to
apply the manœuvres they have mastered on the parade ground
to the actual service. As to the rank and file, they are docile, intelligent and tractable, and if handed over altogether to European
instruction much might be made of them. At present, however,
it seems like crushing a butterfly on the wheel to bring an Anglo-
Indian force with all its modern scientific appliances to oppose the
undisciplined rabble which represents the fighting element of the
Middle Kingdom; but when one reflects upon the various political
complications which are arising, and the diverse occurrences to
which our attention has been drawn of late, all of which bear a
complexion of more or less pronounced hostility to foreigners, it is
impossible to deny that the chances that such a chastisement is in
store for the Chinese, are growing daily less remote.

There is, however, one branch of military science in which the
Chinese have shown themselves fairly proficient; and that is,
fortification. British forces have ere this been repulsed by the
forts at Taku, and at the present moment the defences of the
Hwang-pù river are undergoing a very thorough and systematic
overhauling. A gentleman who lately visited the Woosung forts
has furnished us with some interesting particulars respecting the
really very formidable works now being carried on at the entrance
of the river with a view to fortifying its mouth on modern principles. As is well known, he says, a long range of batteries upon

the old system has existed at this spot from time immemorial, and these same batteries made an energetic resistance to the English fleet in 1841-2. Upon that occasion the guns were silenced with little difficulty, a force being landed from the men-of-war which succeeded in taking them from the rear. These batteries extend a distance of about one mile along the Hwang-pù River, and nearly the same distance up the Yang-tsze. The embrasures must number several hundred, but on very few were guns mounted. Now at last the Chinese are abandoning these old systems of defence, and, under the foreign advice employed by them at the Arsenals, are constructing forts whose solidity will compare favourably with that of many European fortresses. It is true that they have adopted the embrasure system while in the most modern works the guns are mounted behind a parapet and defended inside with traverses over which the muzzles of the guns are presented. But the work at Woosung is being rapidly hurried on. Five thousand men are at work like ants ; some piling, some carrying mud, others mixing concrete for the casemates, but all busy. The forts when completed will contain ten embrasures, each about fifteen yards apart. The casemates are lined with malava wood, and the platforms beneath the guns are formed of massive piles, the quantity of wood used being almost incredible. The whole is covered with a hard composition formed of red, clayey earth, sand, lime, and a paste made from boiled rice; this is spread in layers about an inch thick and firmly hammered down by rows of soldiers holding rams ; and one layer being thus hammered, another is put on. Accommodation for the men working the guns is provided in strong hardwood houses in rear of and between the batteries. The earth for concrete is brought up in papigos from Ningpo. The casemates measure about fifty feet at the base, taken from the top of the berm, and are about fifteen feet high. The embrasures are fixed in a heavy iron frame composed of four three-quarter inch plates, and are protected by iron doors. In rear of the forts are five camps, each about one hundred yards square, giving a clear internal space of ninety yards and holding one thousand men each. The forts are well built with twenty-feet-high mud parapets and bastions, with a wet ditch outside. Within are substantial brick houses forming comfortable quarters for both troops and officers; the granary and audience-hall being in the centre. The soldiers are taken from all the eighteen provinces of China, the greater part, however, coming from Ngan-'hui. In each camp were seen four brass howitzers.

The slight sketch is we think sufficient to show that the Chinese have devoted much time and industry to the subject of fortification, however deficient their armaments may be in other respects: and it is not to be denied that the forts at Woosung, when completed, are likely to prove a very serious obstacle to any invading party that may attempt to enter the Hwang-pù. And this leads us to the consideration of another matter of great importance, namely their Arsenals; the establishment of which is an enterprise which calls for the serious attention of foreigners. In many respects it is one upon which the authorities may claim much congratulation. The Arsenals of China have led to the warm encouragement of engineering science by the official class, and are rapidly bringing about the opening of the vast coal-fields which have hitherto lain *perdus* in the interior of the country. The Chinese Government is generally unfortunate in its purchase of arms through foreign agents, and particularly in its contracts for gunboats built abroad. As we have already remarked, it has to no small extent been the loser, and is learning through much unpleasant experience that the sooner it is independent of its foreign purveyors the better and the cheaper for the country. But its Arsenals, as might be expected, are still grievously mismanaged. It is a well-known fact that the Chinese Government has recently expended immense sums of money in the purchase of arms and ammunition, as well as of ships, from Europe, in anticipation of a war with somebody. This naturally leads us to enquire why, with the four large and expensive Arsenals which have been in operation for several years, China should neither have on hand nor be able to produce for herself, a good proportion of the proper war material required for this emergency. There is evidently mismanagement somewhere, and it may not prove an uninteresting task if we endeavour to point out where the fault appears to be. At any rate, His Imperial Majesty's Arsenals will be none the worse for the little wholesome ventilation we propose to give them.

These Arsenals appear to owe their origin chiefly to the T'ai-p'ing rebellion. It was during the progress of that movement that the fact of the vast superiority of Western arms and ships was forced upon the minds of the dreamy Government officials, and they were led to see the necessity for Arsenals and dockyards like those of foreign countries. Further, the arms required for the suppression of the T'ai-p'ings had to be purchased at very dear rates from the few foreigners who could be found to supply them: while the circumstances attending the disbanding of the Lay-Osborne fleet were such as to point in an unmistakeable manner to the expediency of China being able to build a navy for herself. The main object that was nominally kept in view in the establishment of the present Arsenals and dockyards, was that natives might there learn the theory and practice of the various branches of mechanical engineering. Foreigners were of course regarded as indispensable at the beginning, both to set up and start the machinery and to produce a supply of arms, ammunition and ships for immediate use. At the same time, native workmen and foremen were to be taught thoroughly all that might be necessary for them to know to enable them to manage and carry on the whole work themselves without foreign assistance. It was also contemplated to open coal and iron mines in the vicinity of these Arsenals, at the most convenient places for communication, so that China might not have to purchase these indispensable materials from foreign countries. This idea of future self-dependence was not at all a bad one, and if it had been vigorously and thoroughly carried out China would by this time have been able to produce for herself all the munitions she now requires to have in readiness in case of war.

We believe that the first attempt at an Arsenal was made at Soochow towards the close of the T'ai-p'ing rebellion. A large workshop was started, and shot, shell and war-rockets were made in abundance. Subsequently this establishment was removed to Nanking under the superintendence of Dr. Macartney, where it has gradually increased in size and importance, so that at present it ought to be able to turn out considerable quantities of war-rockets and ammunition of all kinds. Next in order of time comes the Kiangnan Arsenal, which was commenced near Shanghai in the year 1865. It has from time to time been greatly enlarged, and now is perhaps five times the size that it was some seven years ago when first laid out. It has extensive factories for making all kinds of large and small arms, shot and shell, steam-engines and boilers, and yards for building wooden and iron ships. There is also a large dock. At the Lung-hwa Pagoda there are extensive gunpowder and cartridge works in active operation, also under the management of the officials of this Arsenal. There is also a separate factory near the north-east corner of the Arsenal, where are steam hammers and other plant required for forging heavy guns. The Foochow Arsenal dates from 1867, when the buildings were commenced. It is not strictly speaking an Arsenal, but a dockyard, since it is exclusively devoted to the building and equipment of ships. It appears that its director, M. Giquel, undertook that within five years from the commencement of the works, the Chinese officers, students and workmen should learn completely how to build, command and navigate steamships without foreign assistance, and also how to construct and manage the necessary machinery. A large and well arranged dockyard with the requisite buildings and machines has sprung up within the specified time, and a miscellaneous fleet of wooden ships has been built, equipped and manned according to promise. The Tientsin Arsenal comes last on the list, having been commenced about 1868. This place has extensive gunpowder works, and, like that at Nanking, has greatly increased its operations. It appears to be chiefly employed in the manufacture of all kinds of ammunition, and lately of guns and small arms. Arsenals are also in course of construction at Canton, Tsi-ngan Fu, and Hangchow, and the high officials of the other provinces are said to be using great endeavours to induce the Government to allow them to establish Arsenals to supply arms and ammunition for the use of the portions of the Empire under their control.

The above hasty sketch embraces about all that is generally known respecting these institutions. We pause now to ask again why, with such large and expensive establishments in operation for, say, five years, capable, we are informed, of turning out many times as much work as they have done and swallowing up annually millions of taels—why should it be necessary for China at a sudden crisis to have to expend such immense sums for iron-clads, arms and ammunition, instead of being already in great part, if not wholly, supplied from her own resources? We do not hesitate to say that after making all due allowances for the shortness of time they have been established and the difficulties to be overcome, these Arsenals have nevertheless proved to be on the whole a decided failure, and that the Government would have been as well, if not better, off without them, than with them; and moreover, that unless great changes are made in the method of working them in future, they will in all probability continue to be a great drain on the revenue of the country, without producing any proportionate advantages.

In the first place let us consider how and by whom these Arsenals and dockyards are managed. One would have imagined that the Chinese Government before beginning such works as these would have applied to some foreign Power for suitable men to undertake the superintendence, whom they could have consulted with confidence as to what China really required. It is true that such naval constructors as Reid, or such Arsenal directors as Anderson, are not to be easily met with; but still it would not have been difficult to have thus obtained thoroughly experienced practical and scientific men. In five years, if allowed free scope for their talent, they could have made the Arsenals and dockyards of China, as well as their productions, such as would well bear comparison with those of Western countries. But instead of this, the Government seems to have left the establishment and management chiefly

in the hands of a few ordinary native officials, whose chief quali-
fications, in all probability, are a knowledge of the Chinese classics
and the ability to write fine essays and poems. At any rate, they
are ignorant of the first principles of the sciences and arts in which
they ought to be thoroughly grounded to occupy such a responsible
position. These officials are said to engage and discharge foreign
engineers and workmen, to give orders and then countermand
them, and to purchase and use machinery and materials all in the
most random manner possible. If they ever condescend to ask
foreigners for advice, they seem generally to act as directly opposite
to it as possible. At the Foochow and Nanking Arsenals these
eccentricities do not of course exist to anything like such an extent
as in the others, because in the former, M. Giquel, and in the latter
Dr. Macartney, have been more or less associated with the native
officials in the management. But with such drawbacks as these,
can it be wondered at that the Chinese Arsenals are not a success ?

We have for some time past endeavoured to obtain statistics and
information that would serve to institute a comparison between the
money swallowed up by these establishments, and the value of the
things produced. But in this important particular the Chinese
Arsenals are a sealed book. Visitors, it is true, are allowed to go
over any of the spacious buildings full of machinery without let or
hindrance. No attempt is made to conceal the waste of time,
wages, or materials. But the complicated arrangements by which
these establishments are managed, the power that appoints the
officials, supplies and apportions the funds, and explains to the
satisfaction of the Government all the bungles that are made—
these are subjects beyond our power to fathom. There are "wheels
"within wheels." "Let not thy left hand know what thy right hand
"doeth" seems to be the motto. However much we might like to
see a detailed account of the sums reported as expended annually
in these Arsenals and dockyards, our curiosity cannot be gratified,
for no statistics are made public. We do not, however, give the
officials who manage these Arsenals credit for being one whit more
honest or more scrupulous in the use of the money that comes into

their hands than native officials generally are in any other capacity. But we venture to surmise that every ship or gun or rifle that comes from these establishments costs, from one cause and another, perhaps five times what it could be purchased for in Europe and laid down in China, and in this respect China would be far better off without these Arsenals at all.

As regards the quality and suitability of the productions, there are more data that can be seized upon. The Foochow Arsenal, for instance, seems to have spent all its energies in building and equipping a miscellaneous fleet of ships of different size, not one of which is armour-clad, or able to stand before a small iron-clad armed with a heavy gun of modern construction. A few wooden ships were all very well just as despatch-boats or transports; but why not have built, say, two small despatch-boats, two small transports and two large transports, reserving the balance of funds for three or four serviceable iron-clads? Then again the Kiangnan Arsenal has built a few wooden gunboats and certain heavy old-fashioned wooden frigates, such as European nations have long ceased to construct. None of these are armour-clad. The money these next-to-useless encumbrances have cost the Government would, all things considered, have bought two serviceable iron-clads armed with the heaviest guns and able to give a good account of themselves when required. The engines of these frigates are of a still more antiquated form than the vessels themselves, and their consumption of coal will be so much greater than that of modern engines that one can hardly imagine this important item of expense ever having entered into the calculations of the designers. We might go on in the same way to notice the guns and rifles that have been made at these places, and still find the same results of misdirection; but we hasten to show how utterly the main object for which the Arsenals were established has fallen short of being realized. As far as we can understand there is not one of them that can in any department do without foreign employés. How many natives are there in all the Arsenals put together that can design a pair of engines, lay down the lines of a ship or make a working drawing

of a gun and carriage ?   In fact, where brain work is required, and
the faculty of imitation cannot be brought into play, the Chinese
mechanic or draughtsman would most probably fail.   It is seen
in the case of the Foochow Arsenal, where the instruction of Chinese in mechanical as well as scientific pursuits has been carefully
attended to, that without foreign assistance the natives are comparatively helpless.   When the foreign engineers, etc., had completed their term of service and returned to Europe, the establishment
soon went to ruin, and the indispensable foreigners had to be asked
to return.   In the other Arsenals where no definite plan of instruction is pursued, foreigners could hardly be dispensed with for a
single day.   The main object for which these Arsenals were established has evidently not yet begun to be achieved.

In conclusion we may add that if the imbecile Government of
China relies on ignorant officials to manage all affairs connected
with its Arsenals, without having their doings made public, or
kept in check in any way—and if these officials have their own
ends to serve and care not one straw for the success of the establishments they control, beyond what may immediately further
their own private interests,—China will continually have to buy
an undue proportion of her arms and ammunition, as well as ships-
of-war, from Europe.   The Foochow Arsenal has undoubtedly been
the most successful of all, and this is the result of foreign direc-
torship.   We believe that if M. Giquel had been allowed *unlimited* control of that establishment and funds, its success
in supplying the real need of the Government would been been
far greater.   A thoroughly efficient foreigner.put in authority over
all the Arsenals and dockyards as Inspector-General would soon
work wonders ; and if left at liberty to open coal and iron mines
would soon produce all the ships, arms and ammunition China requires, at prices not much above those of Europe.   But this plan
of course would not suit the ideas of Chinese officialdom, for there
could be no peculation.   In short, we are inclined to believe that
these costly Arsenals and dockyards form a most convenient chan-
nel into which a good proportion of the revenue of the country

can be easily diverted and lost sight of in ways that the ignorant
Government is quite unable to investigate. Were this not the
case, we expect that these establishments, so far from increasing
in size and number every year, would soon dwindle into insigni-
ficance, and finally collapse, as Woolwich Dockyard and other places
have done. Other Governments find it far cheaper to have their
ships, etc., supplied by tender from private firms, and China, if
she studied economy, would find the same.

Reverting for a moment to the subject of armaments in general, we must not forget that the Government is even now
engaged in attempting to bring about a great and radical reform
in its military affairs. A year or two ago Tso Tsung-t'ang, the
greatest soldier in the country next to Li Hung-chang, presented
a scheme for the reorganisation of the army which, though almost
audacious in its magnitude, nevertheless recommended itself very
strongly to the authorities. At present the standing army of China is split up and divided among the Eighteen Provinces in a way
which robs it of more than half its inherent strength. It is virtually a number of separate contingents, each under the command of
the local or provincial magnates and practically independent of the
Central Government. Tso's desire is to concentrate these scattered forces, to bring them more under the immediate power of Peking, and so render the army a united and homogeneous force. Li
Hung-chang, the Viceroy of Chihli, and Shên Pao-chên, the Viceroy of the Liang Kiang (Kiang-su and Kiang-si), support Tso in
the proposed measure, although Shên is said to consider the
changes too radical and violent to be adopted suddenly, and advocates a more compromising policy. The Government hesitates to
centralise the army too rapidly towards Peking, not daring to do
anything that will place a fresh accession of power in the hands
of Li, whose headquarters are at Tientsin. But the reforms are
still progressing slowly. Probably Shên is the safest as well as
the most valuable public man now in China. Li is known to look
favourably upon the opening of the country by means of railways ;
but his policy in this direction has for its object the emancipation

of China from foreign influence, and he thinks by adopting foreign appliances in developing its resources to bring about, eventually, the pacific expulsion of foreigners.   But here we are straying from our subject; and the present chapter is, perhaps, already long enough.

CHAPTER VI.

The Kingdom of Liuchiu.

THE relationship of the Liuchiu Islands to the two great Eastern Powers in their immediate neighbourhood for a long time partook of that peculiar vagueness and ambiguity which characterise the mutual rights and obligations of semi-civilised peoples. At the time of the Formosan struggle there was of course more or less interest attaching to the political status of the little kingdom, although it was naturally thrown into the shade by the more important question of the fealty of Formosa; but it will be remembered that the settlement of the difficulty involved a double issue. Not only was it decided that the Chinese held sway over the aboriginal portions of the Beautiful Island as well as over the civilised tracts along the coast, but the very terms of their capitulation to the Japanese implied an acknowledgment that the latter nation was the suzerain of Liuchiu. For many years the question seems to have been a moot point. Owning one lord and paying homage to another is a task calculated to call into play the very highest diplomatic accomplishments, and the attempt is one which can hardly fail to result in a fiasco. The position of such a nation, too, is so utterly and hopelessly anomalous that we, with our European ideas, can hardly understand the possibility of its continuance for a single year. It is very much as though the Gaikwar of Baroda, after receiving his Crown at the hands of a British Viceroy, were to send a deputation the next year to offer tribute and perform acts of homage to the Emperor of Germany, and the Emperor were to receive the Embassy as a matter of course and graciously accept its presents. We therefore think it may not be uninteresting to cast a glance over the past history of the kingdom of Liuchiu, and attempt to form some judgment as to what constitutes one state the vassal of another in the eyes of these Eastern monarchs.

The Liuchiuans themselves are apparently a mixed race, with probably some element of Malayan blood. They are small in stature, and far superior to both the Coreans and Formosans in natural civilisation. The state seems to have been founded about the seventh century by a Prince of Japan, who governed under the title of the Heavenly Descendant (T'ien-sun)—analogous to that of the Tenno or Ten-wo, the title of the present Emperor of that country and the Japanese form of T'ien-wang or Heavenly Prince. As far as we can discover from the meagre details at our command, there seems to have been no subsequent interference with the little kingdom on the part of either China or Japan for several centuries; it was subject to various internal changes, one dynasty succeeded another, the original reigning family was ousted by a rival clan named the Shun-t'ien, but eventually recovered its rights, only however to lose them again shortly afterwards, when a succession of dynasties attained in turn the power of the realm. The name of Liuchiu, or Hanging Globes, was bestowed upon the group by a king who reigned about the middle of the sixteenth century; and it was in the reign of his son, Sio-nei, that the independence of Liuchiu received its *coup de grâce*. The Prince of Satsuma, a warlike and turbulent adventurer, basing his claims probably upon the original establishment of the kingdom by a Japanese, swooped down upon it, overcame the Liuchiuan forces, obtained possession of the King, and carried him off to Japan, where he kept him a close prisoner for four years. At the expiration of this period, however, he restored him to his throne; but the independence of Liuchiu was at an end. Thus far there is no trace whatever of any Chinese claims to seigniory; but it appears that during the latter period of their freedom the Liuchiuans had not been wanting in marks of respect to the great Empire in whose neighbourhood they dwelt. It was in the year 1373 that the first complimentary tribute was sent by the reigning Prince to the Chinese Emperor Hung-wu, the founder of the dynasty of Ming. The Chinese received the Embassy with much complacency, as a proper acknowledgment of the world-wide influence of their monarch, who "overflowed with tender compassion for the "poor savages that dwelt in the unlettered wastes outside the pale "of civilised humanity;" but they neither exercised authority nor extended protection towards them. The Liuchiuans seem to have been actuated not only by the sort of unreasoning loyalty which is the natural sentiment of a tiny state for a gigantic empire, and which was shared by all the petty nations in the far East, such as Siam, Annam, Burmah and Corea, but entertained a very honest admiration for the literature and civilisation of the Chinese. They looked upon the principles of Chinese government as a model of rectitude and enlightenment, and taught the ethics of Confucius in all their schools. Twenty-seven years afterwards we find the Liuchiuan ruler soliciting the confirmation of his prerogatives and his investiture with the kingly power at the hands of the Emperor, thus instituting a custom which appears to have been continued by all his successors down to within a very few years of the present date. The documents which passed between the two countries on these occasions are ludicrous in the extreme as concerns the phraseology employed, but they both contain expressions of mutual regard and kindly sentiment which are not at all unpleasing. The terms in which the Prince characterises the infinite benevolence and power of the Emperor are such as would only be applied by Westerns to the Supreme Being; he "lies pros- "trate under the sense of Imperial favour which in its grand scope "can reach even to look after the glory of distant lands: the Auto- "cratic Virtue is vast and diffusive"—and so on. He acknowledges in his Memorial of Thanks for Investiture "the Dragon-bordered "Proclamation which has caused our national Gods to revive from "their lethargy;" and humbly thanks the Emperor for his 'phœ- 'nix commands.' The Emperor acknowledges grandly the 'palm- 'leaf missive' of the Prince, and returns his 'silken mandates' to

the poor Prince's 'rural hamlet.' But interspersed with all this
Oriental arrogance is much kind and excellent advice as to the government of his realm, and the assurance that in the Imperial Palace dwelt one "who would not forget the kindness" of his vassal.
Such a relation existing between a great power and a small one is
really of a very pleasing and proper nature, stripped of course of
the absurd trappings of Eastern metaphor. Still, the question naturally arises what Japan can have thought of all this, and how, if
she claimed the suzerainty of these Islands, she can have submitted to the holder of her fief receiving his crown at the hands of a
powerful rival; and we frankly confess that we are unable to com-
prehend the anomaly. But although the Liuchiuans are descended
from the Japanese—possessing nevertheless a strong admixture of
foreign blood—and speak a dialect of the Japanese language, they
appear never to have regarded their suzerains with any superfluity
of affection. They have kept up a commerce with Japan, but their
sympathies have always been on the side of China, and their respect for her is unbounded. At the same time there has never been
any agreement between their rulers and the Emperor who over-
flows so copiously with tender compassion for them, which would
justify them in expecting any energetic action in their favour,
should occasion arise. The overtures of friendship have always
come from Liuchiu, and been accepted with much patronising
grace by the superior Power, as the homage due to her rank as the
Central Kingdom; but Japan has been the true mistress of the Islands throughout, and lately, as we know, has asserted her right so
vigorously that the Liuchiuan embassies to Peking will probably never be repeated. For years the tribute-bearers were courteously received, and the Japanese were either too proud or too nonchalant to
interfere. On the last occasion, however, the Japanese Ambassador
expressed his disapprobation in strong terms, remonstrating with
Prince Kung upon having lent his countenance to so irregular a
proceeding; an act on his part which seemed peculiarly ungraceful
to his Japanese Excellency, occurring as it did when the Formosan
quarrel, which originally arose out of the murder of some Liuchiu-

ans, had just been amicably settled. The Liuchiuans were thereupon given to understand that, being formally regarded by the very
terms of that adjustment as under the protection of Japan, they
must discontinue their missions to Peking for the future : an order
which they appear to have taken most grievously to heart. Of
course it was reasonable enough. By full consent of China, Liuchiu
had been declared a dependency of the Japanese Government, and
was now constituted a *Han** or corporation ; any attempt at a
divided allegiance was therefore not to be permitted. But discontent seems to have run so high, that the brother of the Liuchiuan
King lately presented a formal petition to Sanjio, the Prime Minister of Japan, expostulating in the most earnest manner against so
cruel an injunction. "It is now five hundred years," says the
Prince, "that we have enjoyed the kindly protection of China, and
"were we now to discontinue our connection with that Empire it
"would be at once ungrateful and unjust. It is known to all
"nations that we pay tribute alike to China and Japan, and if we
"continued our tribute to China it would not involve us in any new
"tributary relation. Now, if His Majesty the Mikado would gra-
"ciously permit the continuance of our connection with China, it
"would reflect lustre upon the virtues of His Majesty, and the
"world will not say that this is unreasonable." It strikes us that
if the world said anything at all about so small a matter, it would
say that such a request was, on principle, most unreasonable·
"Being a small territory," he continues, "and dependent as tribu-
"taries on two empires, we have enjoyed protection and quiet for
"five hundred years. But if we now suddenly discontinue our
"connection with China, without a sufficient reason, it would cause

---

* The Japanese *Han* no longer exist in the Empire itself. They were all converted into Ken in 1871 or 1872. They were what can best be realized under the English
word *clan*, but did not quite correspond to that. Their names connoted the district
in which the class lived as well as the members of the class themselves. They were
mostly under Daimios, and after the abolition of these latter the Han were also
abolished and their liabilities, &c., taken over by the Imperial Government. The
districts formerly known as Han were called Ken, and the Han organisation, which
resembled a corporation, gave way to the Ken system, which is more allied to the
French system of Prefectures.

" us great inconvenience, and seriously affect our Chinese trade."
He then renews his entreaties that their relations may not be
severed, but that they may be permitted to remain as hitherto.
And if that cannot be, the Minister is urged to negotiate with
China upon the subject, to whose decision the Liuchiuans profess
themselves willing to bow.   But they are much exercised in their
minds at the idea of becoming a Japanese *Han*, and are most anxious,
too, that their ancient form of Government may be preserved to
them.   The Japanese Minister for Foreign Affairs decided three
years ago that neither their nationality nor the mode of their
Administration should be altered, and in 1874, when the supervision of Liuchiuan affairs was transferred from the Guaimusho to
the Naimusho, a verbal order was received from Hayashi Gako to
a similar effect.   Such were the principal arguments put forward
by the King's brother ; and since then the Japanese have decided
to turn the place into a military garrison for the sake of doing
something with it.

The next most natural enquiry is, what is the real state of feeling
with regard to the question, in Japan ; and now we came to the
curious part of the whole business.   It is of course only natural to
suppose that the Government is anxious, for some reason or other,
to retain Liuchiu within its grasp, and to prevent any attempt at
encroachment on the part of China.   There is no doubt that the
possession of a group of islands, situated as Liuchiu is, may be of
immense advantage to a great country in time of war.   Had we only
such a group, where we could station a regiment and which we could
use as an independent house of call in the Pacific Ocean, our position in the East would be materially improved.   But as regards Japan, the public feeling appears to be against it; that is, if we can form
any idea of that feeling from the native newspapers.   The *Hochi
Shimbun* devoted a very ably written and somewhat amusing article to the consideration of the matter, deprecating in the strongest
terms the unprofitable expenditure now incurred.   The arguments
of the writer are tersely put.   He asks what benefit to Japan will
ever accrue from the possession of these islands ; what diminution

of taxes it is likely to bring about; what the Japanese will gain by
garrisoning the islands for their protection against invaders; and
whether they, the Japanese, will be more feared by England, Russia, France or Prussia in consequence? To this last question we
think we may safely hazard a negative reply. The condition of the
Imperial treasury, urges the native paper, is not such as to justify
the Japanese in spending large sums of money on people who dis-
like them, who treat their benefits with ingratitude, who flout their
ambassadors, and whose only true loyalty is given entirely to China.
"And what has hitherto been the result of Japan's beneficence?"
asks our writer, here rising almost into eloquence. "Nothing more
"than this: that last July, when a terrible disease fell upon the
"Liuchiuan pigs and killed numbers of them, the enterprising
"natives salted the poisonous meat, and exported it by junk-
"loads to Japan! Is it not hopeless," he asks, working up to the
climax of his argument in a tone of reproachful indignation, "to
"expect a reproductive outlay from a country whose highest ambi-
"tion is to export diseased pork, from which doubtless many of the
"people have died? Look at the present condition of Japan.
"There is no surplus in the treasury, and there is a multitude of
"reforms which we ought at first to make in this country before
"seeking other places in which to begin them. We therefore say
"to the Government and our countrymen that useful and precious
"treasure ought not to be lavished to maintain showy but useless
"honours."

Such appears to be the opinion of many of the Japanese, and
we confess ourselves much interested in the eventual result of the
dispute. It is nothing to be surprised at when we find a struggling nation like Japan encumbered with dependencies and at a
loss to turn its territorial wealth to good account. Japan is
evidently unable at present to do well by her foreign possessions;
she has quite enough to do to look after her own affairs. As far
as the Islands themselves are concerned, they would be a most
desirable acquisition, both as regards political value (from their
situation) and their exceeding beauty, fertility, and salubrity of

climate. The southern portion of Great Liuchiu can only be compared to one vast enchanting garden, teeming with flowers and fruit, fanned by the purest ocean breezes, and inhabited by a docile, studious and intelligent population. This charming realm, like a floating kingdom in a fairy-tale, is the rightful and undisputed possession of the Japanese; but the natives do not like their lords and masters, and long to be under the Government of the greater Empire, which looks but coldly on their loyalty. China has given no signs of wishing to annex Liuchiu, though she has always treated the little Kingdom with such lofty kindness and goodwill. The Gordian knot might, however, be cut, were Great Britain disposed to enter the market as a purchaser. As the *Spectator* said some time ago, our position in the East will never be assured until we have an island in the Pacific Ocean which we can use as a second Malta, where we can garrison troops and land them in Shanghai in a few days. The English would be able to turn the territory to account where the Japanese now fail; and to reap practical advantage from a possession which, as far as its present owners are concerned, appears to be, not only a white elephant, but a very unmanageable and costly animal too.

CHAPTER VII.

Legendary Corea.

IN the days of yore, there lived a Prince of the Kao-kiu-li in the north-west portion of China, who had in his power the daughter of the Yellow river. He kept her a close prisoner in his Palace; but one day, the Sun, perceiving the beauty of the captive Princess, poured the effulgency of his rays over her with such good effect that she bore to him an egg the size of a bushel; which, when broken, was found to contain an infant Prince of great fairness. When the child grew up, he received the name of Chu-mo-ni, which meant Great Archer, and was appointed Steward of the Royal Stud. One day, when out hunting, the king permitted him to shoot; and the youth acquitted himself so much better than his royal master that the latter determined on his destruction. Chu-mo-ni, learning the murderous designs of the king, took to flight, and left the Court in secret. During his wanderings he came to a river, which he found it almost impossible to cross; and the case was urgent, for every moment brought his pursuers nearer to him. "Alas!" he cried, "shall I, who am the offspring of the Sun, "and the grandson of the Huang-ho, be arrested on the banks of "this river without any power to overcome the obstacle?" But scarcely were the words out of his mouth, than all the fishes that were disporting themselves in the blue depths of the transparent stream entwined their bodies together, thereby forming themselves into a living, silvery bridge, over which he passed in safety. When he arrived on the other side there met him three personages, one of whom was dressed in a garment of hemp, another in an embroidered robe, while the third was draped in river-weeds; and they accompanied him to the city of Ki-chin-kow, where he took the name of Kao, and founded the kingdom of Kao-li.

Thus runs one of the ancient legends respecting the early history of Corea. Like all similar myths, it is fanciful and unmeaning enough; but in the reputed descent of the Corean nation from the amours of the Yellow River's daughter and the Sun, it is not impossible to trace some faint corroboration of the theory that, in years gone by, the present peninsula of Corea was part of the mainland of Pe-chih-li—a tradition which may be found in a certain old Chinese book entitled *Kwan-yu-ki*, where we read that the ancient city where the King of Corea held his court was built in a place which now forms a recognised portion of that province. Many, though vague, are the stories we have been told of this fair, strange land; but of its early history we know little enough. We can only say that it was originally inhabited by several distinct tribes, among which were the Muy, the Han, and the Kao-kiu-li; and that these were afterwards all united under the common name of Kao-li, of which our English word 'Corea' is an obvious corruption. Towards the end of the sixteenth century, and just about the time when they were the source of so much trouble and distress to China, the Japanese invaded the country and conquered it; but the Coreans, assisted by the Tartars, who had then completed the subjection of the Great Empire, shook off their yoke and drove them out. They paid a heavy price, however, for their release, by immediately falling into the hands of their deliverers; although the Manchus found them a difficult people to deal with, for when they attempted to introduce the tonsure among them the Coreans raised the banner of revolt, and it took all the tact and ingenuity of the reigning family to quell their indignation. The native sovereign held his sceptre in suzerainty from the Emperor of China, who generally deputed a Prince of the blood-royal to perform the ceremony of investiture; and, to judge from the memorials addressed by the petty monarch to his Imperial neighbour, the relations between them seem to have been akin to those of a sovereign and his Viceroy.

So far, therefore, the Coreans seem to have a sort of cousin-german relationship with the Chinese. But they have had a good deal to do with the Japanese too, in by-gone years, and a Japanese writer informs us that to the Coreans his countrymen owe a certain amount of their education; just so much, indeed, as they have in common with the people of China. This is a very interesting and remarkable fact. At the time that Corea was divided into three separate principalities, we are told that a certain famous Empress, a sort of Japanese Boadicea, bearing the somewhat comic name of Jingo, went over to Shiura,—one of the aforesaid states; that while there she waged fierce warfare with the two other states, and eventually succeeded in making them tributaries to Japan. This happened in the year 200 of our era. This condition of affairs seems to have continued for about ten centuries, during which time, says the Japanese historian, " the " doctrines of Confucius and Sakya Mouni, the Chinese characters, " and many other arts, *were brought from Corea to civilise this coun-* " *try;* and all that we gave them in return was a lesson how to " take a beating." It is curious to learn from a native of Japan that Corea was the medium through which his countrymen acquired the accomplishments and arts that originally came from China. Then about twelve hundred years after the time of the Empress Jingo, the Japanese ruler, Tai-kee, conceived an intense desire to achieve the conquest of China. To do this, however, it was necessary to pass through the Corean territory, and he accordingly asked permission of the king; but the king refused point-blank, and Tai-kee, enraged at the rebuff, declared war against Corea instead of attacking China, and overran the kingdom utterly. " No bene-" fit, however," says our writer, " accrued from this to us. On the " contrary, indeed ; for we spent a vast sum of money in carrying " on the war, which impoverished us enormously."

Now the communications which have reached us hitherto from Co-rea have been few and indirect. In the truest sense of the word it is

a *terra incognita*, a sealed book, secured by iron clasps which, however, once forced, may possibly disclose treasures of inestimable value. The country was at one time said to be rich in gold, and *so* rich
in silver as to have given rise to the fable that in one of the fastnesses of the interior there lies a mountain consisting entirely of
that precious but now somewhat depreciated metal; while iron,
copper, and salt abound. Nearly every Western expedition which
has been made to its shores has been attended with circumstances
of a more or less romantic nature, and has also proved more or less
a failure. The mysterious visit of the steamer *China*, vulgarised
though it was by the undeniable air of filibustering which pervaded
it, nevertheless gave rise to the keenest interest. Stories and
rumours reached us of clandestine incursions into the country,
under cover of darkness; midnight raids upon royal catacombs,
and the unearthing of golden coffins of priceless worth; with other
marvels of a similarly entertaining and startling kind. The in-
tricacies which were involved in this expedition were simply be-
wildering, and in spite of two political trials to which it gave rise
have, we believe, never been completely unravelled to this day.
The French and American Expeditions were both failures; the
former never pretended to be anything else, while the latter, puffed
though it was by despatches and bulletins couched in imposing
phraseology, and by subsequent photographs of the leaders of the
party standing in grand attitudes, with fingers pointing exploringly
to a map upon the table, can never be remembered as anything
else than a fiasco, reflecting but little credit upon those who placed
themselves in so false a position as to commence an undertaking
they were utterly unable to carry through. But the report which
was brought back by these different spies was a very goodly one.
The land was said to be beautiful in the extreme, rich in the most
luxuriant foliage, abounding in springs, and basking in the smiles of
the bluest of blue skies—more like Italy, in fact, than any other
Asiatic country. It is therefore hardly to be wondered at that the
inhabitants of so fair a realm should have resisted the incursions of
the Western foreigner, of whom they knew so little, and of whom

what they did know was so very unattractive. But the period of Corea's seclusion is now drawing to a close. For some years past a sort of one-sided, hostile courtship has been carried on between Corea and Japan, and an unprovoked attack by some Corean forts upon the Japanese men-of-war engaged in surveying the coast in a particularly dangerous spot at last brought matters to a crisis. For several weeks the storm seemed imminent, and both news and rumour combined to predict a speedy rupture between the two countries. The cause of discontent was a just one. For years Corea had kept herself in jealous isolation from her nearest neighbours, and situated as she is between two great powers on either side of her, it is only strange that she should have preserved this policy so long. Not content, however, with a neutral attitude, she had shown herself in a most ill-conditioned and disagreeable light, and the danger which threatened all vessels which ventured too near her inhospitable coasts was a perpetual source of irritation. At length the climax came, and it is undeniable that through the negociations which ensued the Japanese acted with much credit. On one hand they sent an ambassador to the Corean Court, the instructions given to whom were of a stringently pacific character. The minutiæ of his conduct were laid down in detail, everything he said or did was to be most conciliatory, and he was, above all, to guard against giving offence to the meanest magistrate he might be brought in contact with. Meanwhile another ambassador was despatched to China, the recognised suzerain of Corea, to arrive if possible at a distinct understanding as to the position she intended to take up in the event of hostilities proving unavoidable. It will be remembered that when Yanigawarra sounded the Chinese Government upon an exactly similar point four years ago, the misapprehension which thereupon ensued very nearly brought about a most disastrous war. The Chinese Minister gave an evasive and polite reply, which the Envoy of Japan interpreted as a full permission to chastise the offending aborigines of Formosa, and acted upon it accordingly. In the present instance however there seems to have been no such ambiguity of speech. The Chinese

Government expressed its sympathy with Japan, acknowledging frankly that the Coreans had behaved badly and that China would certainly not interfere with any punishment that the Japanese might deem it right should be inflicted. This satisfactory stand-point having once been gained, negociations on the other side proceeded favourably; a Treaty was concluded, by virtue of which three Corean ports should be thrown open to trade, and Japanese residents enjoy exterritorial privileges; and Japan herself, whose name was formerly a synonym for exclusiveness and conservatism —whose shores it was once death for a foreigner to visit and for a Japanese to quit—now claims the honour of having achieved what France, Germany and America combined have signally failed to accomplish. The victory was a great and bloodless one, and the Mikado's Government deserves the generous respect of all true friends of progress.

It is very possible that the attitude assumed by China may have had something to do with the submission of the Corean king; it is more than possible that the Chinese Government is fully alive to the fact that the hitherto existing relations of Corea to both itself and the Government of Japan are far too equivocal to be preserved much longer. If Corea were situated anywhere else, the eccentricities of her people would be of importance chiefly to themselves : but her geographical position is such as to endow her with an amount of consequence that she otherwise would certainly not possess. It is desirable for many reasons that the relations of Corea with both China and Japan should be kept upon a friendly footing. That there seems to have been no rivalry or jealousy between the two Powers in their discussion of the point at issue is satisfactory, and we fancy that the time is coming when they may not impossibly find it necessary to coöperate, for their common interest, to maintain the integrity of Corea. At present, affairs look tolerably promising. Corea is the acknowledged tributary of China, and has made friends, more or less sincerely, with Japan. Three ports, as we have remarked above, are to be opened to Japanese trade, and whether this step will redound to the interest of foreigners or not, it will bring the Japanese into pretty intimate relations with the Corean Government. The day may not be so very far when Corea will be forced to appeal to either or both of her neighbours for protection against an insidious and formidable foe which is even now gradually encroaching upon her from the North. Bit by bit, the frontiers of Manchuria are being nibbled away, and various 'exploring expeditions,' composed of Russian officers, have been prowling about the territory which lies between Moukden and the Peninsular frontier. The southernmost point of Primorsk even now abuts upon Corea; it needs but little more to tempt the greedy nation to grab at the entire prize. And if Japan succeeds in establishing a permanent footing there, what better excuse will Russia need to do so? The Corean country is a tempting oyster, whose valves it has been a dangerous task to force apart. They are sure to pinch somebody's fingers; and if China and Japan were ever to renew their foolish controversy about an imaginary vassalage, now that the principal object has been in a measure achieved, we should probably see the sprawling arms of Russia reach down and secure the prize. It would be a serious matter for both countries should such an event occur; and frankly, many things have come to pass which once seemed far less probable. It is said that the resources of the Peninsula have been largely over-estimated, and that on neither physical nor commercial grounds would much benefit result from its exploitation; but there might be political advantages accruing from an occupation of the soil to which Russia is probably not blind, and it would be unwise for either nation to close its eyes to the contingency at which we hint, however remote it may now appear. The Corean question may be, and we believe is, a very wide one, embracing issues that may not be recognised at first, but which are none the less important for that; and we therefore consider that the pacific solution of the late difficulty, with its involved concessions, placed the relations of the three countries most concerned on a so far satisfactory basis.

CHAPTER VIII.

Early Japanese Invasions of China.

IF ever a rupture occurs between the Middle Kingdom and the Land of the Rising Sun, such as appeared imminent three years ago, it will only be another illustration of the trite saying that history repeats itself. Few large countries have been troubled with so harassing and restless a neighbour as Japan has proved to China, and few disturbances could happen now between the two Powers which have not had some precedent in ages long gone by. The sixteenth century was perhaps the period when China suffered most at the hands of the sister-kingdom; but two hundred years before then we read of frequent skirmishes, all more or less severe, and generally ending in results the reverse of glorious to China. We therefore propose to take a rapid glance at the mutual relations of these countries for the past few hundred years, leaving it to our readers to draw therefrom what inferences they may with respect to the possible future.

Now as early as the year 1370 of our era, such was the annoyance caused to the inhabitants of the seaboard provinces of China by the piratical incursions of the Japanese, as to draw forth a serious remonstrance from the Chinese Government, accompanied by a strong hint that it would be much to the advantage of the King of Japan were he to pay homage to the Emperor. That monarch accordingly sent over an Embassy, with tribute, returning at the same time seventy Chinese youths who had been previously captured by Japanese pirates. The royal act of submission however had no effect upon the braves who had caused the humiliation of their Sovereign, and they recommenced to infest the coast a couple of years afterwards, burning, slaying, and plundering to their hearts' content.   In the year 1403, when both countries had passed under the sway of succeeding rulers, the King of Japan again tendered his homage and tribute to the Emperor of China, who sent him the Imperial Diploma, by which he established him firmly upon the throne, together with a Golden Seal ; and for nine years there was peace between the two nations. At the expiration of this term, however, the Japanese again broke out, when they made a savage and bloodthirsty attack upon Corea, and discontinued paying tribute to China. This double outrage (for so it was regarded by the Chinese Government) led to the publication of a manifesto, in which the Emperor invited all foreign Powers to present themselves once every ten years to render homage.   He sent a copy of it to Japan by the hand of an Ambassador Extraordinary, accompanying the order in this case with a request that the Sovereign of that country would, in view presumably of the constant troubles arising from the turbulency of its character, station a few decades of soldiers at Peking as hostages.   The unfortunate Ambassador deemed himself lucky to escape with his life, so enraged were the Japanese with this demand ; but the effect of the Ukase held good for some years, and we hear of no very serious disturbances till nearly a century later.

Then, however, the troubles began.   The first feud occurred, as far as we can discover by the old records, somewhere about the year 1523, when a quarrel of a most trifling nature—arising, we believe, from some fancied breach of etiquette—took place between the leaders of a certain private mercantile expedition from Japan, and the Customs officers at Ningpo.   The cause of the latter was naturally espoused by the local military mandarins, and a terrible skirmish ensued, in which the Japanese soldiery utterly routed the Chinese force, pursuing them even out of their own district far into the interior of Chekiang.   They were eventually repulsed, but such was the panic caused by the *émeute*, that China was for a long time closed to foreigners, and the most stringent regulations

were framed against all commerce with any outside nations whatever. These prohibitions were, however, as might have been expected, evaded on all sides; and a very lucrative trade was instituted among the neighbouring islands, which afforded excellent
harbourage for the Chinese merchant vessels. But it was this
commerce that led indirectly to the war which the Japanese subsequently waged upon the coasts of China. A Japanese merchant,
having been pretty severely taken in by a Chinaman in a large
transaction in which the ruler of Japan himself was interested,
gathered a considerable force, and descended furiously upon the
neighbouring parts of Chekiang, where, by plunder, he richly recoup-
ed himself for the loss he had sustained from Chinese duplicity. This
was the signal for war, and in the year 1552 an invasion of a most
formidable nature took place upon the coasts of that province.
The Japanese soldiers, fired with victory, continued their march
almost unimpeded—having taken and looted the towns of Hwang
hien, Siang-chang hien, and Tien-hai hien, and laid waste the
entire surrounding country, before their progress could be stopped.
They made Tien-hai hien their headquarters, and resided there a
year, when they were temporarily expelled. But the next year
they returned in greater force and numbers, and this time they
made themselves masters of Hai-hien, Pingho, Hiuyao, Haining,
Taitsing, Kading and Shanghai. Once more repulsed and driven
out, with terrible bloodshed and loss of life on the side of the Chinese, they again returned to the attack, appearing now in the provinces of Kiangnan and Shantung, pillaging, burning and spreading
terror wherever they went; then, returning to Chekiang they gave
battle to the Imperial forces, leaving many hundreds dead upon
field. Two years later another incursion seems to have taken place,
when the invaders penetrated as far as Nanking and Soochow: but
on this occasion they found the Chinese upon their guard, and
retired without achieving any successes of importance.

Now the continual miseries and anxieties caused to the Empire
by these detested neighbours, seem, about this period, to have
aroused the strongest indignation in the bosom of a certain fair

Princess, who ruled a small independent State in the south of China. The exploits of this Amazon form an element of pure romance in the annals of the Chinese Empire, and her history, as far as it has come down to us, is interesting in the extreme. She combined the virtues of Boadicea with the brilliant seeming of Clorinda, celebrated in the page of chivalry, and wide-spread was her fame in the ranks of both friends and foes. The passion which animated this royal lady was, according to all we are able to gather upon the point, in every way as purely patriotic as that which constrained Joan of Arc to fight for her King and country; and certain it is, that, leaving her infant son to the care of her advisers she placed herself at the head of her troops, and offered her services to her august ally. The Emperor did not refuse; and the *Lang-ping*, or Wolf-soldiers, as she christened her force, soon became known and feared. On her arrival at Soochow, the Princess Hwa-kee (for such was her name) was entrusted with an expedition to repulse the invaders at Sung-kiang. Her success, however, was not so great as she had anticipated—a disappointment which she probably owed either to her inexperience or the fact that she had underrated the strength of her opponents; but so formidable was her array, in spite of this repulse, and so admirable its 'form,' that the Japanese were inspired with a wholesome dread of the now celebrated Lang-ping, and abandoned the siege of Nanking on hearing of their approach. They only changed the scene of their operations, however, and turned their arms towards the south, where they ravaged the fair provinces of Fo-kien and Kwangtung without respite or compunction.

The reigning Emperor, meanwhile, was in every respect a very feeble man. He passed his life in the society of his concubines, and the only thing he seems to have taken the smallest interest in was the discovery of how to render himself immortal. To this end he laboured ceaselessly. Entirely oblivious of the distractions which were rending his Empire in twain, he remained absorbed in studying the secret of immortality, and in his researches after this chimera collected a library of no less than seven hundred and sixty-nine books upon the subject. It may be well believed, therefore, that when such a Prince was appealed to by the agonised inhabitants of the southern provinces, who saw themselves ruined, their friends murdered, their wives and daughters dishonoured, and their fair land laid waste, the results would not be worth much. The Imperial advisers, however, took the matter up, and sent the necessary relief. Once more repulsed, the incorrigible tormentors returned again, in the year 1564, with a force twenty thousand strong: but after a severe and protracted struggle they were at length beaten back, and comparative peace has reigned between the two Empires ever since.

But the ancient feud is not yet completely dead. The old jealousy still smoulders, and may some day burst into a flame again. During the Formosan controversy, the Japanese hailed the comet which then appeared, with its tail pointing towards the Beautiful Island, as a bright and happy omen of their success in the war that seemed on the point of breaking out; while the Chinese found equal reason for encouragement in the fact that, on the very day when the first Japanese gunboat was reported as having weighed anchor for the Island, there occurred a *total solar eclipse*— a phenomenon which, as we all know, symbolises the devouring, by a Dragon, of the Rising Sun.

CHAPTER IX.

Japanese Influence on China.

THERE is one element in the various indications at present visible in the Chinese Government towards a more progressive policy which, we think, has been somewhat overlooked, but which is, nevertheless, extremely interesting. Foreign—that is, Western—pressure, undoubtedly has done much. The Chinese have frequently laid themselves open, by their purblind and foolish acts, to the coercion of the Treaty powers in directions most distasteful to them. They have been forced to do this and to undo that, to concede one thing and atone for another, and each point, as it has been gained by foreigners, has increased the sullenness of the native Government. So far we may claim to have achieved something, though our triumphs have been few and incomplete. Another influence, however, has been and still is at work, and this will prove eventually of the greatest service to us after all; we mean, the force of Japanese example. China is watching Japan as a cat watches a mouse, and every fresh measure adopted by the latter country acts most irritatingly upon the former. The effect of course is good, for the Chinese Government is thereby subjected to a sort of moral compulsion to follow, however tardily and reluctantly, in her wake. It seems to recognise in the steady revolutions of thought in the sister-country the augury of what must eventually follow in China, and the prospect is a most unpleasant one, especially as the undeniable *prestige* which Japan has gained politically during the last few months precludes much of the contempt which the Chinese might otherwise feel for a nation so

renegade in other matters. The Government of Japan often acts
foolishly and has yet much to learn : but the Government of China
has still more, and appears determined to gain its experience at
the highest possible cost. The great railway-question is an apt
exemplification of these remarks ; and we propose to devote a few
pages to the subject.

Now one of the principal features by which the prosperity of a
country may be most fairly gauged consists in its means of internal communication. The great watercourses of China, considered in this light, are perhaps unequalled in any portion of the
inhabited globe ; and the rivers, canals, and creeks which intersect
the country in every possible direction, affording facilities for intercourse between the remotest portions of this vast Empire, cause
it to stand alone and unrivalled in the world. Nature has been
lavish in her gifts, and the Chinese have assisted her and supplemented her favours with artificial devices of admirable ingenuity,
and with much success. Water is in very truth the life-blood of
the Chinese ; and whether for the purposes of travel and transit
on the one hand, or of irrigation and industry on the other, it is
difficult to surmise how, had not China been so favoured, a nation
occupying so enormous an extent of territory and with so few
other means of locomotion could possibly have managed to
exist, either in a physical or political sense. But the mere
presence and abundance of raw material is not sufficient. Unwieldy junks and barges, propelled by the most primitive and
clumsy methods, have hitherto been the only vehicles of transport-
ing either goods or passengers : and every attempt at the introduction of steam into the interior is still regarded by the authorities
with much jealous horror. The provincial mandarins oppose it
because they know that the day the foreigner gets so firm a footing in the country as the innovation in question would afford,
their period of power will be over ; no longer will they be able to
prey upon the unfortunate people they are supposed to guard, and
their best means of preventing an occurrence so fatal is to inflame
the passions of their victims against us meanwhile. As far as the

leading statesmen are concerned, the position is somewhat different. They are fully alive to the benefits which would accrue from the introduction of both steamers and railways into the interior; but they, too, dread foreign ascendancy, and wish to take the matter into their own hands. Some two years ago, only, Li Hung-chäng sent a Chinaman of exceptional intelligence *over to Japan* to study the principles of railways and mining operations, and make a report upon them; a little-known but cogent proof of the Vice-roy's perfect appreciation of the value of such institutions, when they can be availed of apart from foreign influence. Japan is doing great good to China, and here is an illustration of it.

Meanwhile, however, we must not forget to notice, in passing, that a railway on Chinese soil is now an accomplished fact. A private foreign Company, having obtained the requisite land—by a little judicious manœuvring—have lately imported the necessary plant, and a line is now complete between Shanghai and the village of Woosung, some twelve miles down the river. Not the slightest opposition has been met with from the country-people. On the contrary, they take the keenest interest and delight in the novel spectacle, and for weeks assembled by thousands to watch the tiny engine at its work. The scene resembled that of a fair; and men, women, and children came for miles around—many of them from Soochow, about seventy miles' distance—to stare and to enjoy the fun. But the authorities were enraged, and their first act was one of almost inhuman brutality towards an unfortunate villager who had sold, subsequently to the original transaction, a small piece of land to the railway-company. Not to dwell unnecessarily upon the details of so revolting an affair, it is sufficient to say that the man was *beaten to death.* He was sentenced, it was reported, to between two and three thousand blows; but before he had received three hundred his person presented so shocking an appearance that the executioners were fain to desist. But it was too late; the victim died shortly afterwards. Another man, who was a party to the sale, received at different times two thousand seven hundred blows with the bamboo; while a third was summoned thirteen times and had to pay thirty dollars each time. Eventually he was imprisoned, and the same sum demanded as the price of his release.* Then the Tao-t'ai of Shanghai, an unscrupulous person named Fêng, having got into serious disgrace with the Viceroy for having permitted the completion, so far, of the railroad, addressed the following protest to Her Majesty's Consul; a document which will repay perusal. The grounds set forth are these:—

That the construction of the railway between Woosung and Shanghai is against the wish of the Chinese Government, and is a direct insult to that Government on the part of the foreigners. That throughout all the countries in the world, the power of building roads, etc., is reserved to the Government, and in no instance have railways been allowed to be built in one country by the people of another against its will; even in Japan, the railways there, though built with money borrowed from the foreigner, are under the direction of her Government [*lit.* she is free to act as she likes]. If China now allows the people of another country to build roads within her territory, she will not only be laughed at by other countries, but it establishes a bad precedent. That according to the laws of England and America, the making of any railway which interferes with the property in the neighbourhood, or with any public road or water-courses, cannot be carried out without the sanction of the legislature. That when an alien buys land or house property, he must conform to the law of the country, unless it is otherwise provided for in the Treaty. That there is nothing in the Treaty that China made with England which sanctions the purchase of land in the interior by aliens to build railways, nor anything in it which sanctions the building of a railway from Shanghai to Woosung. That the railroad now building is causing much obstruction and damage to public and private roads, while the water-courses

---

* The Chinese have a singular theory by which they explain the recent active measures taken by the authorities. One night, say they, it so fell out that the little Emperor had a very troubled sleep; and in his sleep he dreamt that he saw a *great iron centipede* crawl up his legs—and bite him! He woke from his nightmare in a terrible fright, and, we suppose, told his amah; and this was repeated to the wise men, magicians, astrologers, and soothsayers of the Capital, who held a solemn conclave to discover the meaning and interpretation thereof. At last the secret was disclosed; the mysterious reptile was symbolical of the train of "swift chariots that run to and fro, and turn not as they go," which had lately found its way to—Woosung. The astrologers were triumphant; down came a despatch from the Yamên to the Viceroy, and we know the rest. But the commonly accepted reason among the Chinese, of this step on the part of foreigners, is the best of all. Our real object, we are informed, is to be able to run quickly away from Shanghai next massacre, and retire safely and with all speed into the fastnesses of Paoshan. The thing is clear enough: at least, so says the tea-shop gossip of the place.

have already suffered great injury from it, and great inconvenience has been caused to the houses in the neighbourhood. That the erection of the bridges along the road has interfered with the shipping traffic. That so far back as the 11th year of Tung-chih (1872) representations had been made by two Consuls to the Tao-t'ai of Shanghai, asking on behalf of some foreigners for permission to buy land ; they knew then that if they had not the sanction of the local authorities, they could not even construct ordinary roads ; how much more, then, is permission necessary for the construction of railroads ? Then when permission was granted by the late Tao-t'ai to purchase, it was only intended that there should be an ordinary road. That on the 24th April 1873, when the late Tao-t'ai granted the permission to purchase in his communication of that date, there was nothing in it which could be construed into a concession of additional rights or privileges ; the Tao-t'ai had, moreover, refused to accede to the proposition of a toll-tax being levied. That when the application was made to the Tao-t'ai, the Consuls did not indicate in any way clearly to the Chinese officials what use the purchasers were going to make of the land. If it had been known to them that the purchasers were to run a rail-road, the Chinese officials would never have consented to the purchase of the land. That in the communication of [the English and American Vice-Consuls] the object therein stated was to make an ordinary road, therefore the late Tao-t'ai granted the lease ; but if it were converted into a railroad now, it would be in violation of the original object stated in the communication. Consequently all the leases and proclamations issued on the project of road-building issued by the late Tao-t'ai, will be regarded as waste paper. That inasmuch as the project proposed is one that cannot be permitted in any other country, unless the sanction of the local authorities has been obtained, the writer must object to the scheme, because permission had not been granted by the Tao-t'ai, and any assumption of right must therefore be regarded as pretentious. As to the application by the Consuls for an exemption of duty on the material of the railroad, the communication only stated that the material was intended for the building of a carriage road, and nothing was said about a "steam-engine road." The writer had refused the application. As to the leases sent to him for the purpose of being stamped, he refused also to seal them. Many of the leases belonging to the company not having been stamped, how can the company claim the ground to be theirs ? The writer has objected to the progress of the work, but he has only done so by peaceful means and on principles of right ; he has never used violence or force to obstruct the work. That to sum up his objections, the writer would point out to H. B. M. Consul, particularly to the U. S. Consul, that according to the subsequent convention made by China with Poo An-son (? Anson Burlinghame), article No. 8, it is stipulated that in the construction of railroads the right is reserved to the Emperor of China. Now the Emperor of China has never issued any edict in the matter of constructing railroads. If the Consul persists as before in assisting the Company to carry out the scheme, he commits a breach of international law, as well as of treaty obligations. To assist in an underhand and a deceptive concern causes injury to the Chinese Government and to its people. Such pertinaciousness is clearly detrimental to China in her friendly intercourse with the Treaty Powers. That article 39 of the English Treaty provides that in the shipment and discharge of goods, a permit must be obtained from the Superintendent of Customs ; any breach of this provision renders the goods liable to confiscation. Article 46 says " the Chinese authorities at each port shall adopt the means " they may judge most proper to prevent the revenue suffering from fraud or " smuggling." Then clause 6 of the Articles of Trade prescribes the limit within which goods can be landed and shipped as specified by the Hai-kwan. By virtue of this power the Hai-kwan has fixed the limit to be from the new Dock to the Temple of the Goddess of Heaven, and merchant vessels can alone ship or discharge cargo within the limit. Therefore Woosung is no place to ship or discharge goods. Woosung, moreover, is a sea-beach, which is very essential to the people. Arable ground is held in very great importance in China, and the people are, under no circumstances, allowed to sell Government ground to others to build houses or wharves. Now what is the object of the foreigners who wish to run a train from Woosung to Shanghai ? Woosung not being a place where goods can be landed or loaded, the writer has only to arrest the offenders and to fine them. Such being the case the writer would ask what was the use of the railroad. That the Foreign Settlement extends from Yang-king-pang to Hongkew, and within this limit are the French, English and American Concessions. That Woosung is in the district of Paoshan and does not come within the precincts of the treaty port (of Shanghai). The treaties made with the different countries only stipulate for the district of Shanghai being a port open to trade, and there is nothing about Paoshan district being a treaty port also. The writer would like to know in what concession did the proposed route of the railroad come. That the writer thinks the object of the foreigners in constructing this railway is to shew the Chinese what a railroad is, there being no such thing in China, but if China wants railways, she can construct them herself and she does not require the foreigners to do the initiative ; for instance, the foreigner has steamers and guns, etc., and she has adopted every one of the inventions. Moreover, if foreigners want to build railroads, they will have to go to a great expense to buy land, whereas if China constructs them on her own account, she has nothing to pay for the land. That the undertaking is easy for one and difficult for the other is clear, and if the foreigners wish to make money out of the project is it not an impossibility ? If there is nothing to gain, why, then, do a thing that is contrary to treaty obligations ? The writer wishes to know the object of the projectors, and begs of the Consul to stop immediately the further progress of the work until instructions can be received from the British Minister at Peking and the Tsung-li Yamên, and he has no doubt that satisfactory arrangements will be made there. But if no attention is paid to this request, the writer will communicate the fact to all the treaty Consuls and publish it in the newspapers, so that officials and people alike, throughout the world, will know of it. The Consul addressed being the chief of the treaty Consuls, having been so long in China, knows no doubt fully the exact state of things in Chinese and foreign relations, and understands how to encourage friendly intercourse. In this matter, the writer relies entirely on the Consul for the maintenance of the existing friendly relations, and if the Consul can satisfactorily arrange the affair so as to stop the further progress of the work and to save a rupture, the people in the whole world will be indebted to him and especially will the writer be grateful to him.

Now this is undeniably a very clever document.. Of course it must be borne in mind that its inditement is a purely formal and official act, and the objections therein expressed are simply those of the Tao-t'ai as Tao-t'ai—not in any way those of the man himself in his private and personal capacity. It was necessary that a protest should be made, or Fêng would have laid himself open to severe punishment from the Viceroy of Nanking. Still the paper itself is a very clever one from a Chinese point of view, and many of the arguments are forcibly put. The most cogent remarks are those which deal with the fact of the Tramway projectors having misrepresented the scheme when negociating for the purchase of the land,—with the non-inclusion of Pao-shan in the limits of the Treaty port of Shanghai,—and the illegality of making a railway in any country without the permission of the legislature. These are the most plausible objections, and at first sight appear somewhat formidable. It cannot be doubted that the promoters obtained the necessary land by the exercise of some *finesse*. They did not say they wanted it for a railway, for the reason that if they had they would certainly never have got it at all. But the Tao-t'ai has nobody but himself—or his predecessor—to thank for having been outwitted. The land was stated to be for a ' carriage '-road ; *not* a ' horse '-road (*ma-loo*)—the word which is applied to the streets in Shanghai settlement. Now the very exclusion of the word ' horse ' in favour of ' carriage ' ought to have excited the suspicions of the former incumbent, and rendered it perfectly clear to him, first, that carriages were to be used, and secondly, that horses were not : from which two premises it would not have been absolutely impossible to draw a conclusion akin to the actual fact. The argument about the illegality of landing goods at Pao-shan is flimsier still. It is a mere question of convenience and expediency ; Custom-house officers have often gone down to Woosung and supervised the unloading of cargo outside the limits of the port,

and there is no reason why they should not do the same thing
under the new conditions.   The Tao-t'ai, as Superintendent of Customs in Shanghai, has never interfered with them in this matter,
nor is it likely that he ever will.   All that will be required is a small
Customs station in a convenient spot; and surely, no Chinese
mandarin in the Empire would ever object to an additional Customs
station being built, at Pao-shan or anywhere else.   The Tao-t'ai's
reference to the English law respecting railways is as inapposite as
any of the other points.   An Act of Parliament is only necessary
at home when the proposed railway is to go through other people's
property, and its object is to render the sale of land compulsory;
anybody can make a railway through his own park.   In the
present instance the people have sold their land of their own free
will, and an act of legislature is therefore a superfluity.   The ground
is now the private property of the Woosung Tramway Company,
and consequently, on the Tao-t'ai's own showing, they are at liberty
to do what they like with it; for by Article XII. of the Treaty of
Tientsin British subjects are permitted to acquire land "whether
"at the ports *or at other places.*"   In China we acquire our rights
from the lord of the soil, and hold them in perpetuity.   The other
arguments of His Excellency are mere official bluster, and quite
irrelevant to the subject.   However the Tao-t'ai has done his duty,
and he may now sit and twirl his thumbs with an easy conscience;
feeling that he has relieved himself of all responsibility and ob-
serving with complacency the progress of a work of so much importance to the future welfare of his country.   But for the satisfaction of our readers we will append an extract from the Prospectus
published by the Company, in order that they may see for themselves what the intentions of the promoters really were.   Thus we
read :—

This Company has been formed for the purpose of constructing and working
a Line of Railway between Shanghai and Woosung, a distance of about ten
miles.

The projectors believe that the present time is favorable for the introduction
of Railway Enterprise into China, and they appeal to the Foreign Community
of Shanghai to assist them in carrying out a scheme, which they confidently

expect will lead to the early development of railway communication with the interior, and to the opening up of the mineral, and the other resources of the country, affording at the same time a new field for the employment of foreign capital, and giving a fresh, and much needed impetus to trade in manufactures, and native produce.

With these objects in view, a continuous strip of land, suitable for the proposed Line of Railway, extending from the Northern Bank of the Soochow Creek to Woosung, with space for the erection of termini, sidings, &c., &c., and containing 346 *mow*, 8 *fun*, 6 *li*, 1 *haou*, has been acquired by the Provisional Board of Directors, for the sum of *Fifty Thousand Taels* (*Tls.* 50,000), to be paid in the Company's stock at par.

This land is held under the usual foreign title deeds.

The projectors do not advance this scheme as one which will yield a handsome profit to investors, (though careful investigation leads them to believe that the traffic on the proposed Line will leave a fair margin over working expenses); they bring it forward with the hope that all persons having permanent interests in Shanghai, will co-operate in the introduction of the First Railway in China, looking to the future development of the commercial interests of the country, rather than to an immediate return upon their investment.

Should their expectations be realized, and other Railways follow, the proposed Road will form the first section of a main line, by the most advantageous and practicable route, from *Shanghai* (via *Paou-shan*, *Tai-tsan*, *Ka-ding*, and *Quin-san*) to *Soochow*.

The simple truth is that the Chinese are not so obtuse and so blind to the advantages of foreign institutions as they are sometimes made to appear. To give a few instances of what we mean, even if we have to descend with a rapid motion from the sublime to the comparatively ridiculous in doing so, one has only to look at the extraordinary patronage accorded by well-to-do Chinamen in Shanghai to the much-spoken-against Japanese carriages known as jin-rick-shas.* When this innovation was first agitated, there was a dead set made against them by all classes, and the proprietors of the wheelbarrow-hongs threatened no end of ruin and destruction to the originators of the scheme, as well as to the coolies who were to be employed in it. At the present moment wheelbarrows are hardly ever used, while jin-rick-shas are not only a nuisance from their very number, but are extensively patronised by the wealthy compradores, merchants and brokers of Shanghai, who may be seen, night after night, lolling luxuriously upon the cushions on their

---

* A commodious but insecure vehicle, pulled by a coolie. 'Jin-rick-sha' is a Japanese corruption of *Jin-li-ch'é*, or 'human strength carriage.'

way to the theatres and restaurants which they may particularly affect, not unfrequently accompanied by the gorgeously tricked-out damsel, with her elaborate *coiffure* and enormous golden finger-nails, in whose insipid smiles they purpose to bask for the evening. They have simply discovered that a jin-rick-sha is a more commodious and expeditious vehicle than they have been accustomed to, and consequently adopt the use of it in the most natural manner possible. Another and more apposite example of what we mean is to be found in the universal advantage taken of foreign steamers, not only by the masses, but by mandarins of the highest rank; for we find the Fu-t'ai of This and the Hoppo of That voyaging constantly from port to port in the ordinary steamers plying upon the coast. Moreover the Chinese are now building both merchant-steamers and men-of-war themselves, by the dozen; and these enterprises are not undertaken by the mercantile classes alone, for the sake of private gain, but are and have been superintended and encouraged by men of rank and influence like the late Tsêng Kuo-fan, Li Hung-chang, Ting Jih-chang, and Shên Pao-chen. Here in fact is another illustration of what we have elsewhere affirmed, *viz.*, that the one bugbear to a Chinaman is, after all, dread of foreign ascendency. He has no objection to foreign institutions, as such; it is only in so far as he fears foreign power and foreign interference that he fights against the inventions and innovations of the West. Apply this to the question of railroads. A Chinese would travel by rail from Shanghai to Soochow in preference to going in a slow uncomfortable boat, for exactly the same reason that he now travels in a foreign steamer from Shanghai to Canton instead of beating about the coast for a month in a clumsy, unsafe, and incommodious junk. The land journey would take him at the outside three hours to perform, whereas the water route now consumes from three days to five, according to the state of the weather; and there can be no reasonable doubt that were a railway between Shanghai and Soochow once set going, the number of passengers would before long be almost too great for the accommodation provided.

As a particular instance in proof of our theory respecting the willingness of the Chinese to adopt foreign institutions so long as they are not personally interfered with, we may recall a certain little incident recorded in the *Peking Gazette* in August 1873. A report upon the navigable capabilities of the Yellow River and the Grand Canal was demanded of the Great Council, the Six Boards and the Nine Offices, with a view to facilitate the transit of rice from one part of the Empire to the other; and the required report being submitted, the question was referred to Li Hung-chang, the Viceroy of Chihli, who with one stroke of his pen vetoed the whole business. His arguments were plausible; and the point he then gained was one not only of great importance to the internal economy of the Empire, but also of considerable value to his own private exchequer. The thing is clear. There were only two routes by which the tribute grain could be conveyed to the Capital; and the result was that all such cargoes as would have been transmitted to the Northern provinces by the great internal highway, were sent from Shanghai to Tientsin by the boats of the China Merchants' Steam Navigation Company, of which the powerful earl is the promoter, and in which he is largely interested. By this policy he succeeded in doing a very good stroke of work for himself and the shareholders; and it is suggestive of the great influence which may be brought to bear upon the mercantile interests of a country in the transition-state of China, when her leading and most influential statesman, who can by a single word overthrow the plans of Councils, Boards, and Offices, has an eye to the main chance, and forces a policy upon the Emperor which conduces at once to his own personal benefit and the furtherance of legitimate trade. It is rare indeed that we see the private interests of a politican coalesce with the public interests of the country which he serves; perhaps, because it is equally rare in the East, or has been hitherto, for the great ones of the earth to engage in commercial enterprise. There is nothing more likely to lead to the opening-up of China than this very spirit, which we find so openly displayed in the doings of Li Hung-chang; and should ever a railway company be started to run from Peking

to Canton with native capital and under native supervision, the
name of the Viceroy of Chihli would most infallibly figure in a
prominent position upon the Board of Directors. It must come,
sooner or later. Free transit through China is an eventual necessity, and, this once acquired, fast transit will be the natural result.
The lumbering waggon and unwieldy junk will be inadequate to
meet the requirements not only of foreigners, but of all who are
brought in any way under foreign influences or control. Of
course, the first railway that is laid down in the wilds
of the interior will prove a hornets'-nest to everybody for
months. It will interfere with Fêngshui, it will desecrate
the peace of homesteads, it will disturb the potted joys
of China's ancestry, it will be looked upon as the incarnation
of devilry gone mad. The West and East will take many years to
shake down together; it is useless to look for a millennium of
prosperity from the moment that the bar of entrance is removed.
We have mentioned a few of the difficulties that will arise,
by way of suggestion; many others will doubtless occur to our
readers. But the sooner they are grappled with the better. The
eventual result is too great, too heavily fraught with good to
thousands, to permit for a single moment a discouraging thought.
The opportunity is one that we have been working and striving
after for many years; when it comes, it will be for us to take the
fullest advantage of the means within our reach, and to use them
for the good of China as well as for our own.

Here, too, the argument to be drawn from analogy is very strong.
It has been much the fashion lately to speak with unqualified admiration of the progressive policy of Japan, and her evident desire
to compensate, in as short a time as possible, for her long period of
darkness, inactivity, and seclusion. The puerile features that have
been manifested in the recent changes, the petty and harassing
legislation, and the monkeyish mimicry of foreign dress and manners that have formed part of the Governmental measures are
looked upon as unfortunate concomitants; but what is applauded
is the spirit of candour and liberality displayed. Now when we

survey these innovations; see foreigners and Japanese travelling cheek by jowl in a railway-carriage,—residing in the Capital,—gazing unmolested, nay, invited, upon the sacred features of the once mysterious Mikado, in his unbecoming foreign uniform—and mutually fraternising upon terms of the most cordial intimacy, it seems almost incredible that, such a few short years ago, it was death not only to any foreigner who was caught upon the soil of Flowery Nippon, but to any Japanese who dared to leave it; that the very name of foreigner was to a native of Japan more exasperating than a scarlet cloth to a rabid bull; and that the Mikado was veiled in mystery from the vulgar gaze, while, in order that no unhallowed eye should pollute him with a glance, he never quitted the precincts of the Palace,—the very Sun being deemed unworthy to shine upon him. Japan was regarded as the emblem of all that was quaint, and unknown, and vaguely beautiful. It was the Atlantis of the East, shrouded in mystic splendours, and invested with a keener and more delightful atmosphere of attractiveness from the extreme danger which attended the incursions of adventurers. Things were never quite so bad as this in China. Is there not something to encourage us in the contemplation of the fact ? Nay, more: if China is likely to be slower than her flighty neighbour, she is all the more likely to be surer. And the influence of Japanese example is working upon her to a degree that foreigners do not and perhaps cannot appreciate. We don't expect, and we don't want, the Chinese to discard their chopsticks, repudiate the various elegances and excellences of their social life, and take to paper-collars and stove-pipe hats;—nay, Heaven forfend ! but we do hope and believe that in course of time they will gradually be brought to see that, in the adoption of Western civilisation, in its highest sense, lies the safest and only way to power and freedom, and true and lasting welfare.

CHAPTER X.

The Extension of Foreign Trade.

MANY and bitter are the jeremiads which have been sung over the stagnation of trade in China. Year after year we have hoped against hope, we have wondered in piteous perplexity how long so dark a time could possibly last, and often have we hailed an imaginary streak of sunlight; but the gloom which settled upon our commercial horizon five years ago hangs sullenly over it still. People cannot understand it. Everybody is more or less familiar with troublous times and days when trade is lax, and even with periodically-recurring panics; but this long period of depression puzzles us, and people are fain to exclaim with weariness that China is played out, and that they had better try their luck elsewhere. This despondency, however, though natural enough, is apt to lead us astray, even with such hard facts staring us in the face; and while we acknowledge how very natural the feeling is itself, we yet hope to show, as briefly as may be, how natural also are the conditions which have led to it, and how very far from hopeless the prospects of China commerce really are. Of course the great trouble is the almost unprecedented fall in the values of produce; a fact which there is no blinking. To bring forward an array of figures to illustrate such a statement would be simply superfluous. The two great staples of export have fluctuated to an extent which has become proverbial, and which in spite of the brilliant fortunes recently showered upon the few who were bold enough to specu-late largely in raw silk, has crippled the resources of some of the wealthiest and most respected of the China firms: ma-

nufactured goods have shown a certain and unvarying loss to
the importer in almost as great a degree as export produce; while
local securities of every description have been subjected to more
violent convulsions still. We grant that it is impossible to over-
state the case, or to present its actual features in a darker or less
promising hue than really belongs to them. But severe though
the pressure be, it is *not* the index of so disastrous an internal and
radical state of commerce as is generally and superficially imagined;
nor does it in any way necessarily betoken even a decline in
prosperity, in the widest sense of the term. These may perhaps
be considered bold words; but one is so apt to take a narrow and
restricted view of things in China, it is so natural for foreign merchants to see the world solely from their own standpoint and to
compress into a minute focus the vast area of general commerce,
that they lose sight of much that has a most important bearing on
the question. Why, the fact is that the years which have been so
disastrous to merchants engaged in the China trade have been
particularly prosperous years to the world at large, and indeed to
the Empire of China itself. Crops have been fine and plentiful,
new sources of mineral wealth have been discovered, and money
has been abundant. This of course does not alter the fact that
China merchants have been more than half ruined. But the reaction is one which might have been expected, and which must
have come sooner or later. The sinews of trade had been stretched
to their utmost; prices had been run up to a height which was
unhealthy and unnatural in the extreme, and consequently, while
they stimulated production to an abnormal extent,—in fact to an
extent far in excess of the world's requirements—checked consumption, and flooded the markets with superfluous and expensive
goods. Naturally a reaction set in, and the fevered pulse sub-
sided into exhaustion; but the very principle which caused the
catastrophe will prove itself the healing power, and 'ruinous'
prices will bring about the double effect of stimulating consumption and curtailing the supply. In the meantime, however, we
must not forget that it is upon the merchant and the merchant

exclusively that the brunt of all this falls. He is the real scape-goat, while the producer and consumer of the article reap the benefit in the long run. And here we find the true cause of the terrible sensitiveness of Shanghai to the commercial barometer· In Shanghai, as in every other open port, the interests of commerce are represented entirely by the mercantile classes—the middle-men. There are no producers, no consumers. Neither foreign nor native manufactures exist, and the balance of trade seems therefore to be cruelly upset, because we see only those who suffer most. Shanghai stands alone—an oasis of activity in a desert of stagnation. If, on the contrary, Shanghai were the seat of manufactures, or the centre of a non-Asiatic country with powerful, though lesser, centres of movement in surrounding provinces, the severe depression now existing would not be felt so keenly. At present the foreign merchant in China has no other resources for his energy and his capital than the mere exchange of produce and sycee, while in other countries new modes of utilising both energy and capital are continually arising. His capital being limited to one or two outlets, these outlets become choked : and unless they are rapidly cleared a commercial crisis comes, and much disaster follows. It is clear therefore that the remedy lies in fresh channels, as the present do not suffice. New fields of industry must be opened up, and 'free transit through China' and free residence *in* China, are the only means to preserve commercial prosperity and international peace. The opening-up of the country and the permission to foreigners of respectability to settle in the interior, we believe to be the great panacea for the ills now suffered. That such foreigners should live under strict Consular supervision would be of course a necessity ; but we are convinced that until fresh fields of enterprise and new scope for talent are thrown open, the trade of China will be subject to periodical fluctuations. far exceeding in severity those to which ordinary trade is liable. As long as investments are limited to the old paths, warnings to be cautious will fall upon deaf ears ; the capital afloat must find employment, and, in default of discovering new fields to irrigate, go to swell the already overburdened channels of what is now called legitimate commercial enterprise.

Before commenting further on what appears to us to be the natural remedy for this diseased condition of our trade, we wish to call attention to a system, written about *ad nauseam*, but which is incontrovertibly sapping the foundations of foreign commerce, and wresting it quietly, unobservantly, yet surely, out of the hands of foreigners themselves. We refer to the open and daily violation of Treaty rights by the authorities in the interior of China, in levying illegal taxes upon foreign goods *in transitu*, in addition to the legal and recognised inland dues.* The importance of this subject is supreme; for, connived at by the Government on the one hand, and virtually fostered by the fatal apathy of foreign representatives at Peking upon the other, this crying abuse is putting a certain, though gradual, end, to the use of foreign goods altogether, and therefore to foreign commerce generally. One is so apt to turn petulantly from the continual discussion of Treaty rights, as though one had no interest in them whatever, but as being something for Ministers and diplomatists exclusively to trouble their heads about, that it is perhaps difficult at the first blush to realise the enormous stakes involved. There are influences at work in high places, of which the general public know nothing; influences which permeate the entire economy of Chinese official life throughout the Empire, and which are hostile to the foreigner. Li Hung-chang is notorious for his anti-foreign prejudices, and he is working with an anti-foreign object in view. Chung-how, whose name has been mentioned as the possible successor of Mr. Robert Hart, the present Inspector-General of Imperial Maritime Customs, is known to be an urgent advocate of the establishment of native cotton-mills, with the avowed intention of rendering the Chinese independent of foreign manufactures. The aim of this policy is clearly to starve the foreigner out of the country. Meanwhile no restriction has been placed upon the illegal

---

* The abuses here referred to will, it is hoped, be somewhat mitigated when Sir Thomas Wade's Chefoo Convention comes into force.

taxation of foreign goods, which are burdened with imposts and exactions of which we never dream; and the consequence is, that, the facility of transit being stopped, the issues of trade are stifled and commerce languishes and dies. Small wonder, indeed, that the importation of goods is attended with such disastrous results. The people simply cannot afford to buy them, and for reasons the most obvious to all. When therefore our eyes are opened to such a condition of affairs as this:—when we see our treaties ignored, our goods burdened with squeezes, consumption falling back upon native produce, and, in a word, *trade passing slowly but surely out of our hands*, we are tempted to ask: To whom are we to look for the protection of our interests; and, would it not have been better for the British Minister, previous to the impetus he received by the outrage in Yunnan, to have eschewed the study of Chinese ethics in favour of the more important duties which called so loudly for his care?

It is clear, therefore, that the remedy for all this lies in the opening-up of China. This is a proposition which probably no one will dispute. But we submit that the manner in which this step will eventually be brought about is very different from the popular idea, which is about as unreasonable as it is vague. So great and radical a change must come gradually; and the only way in which it ever will come we believe to be the throwing-open of new seats of trade. Supposing the Chinese Government were to proclaim suddenly that any foreigner who chose might go anywhere into the interior and do there whatever he liked, what practical benefit should we gain? The mere legalisation of an impossibility is no use. Bare permission solves no difficulties. And this is what so few people really see. Yet the very same persons look upon the multiplication of open ports as after all of doubtful practical value to foreign commerce, although the step may be accepted as an indication that the Central Government is becoming more amenable to reason and to the considerations of industry and progress. Surely, this is a very superficial view to take of the matter. In the first place a good deal depends upon the situation of a newly opened port. One town may not be worth opening. Its surroundings may be agriculturally poor and industrially insignificant. There may be no enterprise already existing, little or no consumption for the goods on offer, no productions worth the name. Both geographically and commercially every avenue branching off from the centre itself may be a *cul-de-sac*, leading nowhere and to nothing further. This is to a certain extent the position of every open port, and will be until more ports are open. But every fresh concession of this nature is a step in the right direction. Lately several more towns have been added to the list, among which are Ichang, Wuhu, and Wênchow. Will this prove useless? Look at the position of Wênchow. It is a sea-port city in the province of Chekiang, situated just half-way between Ningpo and Foochow, and embodying in itself the elements of much commercial prosperity. It has been said that the opening of Wênchow to foreign trade will have a serious effect, sooner or later, upon Foochow; but we believe that the only places at all likely to suffer at first are a few neighbouring coast-ports of insignificant standing, which during the last sixteen years have attracted the legitimate trade of Wênchow to themselves. This remark refers almost exclusively to the trade in tea. " Previous to the year 1861," says Mr. Bowra, late Commissioner of Customs at Ningpo, " this " was the only port in the department at which tea was allowed " to be exported ; which, in a measure, made it the market for the " trade of the surrounding country. The city was then in a " flourishing condition. But in order to prevent the teas from fall- " ing into the hands of the T'ai-p'ing rebels, who overran the whole " district during that year, this regulation was exchanged for the " one now in force, which authorises the exportation of tea at any " of the Custom-houses along the coast ; consequently, the enormous " trade formerly concentrated here now finds its way to all the " minor ports on the seaboard." The opening of the city will therefore re-divert this lost trade to itself again, and Wênchow will probably become an important emporium for the purchase and export of tea. Besides this, it is supported by a commercial basin in the immediate neighbourhood, lying between the great tea-producing countries of Northern Che-kiang on one side and Fuh-kien to the south; so that even in its present condition it contains great capabilities of development. Agriculture flourishes in the department where it lies. Twenty-seven miles north-east of the *fu* city a peculiar description of tea is grown called An-shan, celebrated throughout the Empire for its delicacy of flavour, and purity. In addition to an inexhaustible supply of alum, there are fields of iron and silver, which however have never yet been properly worked. Is not this place worth opening? Then look at Wu-hu. This is a district city in the prefecture of T'ai-p'ing in the province of Ngan-'hui, and lies a few miles up the Yang-tsze beyond Nan-king. It is the centre of an extensive trade, and, like Shanghai, boasts a Tao-t'ai for the supervision of its commerce. Long before it was formally opened to foreigners, river-steamers were in the habit of calling there to land and take up passengers, and its complete unclosing will develop commercial possibilities of no mean extent. Lastly, think of all we may look forward to from the opening of Ichang, a city which is situated in the very heart of the Empire, and to-day the centre of a thriving trade. When Ichang is opened it will be the source from which a new tide of commerce will flow and mingle with the currents already permeating the Empire from other markets. Here, again, we must not forget that we have lately secured the opening of a trade-route *viâ* the Burmese frontier; thus the opening of Ichang will help to spread the tide of business in this direction, and meet the influx of trade through Burmah half-way. Lately the French have gained an important footing in Tongquin, and it is impossible not to feel a keen interest in their future fortunes in that country, for we have an indirect stake in them ourselves. At present their prospects are not brilliant. The commercial regulations of Haiphong are unnecessarily stringent, and the infringement of any article entails a severe penalty. The spirit in which they are drawn up is essentially narrow, and betrays much ignorance of the exigencies of Eastern trade. Too much protection is the very curse of commerce in the colonies of France; the merchants are absolutely strangled with being over-cared-for by their Consuls. This is particularly unfortunate in the case of Tongquin, as the trade of the country requires development before it can assume any considerable proportions, and any unnecessary stringency will be fatal. Of course, it is not only on account of its own commerce that we should like to see freer play given to enterprise in Tongquin. Its chief importance to us lies in the fact that the river on which Haiphong is situated forms the link or highway between the open sea and the province of Yunnan, and it is this fact which makes us jealous of over-zeal in the administration of its commercial affairs. Now that Consular agents are to reside in Chung-king and Ta-li Fu, we trust that some time or other the French and English may coöperate at Peking to bring about the opening of the frontier between Annam and Yunnan, as well as that between Yunnan and Burmah. This we believe to be the most important advantage likely to be gained by the establishment of French authority in Tongquin : and we trust it will not be lost sight of by those most interested in its ultimate achievement. The object of several Expeditions, all failures hitherto, will be attained, and it will eventually be found necessary that the country between Tongquin and the main body of the navigable Yang-tsze-kiang shall be surveyed by competent engineers with a view to the rapid and unhindered transit of passengers and goods. Thus we shall have a clear and uninterrupted passage straight through the Empire, from Shanghai to the Western frontier of Yunnan, and the largest foreign mart be directly connected with one of the wealthiest and most fertile provinces. The difficulties in the way of this project are chiefly those connected with the engineering that would be necessary for the construction of a better highway than at present exists through the rich though rugged country of Szechuen : but all diplomatic difficulties have now been overcome. The opening of this trade-route will, we believe, solve the difficulties to which we have referred above, and place at our disposal fresh channels for the distribution of foreign goods and fresh fields of employment for both foreign labour and foreign capital. When this new outlet is provided, the balance which has been lost for so long will be readjusted, and a season of healthy prosperity set in. The province of Yunnan itself is one of the most fertile in the Empire, alike in soil and in mineral wealth. The sparkling grains of gold-dust which are washed down in the sand by the rivers and torrents that descend from the mountains and water the entire country so plentifully and with such fertilising effect, give fair promise of mines of the same precious metal in the elevations whence they spring. Copper is abundant, both red and white; the necessaries of life are cheap and plentiful. The inhabitants and soldiery appear to have rather changed in character since Du Halde described them as being " of a mild and affable " temper, and fit to study the sciences;" although on the old principle familiar to us in our schoolboy days, respecting the faithful cultivation of the ingenuous arts and its effects upon one's manners, they may at any rate be considered in a state in which the study of the sciences might be beneficial. The exploitation of this fair, lawless province will doubtless be attended with many dangers at first; but the prospects of the future are too bright for us to allow the risks inseparable from all enterprise to paralyse our intentions and our hands.

In conclusion : we must not forget that the extension of trade in the opening-up of China has a double aspect. It is a mistake to regard the subject simply from an outside, and, we may add, selfish point of view : the enlargement of commercial enterprise in China is calculated to benefit the Chinese themselves, and this is a fact which should not be lost sight of by the mercantile portion of our communities. It is natural, no doubt, for foreigners to fret and fume at the slurs which are occasionally cast upon them by home writers, and the charge of selfish aims and narrow, unscrupulous views which is so frequently brought against them : but it behoves them to guard against laying themselves open to such inuendoes, and it is difficult to deny that, as a rule, the element of selfishness does enter, perhaps more than it should, into their calculations. We may therefore venture the remark that, as a fact, the inhabitants of many commercial districts in China have been most anxious that their trade should receive the impetus of an influx of foreign enterprise; and we are glad in the interest of the Chinese nation at large whenever the Imperial Government so far extends the provisions of the foreign Treaties as to throw open fresh ports to the healthy influence of outside commerce. Free trade is the backbone of a nation's prosperity: so that the interests of the foreign merchant are, in point of fact, identical with those of China itself. Sooner or later, we doubt not that the barrier which divides the Middle Kingdom from the outer world will be broken down, and the oldest nation upon the face of the Earth be forced to participate in, and contribute to, the universal weal. Recent events that we have witnessed, and coming events, the forecast shadows of which we all of us recognise, point to the conclusion that the final opening-up of China is not far off. The free transit of foreign goods through the interior will, when achieved, necessitate the working of those rich and various mines in which the soil of the country so greatly abounds; the introduction of railways, a beginning of which has been already made, will exercise a purgative influence upon society, upsetting the venality of the mandarins and the corruptions of the Government: a way will be cleared for the full ingress of Western civilisation, Western commerce, and Western truth: and then, but not till then, will China be great, and noble, and free.

CHAPTER XI.

The Doctrine of Previous Rights.

EVER since the summer of 1875, when general attention both in China and at home was fixed upon the political crisis in the North, a good deal of comment has been hazarded with respect to the stipulations embodied in the Code of Demands presented by our Minister to the Chinese Government. Not the least important of these stipulations was the opening of the trade-route between Yunnan and Bhamo; and upon this point a certain amount of wariness, the result of some not unnatural misapprehension of international law, characterised the utterances of the public. There seems to have been a general impression that the requisition could have been obtained through the Indian Government; although it was a moot point with many whether, according to the strict letter of the British Treaty with China, it was a concession to be negotiated for, or a right to be enforced. A perusal of the Treaty of Tientsin will be sufficient to convince the reader that no such provision is therein contained, and that every article which touches upon the right of entry and travel in the Eighteen Provinces presupposes, apparently, the Treaty-ports as the exclusive and only places from which foreigners can claim any permission to start. Hence it follows, upon a superficial view of the question, that any attempt at entry from the Western or any other frontier than that where the Treaty-ports are situated, is, in our present relations with China, illegal, or at least not provided for by Treaty of Tientsin; and to become law must be made the subject of a new convention. But looking a little more deeply into the argument, we

think we are in a position to take up a somewhat different standpoint. It will be conceded on all hands that there are certain
tracts, so to speak, of common understanding between all nations,
the proper recognition of which by both contracting parties is the
only and acknowledged basis of diplomatic intercourse and of special
and further reciprocities. All international relations rest upon
what we may term, for want of a better word, the theory or doctrine
of Previous Rights; and it may be laid down as a broad axiom
that a larger proportion of the wars which have been waged by
enlightened nations against the semi-civilised peoples of the East,
have arisen from infringements of these pre-existent privileges, or
refusal to acknowledge their justice, than from open breaches of
specific stipulations. The existence of Previous Rights is acknowledged in the fullest way by Wheaton, in his 'International
'Law:' there must be a common ground to start from, a natural
law recognised by all nations, on the basis of which *only*, says this
authority, can war be waged, treaties concluded, and commerce
carried on. We fully agree with the Baron von Gumpach in the
view he took,* and to no point is the theory more admirably applied
by him than to the one we are discussing. It requires no diplomatic education to prove to us that the Earth was not intended by
the Almighty to be portioned out to such and such races, much less
to such and such dynasties, to hold as their own personal property.
However widely private territorial possessions may have been extended, among civilised nations, they nowhere and in no case
include mountains or rivers, highways or byeways; and every
educated people of the present day,—we quote the Baron's words—
"recognising, whether consciously or not, the great principle that
"the Earth is the Lord's and by Him given to *man*—freely throws
"open that portion of its territory, to which under its own laws
"the public rights extend, equally to the foreigner and the native
"for the purposes of commerce, science, instruction, and all other
"peaceful and legitimate pursuits."

---

* *The Treaty-Rights of the Foreign Merchant, and the Transit System, in China.*
By Johannes Baron von Gumpach.

It may be open to question, which is the more cogent plea; a moderate and sober argument, put forward by a man of notoriously extreme views, or a startling and, at the first blush, violent theory, advanced by a usually reserved and timid thinker. That the extract we have given from the Baron von Gumpach's posthumous work answers to the former description few candid readers will deny; while as an instance of the second, we think we are justified in citing a passage from a recent article from the pen of Sir Rutherford Alcock, headed 'The Future of Eastern Asia.' Referring to the "restrictive and injurious policy" of China in the very matter under discussion—the barring of our road to Yunnan, either from Bhamo or Ta-li Fu, Sir Rutherford thus proceeds : "Why should "Great Britain submit to it any longer ? Existing treaties may "not give such rights; but international law and usage among "civilised nations acknowledge no absolute right of exclusion. On "the contrary, any act of this kind is justly regarded as an evidence "of enmity, if not an overt act of hostility, and the nation delibe- "rately adopting such policy must bear the responsibility and "accept all the consequences. Hostility begets hostility, and in- "jurious action along the whole of the Chinese inland borders can- "not be compensated by a forced admission of a right of trade on the "coast. The manifest contradiction between the two only tends to "prove a total misapprehension on the part of China of the rights of "nations in mutual intercourse." Such an expression of opinion as this from a statesman who has been often singled out for reproach as being too indulgent in his dealings with the Chinese Govern- ment for the due preservation of foreign interests, gleans, from that circumstance, fresh force. The vacillating and timid Minister now points to the non-concession of a right ignored by Treaty, as a just occasion of hostilities; an apparent change of creed on his part which may almost be regarded as a perfect political conversion. Those disposed to cavil will of course express regret that Sir Rutherford's views with respect to the importance of Pre-existent Rights did not extend to those specific privileges secured to us by Treaty, as far as we may judge from the results of his administration, or that they had not reached their present excellence when he drew up his unfortunate Convention. But now that he is in a sphere where his influence may be propitious while his personal intervention is impossible, we hail with pleasure so sound a declaration, in favour of foreign interests, from his pen.

This point being once established, the results accruing from its practical application are overwhelmingly important. There are many politicians who look upon the annexation of Burmah, if not as virtually an accomplished fact, at least as a highly probable contingency, and we may therefore be permitted to take it into our calculations in weighing the probabilities of the future. As soon, then, as this object is attained, we shall have a double claim; for then our rights of free trade across the frontier of Yunnan will immediately accrue from the application to ourselves of the stipulations in the Russian Treaty, by virtue of the Favoured Nation clause. A careful study of this document will show that the Russians have great privileges of frontier trade, and on no single article of commerce along the entire frontier-line is any duty leviable. Thus the Russians are in the full enjoyment of free-trade with China from the North-west and West, by which they naturally derive no small advantage over the other nations whose commerce has to come coastwise and to pass through the foreign Custom-house; therefore, when we are established on the frontier too, by the occupation of Burmah, we shall by right be in a position to claim the same immunity. An attempt was made some time ago to establish Custom-houses on the North-western frontier, which was resisted by the Russian Government; indeed, the project went so far that officers were already appointed at Urga; but the opposition of the Russians rendered the scheme abortive, and it is at least presumable that, when we occupy a similar position in the South-west, the Chinese will perceive the futility of endeavouring to foist the same restrictions upon English trade. This is a point however which lies almost beyond the scope of the present chapter. Meanwhile we look for the reformation of the past, and the promise of the time to come.

CHAPTER XII.

Opium.

THE Opium-trade between India and China has, for the last twelve years, been undergoing a steady and radical change. For a long time after its first introduction, the Chinese were quite willing to receive the drug into the country as one of the ordinary articles of import, calling it the "foreign medicine"; and from being used, at first, for remedial purposes, it developed into a source of sensual enjoyment—questionable or no is not our present business to discuss—and grew fast in popularity and demand. The warnings of philanthropists and the resistance of the native Government were alike powerless to arrest the rapid extension of the now increasing trade; the Chinese had smoked opium, and, like the animal who has once tasted blood, had created or discovered a passion which, once aroused, was not to be quelled without the gratification it demanded. The drug was imported largely, but the consumption was never unequal to the supply; and at the present moment the opium smoked yearly in the eighteen provinces of China exceeds the correlative amount of twenty years ago, by exactly three times the quantity. It is to this enormously increased demand that may be traced the change that has come over the trade at large, and that has given an entirely new aspect to the much vexed opium question. The importation has not kept pace with the requirements of the people, and the consumers of the drug have resorted to the natural remedy of cultivating the poppy for themselves.

Now a very few words are necessary to show the immense hold that the consumption of opium has gained upon the people in

their social character, and the importance which attaches to its
cultivation from the standpoint of political economy. There is no
doubt about the wide and growing extent of the land devoted to
the purpose. In fact this new branch of agriculture is increasing
everywhere, and although we have found it difficult to obtain
trustworthy information from native sources it cannot be denied
that the poppy is fast becoming a regular domestic crop, and in
many districts is entirely superseding the growth of cereals. This
is principally apparent in the provinces north of the Yang-tsze
river. In Kwangsi, Fuhkien, Hunan and Kwangtung, the cultivation of opium is meagre and in its infancy; it is carried on, to an
equally small extent, in the province of Chekiang; but in the
north, acres upon acres, which till recently were clothed in the soft
green of the springing corn and rice-plants, are now all ablaze
with millions of scarlet flowers. The practice has even spread so
far north as the steppes of Mongolia and Manchuria; but Szechuen
seems to be at present the foremost producing province. The
climate is warm, and the soil so rich and fertile that no less than
three crops may be obtained annually, besides grain and pulse, the
maturing season of which is sufficiently early not to clash with the
larger, and now more important, harvests of the drug. Sown early
in February, it blossoms in April, and before the end of May the
fields are cleared, ready for the sowing of rice. Before the poppy
has arrived at maturity, an intermediate crop of Indian corn, or
cotton, or tobacco may be sown, which commences to peep out of
the sod by the time the old poppy-stalks are ready to be cleared
away. A great quantity of opium is also produced in the province of Yunnan, where, as in Shensi, not only is the native
opium a serious rival to the foreign drug, but, as Baron von
Richthofen informs us, the poppy actually takes the place of
the ordinary uncertain crops of wheat, beans, or rape-seed. This
eminent traveller goes on to remark that about a fiftieth part of the
entire acreage, as far as he can judge, is taken up by this branch
of agriculture, and the poppy is in nearly all instances sown upon
the richest soil in the provinces. The testimony of Dr. Legge,

who traversed the opium-country in the spring of 1873, is very striking. We learn from this traveller that from Tan-ngan Fu down to Tsing-kiang Fu opium is extensively cultivated, and that the temptation it offers to the farmer is very great. A *mow* of land is at least twice as profitable, and in many places productive of three, four, and even six times the revenue, to the peasant, if sown with poppies than if sown with grain. The production had only commenced two years previously, but had taken already a firm hold. This testimony is confirmed by the correlative observations of Mr. Ney Elias, who reports that even six years ago, the cultivation of opium along the line of the old Yellow River in Honan was steadily increasing—wheat and opium being in fact the only winter crops to be noticed in the districts of Kwei-tien Fu and Sui-chow. The southernmost limit of opium-cultivation (we revert to Dr. Legge) is at a town named Tsing-kiang-pu, situated just where the Grand Canal meets the bed of the old Yellow River, but now occupied by the river Hoei. This is the key of communication between Chinkiang and the northern provinces, and through it passes all the foreign trade of that port with the north and north-west. It is, moreover, only about a hundred miles from the Yang-tsze, and within the province of Kiangsu, where Shanghai and Chinkiang are both situated.

The portion of the Empire where, we believe, the influence upon foreign trade of the native growth of opium will be the soonest felt, is Manchuria; in which neighbourhood the cultivation of the poppy is spreading with a rapidity that is simply marvellous. Every farmer, every cottager, however poor, now grows his little plot of opium, which yields him treble the return which cereals have hitherto produced. The soil, not being so rich as that in the southern provinces of China, may not give him three crops a year; but two may generally be counted upon, and the income of the farmer is thereby increased eight, nine, and even ten-fold. The labour involved is light, and not in any way unpleasant; and the only drawback, as far as we can discover, to the new culture, seems to be a tendency on the part of the poppy-plant to impoverish the soil. This, however, may be obviated to a great extent by occasionally sowing an intermediate crop of millet or some other cereal, the roots of which, decaying in the earth, enrich it and provide a stratum of good manure for the succeeding crop of poppies. And whatever the Government of China may think or may have thought about the question of the opium-trade and the consumption of the drug by its lieges generally, we have reason to believe that it is fully alive to the fact that the habit has already taken root too deeply to be incontinently put a stop to. Therefore we find Li Hung-chang, as Governor of Chihli, giving every encouragement to the cultivation of the native plant, and aiding its production to the utmost of his power. Only last year, the poppy-fields of Manchuria yielded no less than four thousand piculs of opium, and had not the weather been unpropitious the harvest would have been more than doubled. Had ten thousand piculs been thus produced, what would have been the fate of the foreign opium-trade between Newchwang and India? Or rather, what is perhaps a still more practical question, what are the future prospects of that trade? The native drug will soon be almost, if not quite, equal to Malwa. Hitherto this branch of agriculture has been in its infancy, and the drug has been clumsily prepared for consumption. Leaves and other unsuitable elements of adulteration have been boiled down in it, and the result, as far as flavour and effect are concerned, has been a failure. But the native growers are getting wiser in their generation, and are taking other and more suitable leaves out of the book of their Indian colleagues. They are now acquiring the art of adding a judicious admixture of sugar, cardamums and other ingredients of similarly agreeable taste, which impart the favourite smack to the Indian drug; and, as the cultivation becomes more and more extended, and more generally recognised as a branch of industry in the country, the greater care that will be taken in its doctoring, and the greater skill acquired in its growth, will combine to produce a very serious and radical change in the prospects of the Indian trade.

Considered in a domestic light, the subject is also full of interest. Now there are not only two, but often several, sides to a question, and we believe that the use of opium by the Chinese is not altogether an unmixed evil. One is apt to overlook the fact that opium is almost the only stimulant the Chinaman has. His tobacco is both rank and weak. Samshu is not indulged in by him to the same extent as wine,·beer and spirits are with us; and it may be a question how far such a stimulant is not almost required, in moderation, by certain constitutions in a malarious climate like that of China. We do not for a moment defend anything like excess in opium, any more than we should defend excess in absinthe or tobacco. But while there are those who see a drunkard's grave looming in the distance for all who take a glass of sherry-and-bitters before dinner, and can talk piously about trembling hands and enfeebled brains to a healthy man who smokes his half-dozen or so cheroots a day, it is not to be wondered at if the same exaggerated arguments are applied to the moderate indulger in the soothing drug. In fact the growing universality of the practice is almost sufficient to controvert such indiscriminate censure. In many of the districts to which we have referred nearly all the guest-rooms in the various houses are provided with opium-pipes and tables, and each visitor is offered a whiff on entering, in exactly the same way as he is served with a cup of tea. If therefore the use of opium in any quantities, however small, were so fatal in its results, we should have a country populated by feeble, emaciated creatures, with the sunken cheeks, clay-like complexion, and hollow eyes that we know, alas! so well, to be the dire effects of immoderate indulgence. But without discussing the *morale* of the question at present—which we touch upon hereafter—let us confine our attention to facts; and we here find a state of things with which the Government has proved itself utterly unable to deal, even if it wished. Supposing the importation of Indian opium to cease to-morrow, there would hardly be a smoker the less; and the only effect of the successive edicts issued by the Government has been to place fresh power in the hands of the local mandarins, to squeeze and extort illicit taxes from the traders. For curiously enough the trader is the scapegoat, while the cultivator—whether on account of a farmer being more highly considered than a merchant or no, we cannot say—is let off with greater leniency. In fact, in spite of its moral homilies and fatherly advice, there is no doubt the Government connives at the cultivation of the drug, which is after all a great source of revenue to the country. Not, however, that it very much matters whether the Government connives or not, or what action it takes in the affair. Practically speaking, it has no settled and specific policy with regard to it, excepting a general desire to shake itself free of all foreign importations whatsoever; but even if it had, it would be powerless to put it in force. Its own paid officials could not be depended upon to second its efforts or carry out its behests; and such are the fiscal arrangements of the country that the interchange of this and many other trade commodities between one district and another is prevented or hindered by a system of cumulative taxation almost prohibitive in its results on legitimate trade. It is simply impossible for goods to escape this vicious organisation, during their conveyance upon a long line of traffic. The squeeze-stations are at a most trifling distance apart, and the trader is just at the mercy of the officials, each of whom has practically purchased his post, and has to look to his depredations to recoup himself for his outlay. Now the Commutation Clause, as it is called, in the Treaty of Tientsin, by which all foreign goods imported by British merchants were (supposed to be) protected during their transit through the interior, leaves foreign opium entirely out in the cold, and excludes it from all participation in the theoretical advantages of the system thus instituted. In fact there is virtually no check upon the amount of extortion and squeezes which are practised by the petty local authorities. The *likin* tax, which is levied upon the drug before it leaves any open port, varies from thirty to sixty taels per chest, according to the convenience of the mandarins. But as soon as it gets past the boundary of the foreign settlements,—which, by the way, has never been properly defined, and it is rather a difficult question to answer

where the 'interior' of China, politically speaking, begins,—then
the extortion system sets in in full force, and there is no limit to
it but the exigencies of the mandarin.* The effect of this is to
confine the internal consumption in no small measure to the native
product; and it is only owing to the enormously increased demand,
and the inferior quality of the Chinese drug in its natural state,
that the Indian trade has not been affected more seriously than is
actually the case.

Now all this not mere theory. At present of course the injury
to foreign commerce is a mere flea-bite. But we have to look to
the future; and when we see the native produce, even now, surely
though slowly elbowing the imported drug out of the market—
supplanting it in the estimation of the common people, creating a
demand which at the same time it supplies in all abundance, offering a cheaper luxury than has hitherto been obtainable, opening
up a new and eminently lucrative field of labour to the husbandman, and, above all, encouraged by the Provincial Government,
does it require the gift of prophetic sight to foretel the inevitable
result in the course of ten or fifteen years? There is not the
slightest reason why China should not grow for herself all the
opium that she can possibly consume. Her acreage is broad
enough; her soil is rich enough; her peasantry are eager, to all
appearance, to cultivate it for themselves. If, then, in these ten
or fifteen years we lose a portion of our trade with China which
has hitherto been worth six millions sterling a year to England, and
gone so far towards increasing the stake we at present hold in
China, what is likely to be the natural result? With an interest
amounting to upwards of 80 per cent of China's entire foreign trade,
we have far more influence to-day than we should have were
we to lose so large a slice as that which seems to be threatening to
slip away from us. China has everything to gain by making the
change that now impends—we have everything to lose. Of course

---

* Since this was penned, the position of opium has been somewhat modified by
the Convention recently concluded between Sir Thomas Wade and the Viceroy of
Chihli at Chefoo.

the resources of India could be developed in other directions; and, though this would doubtless be a work of time, we imagine that the revolution will prove sooner or later inevitable. As far as the Government of China, and its action in the matter, are concerned, we simply see another proof of the continuous and unceasing efforts it is making to shake off the influence of foreigners generally and the English in particular; and it could hardly have selected a more practical method of doing so than by encouraging the Chinese people to grow for themselves an article of consumption, the trade in which has been so lucrative to the British nation and which has formed, so to speak, the most galling link in the chain of intercourse they seem so anxious to break in twain.

But it must, of course, be clear to every candid mind that the policy of the Chinese Government with regard to the importation and growth of opium has nothing whatever to do with the morality of the opium-trade itself. It is often said that while the Government fosters the native cultivation of the plant, it is absurd to charge England with forcing on the Chinese a deleterious drug for the mere sake of a profit to the Indian exchequer; that the occasional protests of the Chinese Government are feeble and insincere at best, and that it would be the height of Quixotism to abandon so valuable a branch of commerce on the bare grounds that many Chinese smoke opium to excess. However undeniable such facts as these may be, the chain of argument into which they are often spun is faulty to a degree. We cannot but consider it proved beyond reasonable doubt that the only objection entertained by the governing body in China to the opium-trade is the enormous amount of foreign influence to which it opens the door; and, recognising the fact that the use of opium has now taken too firm a hold upon the nation to be easily shaken off, it now attempts to supply the demand from the fields of China herself, with a view, in time, to get rid of all dependence upon the imported drug whatever. This is the secret of the Government's so-called opposition to the foreign opium-trade, and it is this, and not the paternal benevolence about which such a maudlin fuss is often made, which lies at the root of the Imperial proclamations upon the subject. But of course we cannot point to such a policy as this as a justification of what is considered by many an immoral trade. If it is immoral to supply the people with an alleged poison, neither the approval nor the disapproval, the honesty nor the insincerity, of that people's Government affects our own position one *iota;* and any attempt to defend the action of the British Government upon this ground, must inevitably prove a failure.

We cannot but think, however, that it is quite an open question whether the Government thus hotly assailed requires any defence at all. The accusation brought against us is that we derive an enormous addition to our revenue by legalising a system which is a curse and a blight to the Chinese; that we, a Christian nation, pander to the indulgence of a vice by a heathen country, for the mere sake of filthy lucre; and we are told that as long as we are guilty of this national sin, so long have we no right to expect the blessing of Heaven. The argument is very plausible, and when taken in conjunction with the moving picture often drawn, of China imploring us to leave her alone and not supply her millions with what is ruining them in body, in intellect, in morals and in purse, assumes the guise of a very solemn prophetic warning. There is quite a flavour of Jeremiah or Eze kiel about the appeals of the opium-Crusaders, and it is not surprising if a good deal of gushing but we think somewhat misplaced enthusiasm is evoked thereby. It all arises from the use of that most stupid and misleading word, *legalise.* To ' legalise' a practice need involve neither protection nor approval. The trade exists; and it cannot be destroyed. Is its taxation, therefore, a tacit proof of Government approval? Does a Government lay heavy taxes and burdens of a fiscal nature, upon any enterprise it wishes to foster and encourage? Surely not. That the Indian authorities should absolutely prohibit the growth of opium can hardly be expected; the most ardent philanthropist can but advocate that the industry and commerce resulting therefrom should be somewhat heavily taxed, and such is, in actual fact, the present condition of the case.

To say that taxation, and such almost prohibitive taxation too, is an encouragement to trade, appears to us a contradiction in terms. So far from the opium-trade being fostered by the Government, it is really subject to restraint. It is clear that, were there no taxation, the export of the drug would increase indefinitely, and it is only by virtue of the wise restrictions placed upon it by the Indian administration, that it is kept in any way within its present reasonable bounds.

As to the question of the alleged deleteriousness of opium, we are fain to express ourselves with caution. That it is a source of ruin and misery to thousands, cannot for a moment be disputed. Yet so is alcohol; and we have the authority of the present Bishop of Victoria for opining that, of the two evils, opium is, in his view, the less. Few missionaries, perhaps, could be led to express themselves thus candidly. They are apt to see this evil in a somewhat exaggerated light, simply because they are brought into such very intimate relationship with the sufferers; and their view lacks breadth in consequence. But there is at the same time no reasonable doubt that the abuse of opium does, in a very great degree, outweigh the benefits derivable from its use. The problem to be decided is: which side preponderates,—the evil or the good ? and common candour compels us to admit, in the face of all the *arguments* on one side and the *evidence* on the other, that the balance is against the drug. The amount of solace and reasonable pleasure derived by the moderate smoker from his daily pipe, is far surpassed by the ruin and desolation caused by excess in the indulgence. We have weighed the matter conscientiously and, we trust, impartially, for a long time past, and this is the conclusion we have come to, making the fullest allowance for all the prejudiced opinions and highly coloured representations offered on one hand and on the other. Opium is not an unmixed evil; but the bad results of it certainly appear to be very much in excess of the good. And what is more, the Chinese themselves are fully alive to the fact. We have nothing to do with the insincere and shuffling policy of the Government; but the vote of the people deserves record.   Of this vote—calm, deliberate, and earnest—we have a cogent illustration in a certain very remarkable Appeal made to the Chinese in the form of a public proclamation, issued by a native philanthropical society and scattered far and wide over the interior.   A copy of this document was seen by a recent traveller in Shantung, on the banks of the Yellow River, and we now present to our readers the translation with which this gentleman has favoured us.   It runs as follows :—

Opium-smoking is a very demoralizing habit ; it leads many of our fellow people astray, causing trouble and dissension in families, and the separation of parents and their children.

We are moved by a sincere and earnest desire to endeavour to stop this destructive practice, which is so rife amongst our fellow-countrymen ; therefore we make this appeal, and communicate a remedy which will stop the indulgence ; by doing which, we trust we are giving no offence.

Safflower 3 ounces, China root ¼-oz., rhubarb ¼-oz., 8 red dates, orange peel 3½ oz., Pe-chuck, 4 dried olives, linseed ½-oz., Canton orange peel 1½ oz. Boil these together and take a dose twice-a-day ; in the morning at rising, and in the evening at going to rest.

So, dear friends, we hope you will bear this mind and resolutely overcome this ruinous habit.

TSEN-SI TAN, Shantung,
(Charitable Society).

Comment upon this is unnecessary.   It is simply, as it stands, an urgent appeal on the part of a body of public-spirited natives to their fellow-countrymen to break off a habit so fatal to their peace and welfare ; and the earnestness, indeed pathos, of the apostrophe would only be injured by dilation.   But it will never lead to any distinct results as long as the Government of China promotes the growth of opium as energetically as it is doing now, even if the taxation by which the Indian Government checks its export so considerably were doubled or even trebled in extent.

CHAPTER XIII.

The Rival Evangelisers of China.

THERE are few callings pursued by foreigners in China more coldly criticised than that of the Protestant missionary. The very
world 'missionary' is seldom uttered in general society without
a covert sneer. His intellectual inferiority to the Catholic propagandist is, justly or unjustly, proverbial. He belongs to a slighted
class. The Protestant missionaries who enjoy the respect of
their compatriots are the exception, not the rule, and owe their reputation more to sinological accomplishments than to ecclesiasti-
cal *prestige*. The fruits of Protestant labour are confessedly discouraging, in spite of the rosy reports so greedily swallowed by
Exeter Hall, and the position which all sympathisers with mission work are forced to occupy is unfortunate in the extreme.
Disposed upon the highest grounds to afford all possible encouragement and assistance to the pioneers of Protestant Christianity
in China, their ardour is checked and chilled by the apparently insignificant results that are achieved, and they chafe helplessly under the sceptical laugh of the unbeliever. Missionaries on the
other hand make no secret of their mortification at the lack of the
sympathy they so much desire, and appear bitterly aggrieved
whenever they hear a Roman Catholic fellow-worker spoken of
with approval. We have no wish to exalt either at the expense
of the other. The system of neither party is perfect; but we very
sincerely believe that, of the two, the principle on which Catholic
missions are conducted is far and away the better, both on ethical
and diplomatic grounds. The difference does not consist altoge-

ther in the higher discipline or more perfect organisation of any
special Order of the Church. It is not entirely owing to the fact
that while Protestants are content to effect questionable conver-
sions of grown men with settled opinions and an eye to the main
chance, Roman Catholics cultivate virgin soil by buying infants
and educating them from childhood in the Western faith. The
superior success of the Romish party is not even due to the imposing ceremonies of their religion, the similitude between their
ritual and that of Buddhism, or any inherent attractiveness of their
creed alone. It must be traced primarily to the great fact of their
utter renunciation of family, fortune, and everything else that
makes the world worth living in, so that, in accordance with the
command of Christ, they have left all, and followed Him.

Now it is not difficult to understand that the enunciation of such
a comparison as this between the Protestant and Catholic missionaries should be particularly unpalateable to the former. It is easy
to rail at the bigotry of the Catholic, to express holy horror at the
assumption of Papal Infallibility, and to explain away the results of
Catholic missionary labour. We are not writing at random when
we record our firm belief that there are many Protestant missionaries of limited education and contracted sympathies, who absolutely refuse to give Romish priests credit for believing their own doctrines. The sneer of sectarianism and only half-veiled anger is immediately observable when the Catholic missionary is so much as
referred to in their presence ; a sneer every whit as bitter as that
of which they themselves complain as being levelled at them by the
unbelieving world. Every word of admiration applied to the Catholic in their hearing is taken as a personal affront, and the speaker
is set down either as a confirmed sceptic, or as an enemy of the
Truth with sentimental proclivities towards the "Apostate Church."
In fact, bigotry is the same all the world over, whether it flourishes
in the bosom of a Moslem or a Protestant, a Greek or a Roman Catholic ; and had been so, long before St. John forbade the man to
continue performing his works of healing love because he followed
not with them. We are not disparaging the Protestant—the pio-

neer of our own religion. But we do say that, in the point of self-denial, the Catholic outshines him far. The one may have left a few of his worldly comforts behind him—though his sacrifice is not greater than that of the majority of his fellow-countrymen in China—to teach the Chinese Christianity; but the other has renounced all—home, country, friends, fortune, nay, even his own identity—for ever, to be Christ to the perishing and poor. His faith has led him to follow his Master's commandment to the full, and to give up *all* for Him. The Protestant gives up half; and is rewarded for the meagre sacrifice by the admiration of audiences at Exeter Hall during his ocaasional visits to England, and by a stipend sufficient for the respectable maintenance of himself and family in China or elsewhere. Can he wonder therefore if the results are meagre too? We say nothing against the man; but we do condemn his system as entirely opposed to the expressed commands of the Great Missionary himself. There is not a sleek bishop in the House of Lords, ranking with an earl and having a sumptuous mansion in St. James's Square, who is less like the simple fishermen whose successor he pleasantly claims to be, than the worthy missionary gentlemen of here and elsewhere are, in the rules and conduct of their avocation, like the earliest pioneers of Christ's religion. No, the system is a bad one. It may be a very laudable, and in a great degree useful, way of earning one's daily bread; but it is no more like Christ's Ideal than it is like the moon. We are convinced that if only the purity of primitive Christianity, which we believe is to be found in the New Testament, and in the New Testament only—were *combined* with the utter self-abnegation seen in Christ and His Apostles, and which has been so ably emulated by the emissaries of the Catholic Church from the time of Polycarp down to the year of grace 1876, no power in the Universe would be able to resist the overwhelming force of the One and True Religion among the nations of the world at large.

The Catholic missionaries, again, are one and all picked men; and, in most instances, gentlemen of culture and breeding. They are highly proficient in science, and their accomplishments are all devoted to the great end they have in view. With the Protestants it is different. True, there are numbers of great men still among them, and while we find such honoured names as Martin, Edkins, Williams, Muirhead, Legge, Moule, Burdon, and Russell, upon the muster-roll we cannot but speak with respect of the entire body. But there are others whose claim to set up as teachers and preachers it is difficult to divine : men with little or no education, utterly devoid of either culture or address, and fresh, apparently, from the village workshop or blacksmith's forge. These gentry, actuated doubtless by worthy though sadly misplaced motives, come to China, unhesitatingly—we had almost written unblushingly—style themselves 'Reverend,' and attempt to instruct the Chinese in the ethics of Christianity. If they do any good, we can only say it is a wonderful instance of the Almighty having chosen the foolish things of this world to confound the wise ; but we fear that the cause of missions generally has but little to thank them for. We are glad however to believe that the bulk of missionaries in China are formed of very different clay ; though it is possible that this defect in Protestant missionary organisation may in some measure account for the lofty and almost insolent contempt with which they are regarded not only by a certain section of the public, but also by the Catholics. A curious and at the same time somewhat amusing incident illustrative of this feeling occurred some time ago in the province of Shantung, and before proceeding to consider the subject of Catholic missions at large we may be forgiven for introducing it *en passant*. One fine morning, good Father X—— was surprised by a visit from several well-dressed and intelligent-looking Chinese, who courteously requested a little conversation with him on religious matters. The worthy Father was enchanted, and in answer to their enquiries held forth for a long time on the doctrines of the One True Faith. The deputation listened with respectful attention, and then said— " But there is another missionary living not far from you, Sir, who " also preaches the religion of Jesus, though he does not belong to

"your particular communion. How about him ? Do you not re-
"cognise him as a fellow-Christian ?   Can he not also be 'saved,'
"although he differs from you on various minor points ?"—referring
to a neighbouring Protestant clergyman, an exception to his brethren
on the score of liberality.   The Father replied in the usual strain of
reputation; Protestants were worse even than the heathen themselves: there was not, nor ever could be, the slightest sympathy
between them: and neither the Rev. Y. Z—— nor any of his co-
religionists had any chance of salvation as long as they perversely
remained out of the pale of the Church.   His visitors listened
quietly, and then remarked that it was very odd; for they had just
been 'interviewing' this very man on the same subject, and
in answer to their enquiries about him—Father X——, Mr. Z. had
told them that, although they differed on certain matters, he looked
upon the priest as quite as good and sincere a man as himself; and
of course with as good a prospect of getting to heaven at last!
"Therefore," concluded the deputation, "we think that his form of
"religion is, on the whole, a better one than yours; and if we be-
"come Christians we certainly shall not embrace Catholicism."
The Father was dumb with surprise and indignation, as the visitors
withdrew; and ever since he has cherished bitter feelings against
the Protestant for taking so mean an advantage of the Church.

Now the Catholic system of propagandism, like every other system in the world, has its bad as well as its good side.   The Catholics have undeniably done more for the enlightenment of China
than any other class who ever visited its shores or professed to
have the interest of its people at heart.   But they not 'infallible;'
and one of their weakest points is an undue and quite unreasonable love of persecution.   We treat this peculiarity at present as a
simple error of judgment, and one which, in its exaggerated form,
is certainly confined to Roman Catholics.   They seem to enjoy
being maligned, and positively luxuriate in being beaten.   Of
course we know that persecutions have always been regarded by
the Christian Church as a special sign of the Divine favour, a special opportunity for the manifestation of Christian fortitude, and a

special means of showing forth, in the resignation of the persecuted, the triumphant power inherent in religious Faith. It is an incontrovertible truth that the Church has never flourished so truly as when watered with the blood of her children; never has her faith been so pure or her zeal so fervent as when put to the test of fire or of sword. The martyr's crown has been the highest ambition of the most ardent souls, and men have embraced the stake, refusing every compromise, that they might obtain the coveted reward. But this over-eagerness, as one may call it, to suffer persecution for conscience' sake, involves one or two minor results which somewhat interfere with the high object held in view. In the first place, missionaries, upon whom the honourable scourge is most apt to fall under the present conditions of society, are tempted almost unconsciously to exaggerate the trials to which they are exposed, and claim sympathy for dangers and misadventures which could sometimes have been averted by the exercise of little common prudence. Nor is this all. By so doing they involve their own authorities in unnecessary trouble, and, while they stoutly proclaim their dependence upon Him in whose work they are engaged, do not disdain to rely upon the practical protection of a gunboat by way of a second string to their bow. It may seem a trifle inconsistent for those who profess to go forth with their lives in their hand, to appeal to the secular arm, and we are inclined to think it is so; but we do not care to discuss this point at present. Besides which, whatever may be the nature of the criticisms that have been passed upon Protestant missionaries, it is impossible for us to deny that such faults on their part as have given rise to disturbances have been of the most venial description. Their system may not be so good in some respects as that of their Romish colleagues, but there is nothing in their method of working to excite the hatred and jealousy of the official class, or the ill-will of the populace. We have occasionally stated in public wherein we consider the Romish system superior to that of the Protestants, and we have been roundly abused for our candour in so doing. We have been suspected of

being secretly devoted to the interests of the Papacy, and a few critical though we hope temperate remarks upon a wholly unpolemical
question taken as a proof of our hidden belief in the infallibility of
the Pope. Our present readers might as well suspect us of being in
the pay of the Chinese Government on account of the admiration
we have sometimes been led to express at the native system of banking. Absurd as all such misapprehensions and false deductions are,
we still feel an unwillingness to be misunderstood, or to have our
impartiality so egregiously misconstrued. The remarks that we
have to make may therefore cause some surprise to our Protestant
readers; not however that there is anything new in what we are
about to say, but because it may seem strange to them that anybody who is so perverted as to see anything whatsoever to admire
in the Romish system of working can possibly admit a flaw. But
there is one practice indulged in by emissaries of the Catholic
faith which has hitherto received little attention from the general
public, and which we think cannot too strongly be condemned.
We refer to the assumption, by Romish Bishops, of the titles and
honours of the mandarinate; a policy which on both religious and
political grounds is reprehensible in the very highest degree. We
have every respect for the missionary, be he Catholic or Protestant, who leaves the softnesses of life, and, Cross in hand, follows
single-hearted and in poverty in the footsteps of his Master and
the Apostles. To such a man, if persecution comes, it comes in a
path where he can meet it with a pure conscience and unwaver-
ing faith, assured that it is by no sin or folly on his own part that
he has incurred the peril. He can meet it as S. Paul met his pe-
rils, counting not his life dear unto himself, and may look forward
to the martyr's crown hereafter. But we should have had neither
sympathy nor respect for S. Paul if he had arrogated to himself
the rank and honours of a heathen tetrarch, and disputed with
Porcius Festus or Agrippa the right of judging his own converts.
How then can we sympathise with a modern Bishop in Chihli or
Szechuen who constitutes himself the head of an *imperium in im-
perio*, who receives the same honours as a Fu-t'ai, who rides pom-

pously in a green official chair preceded by yamên-runners and
outriders in official costume, who is received with a salvo of artillery on his arrival in a town or village, who accepts the *ko-t'ow*,
who claims the right of jurisdiction over the native Catholics, and
interposes his authority between the people and their rulers?
Where shall we find any precedent to justify such strange presumption? Certainly not in the traditions of the Early Church;
certainly not in the acts of the Apostles themselves. In the Scrip-
tures? Hardly; for there the chief of the Apostles, he who was
pre-eminently the Apostle to the Gentiles, is careful to incul-
cate submission to the authorities and honour to the King, and
nowhere do we find him permitting his converts to resist the powers that be, but rather to suffer persecution. The idea of a Christian priest arrogating to himself and aping the honours of a Pagan
magnate is indeed an anomaly in the sight of sceptics and believ-
ers alike. The pomp and luxury of Cardinals, those "Princes of
"the Church," constitute the only precedent, as far as we can see,
for the pretensions of the Bishops in the East; and a miserable
precedent it is. "On my arrival at Ting-lan," writes a certain Vicar
Apostolic in the *Annales de la Propagation de la Foi,* "I was salut-
"ed with a discharge of eighteen guns, to say nothing of fireworks
" . . . . Some of the natives tied a long rope to the poles of
"my palanquin, as is done when great Chinese dignitaries travel
"abroad, and began to pull with all their might . . . . At the
"head of the procession were the trumpeters, and behind and before
"were the musicians." Is it any wonder, therefore, that we hear
from time to time of the "persecution" of Roman Catholics in Szechuen? Is it any wonder that the mandarins regard, not only with
jealousy, but with fear, the arrogant behaviour of these foolish
priests? About a year ago, a French Bishop presented himself at
the gates of a city in Chihli called Yen-p'ing Fu, riding in a
green official chair and accompanied by a numerous and imposing retinue. The gate-keeper, however, took upon himself
to shut the door in the face of the holy father, who sent an
interpreter on to the Chefu to announce his arrival and request a

more courteous reception. Whereupon the mandarin asked the delegate who he was : what business he had in hand : and whether his master had anything particular to say to him ? And the replies of the interpreter being unsatisfactory, he coolly threw him into prison. On this news reaching the ears of the Bishop he was much grieved, and sent again another messenger to demand the release of the first. This after a time was granted, but only on condition that the Bishop took himself off there and then; which it seems the Bishop found it advisable to do. In fact he had no choice. And why was he refused admission ? Not because he was a Bishop, but because he travelled with all the state and paraphernalia of a high mandarin. It is a shame that Christianity should be saddled with odium which is simply the result of political intrigues; and it is vain and worse than vain on the part of the Catholic Church to appeal for sympathy or lay claim to the crown of martyrdom, on the ground of persecutions deliberately provoked by actions so thoroughly opposed to the spirit and teachings of our faith.

The *political* danger that is thus incurred is a theme which has already received attention from diplomatists. The present tactics of the Roman Catholics in China have been denounced by several of our representatives, as may be seen by reference to the Blue Book (China—1, 1872), where Earl Granville, Sir Thomas Wade, and Mr. F. F. Low express themselves strongly and sensibly upon the subject. It is no cause for surprise that the mandarins of China—we trust none of our friends will suspect us of being secretly devoted to the interests of the Mandarinate—regard the tactics of the Jesuits as far more political than religious; neither need we be at all astonished if they take stringent measures every now and then to stem their growing influence. We know pretty well the plea of "expediency" that would probably be put forward by the Catholic; but it is false and shortsighted policy at best. "The "assumption of the insignia and paraphernalia of authority to "which they can have no possible right," said the *Pall Mall Gazette*, in commenting upon the state of propagandist labours in the West of China, "and the habit of using their advantages to ride rough-

"shod over the prejudices of the people, are weaknesses to which
"the Roman Catholic missionaries are, by their own account of
"themselves, much prone, and they are weaknesses which give
"strength to their opponents."

And yet, not only have Jesuits contributed more to the instruction and enlightenment of the Chinese than any other body of
men, but there are few phases in the history of China more interesting than that in which we have the early Jesuits presented
to us as playing so prominent a part in Court politics. It was
perhaps during the reign of the great Emperor K'ang-hi that they
flourished most vigorously, and attained the greatest height of
popularity and power. They had worked their way upwards by
the graceful courtliness of their address, the æsthetic accomplishments which they possessed, and the very high position in science
to which they had attained. Skilled as they were in the practical
sciences of astronomy, geography and mathematics no less than in
the arts of painting, architecture and music, the enlightened mind
of the reigning monarch appreciated to the fullest extent the value
of their services; and the high esteem they earned for themselves
among the hierarchy of China, while fraught with danger, at the
same time secured for them the respect of their bitterest foes.
Occupying thus a position where they might be, and indeed were,
hated, but could never be despised, it is not to be wondered at if
numbers of the educated classes first examined and then embraced
the doctrines which they came to preach. The principal source of
hostility seems to have been the Li-pu or Board of Ceremonies,
and, worried by its importunities, the Emperor at one time issued
a proclamation against the Christian religion; but the missionaries,
in addition to their other attainments, proving themselves political
diplomatists of no ordinary skill, and rendering the Court certain
services in connection with Russia which laid the Emperor under
exceptional obligations, the manifesto was rescinded shortly after
its promulgation. The Jesuits were loaded with honours: they
united the grace of courtiers with the erudition of philosophers,
and their influence became so great as to intensify the jealousy of

the native mandarins and princes. Having achieved a position at Court unrivalled, indeed unapproached, by any other foreigners in the world since the Israelitish shepherd became the Prime Minister of the proudest dynasty in Africa, and Daniel and the Three Children found favour in the eyes of the Babylonish monarch, the Jesuits were eventually driven from Peking because of their meddling and intrigues. Their expulsion was the natural reaction from the undue reverence in which they had been held, the result of annoyance at the political schemes in which they were constantly engaged, and of dread at the ultimate issues of their growing power. Their ascendancy proved their ruin : their fatal aptitude and fondness for intrigue undid much good that they had accomplished. But, apart from politics, the Jesuit plan of working is unique, magnificent ; it combines the inculcation of precept with instruction in every useful science, and its success attests its merits. Take as a sample of their missionary enterprises the Jesuit College at Sikawei, a village about six miles west of Shanghai : an establishment which it is impossible to visit without being deeply impressed in more ways than one. So admirable is its organisation, so complete the development of the scheme, so perfect are all the arrangements and so wide is the scope of the undertaking, that whether it is regarded from the standpoint of missionary, educational, or political enterprise, the ideas suggested to any thoughtful and reflective mind are, we think, of sufficient importance to warrant us in bestowing some consideration upon it as we pass. The institution has been in existence for twenty-seven years, and consists of several departments : including seminaries devoted to both the elementary and more advanced branches of literature, science, and the fine arts, and containing Chinese and foreign libraries of no small value. The Orphanage connected with the College is, however, the most interesting portion. The pupils are the children of pagan families, who have been left in destitution. All are welcomed and cared for, clothed, and fed, and educated. Knowing neither home nor friends themselves, they naturally look upon these benignant foreigners, who speak their language and wear their dress, as their natural protectors. Nor is this all. Every one of these children is taught a trade; and we have seldom seen a more interesting sight than when we visited the rows of light, airy, well-built houses that form the workshops of the establishment. Each branch of industry is here represented; and no lad leaves the Orphanage without having some one trade at his fingers' ends, by which he will be enabled to earn an honest and comfortable livelihood. Tailors, shoemakers, carpenters, joiners, carvers, printers, painters, sculptors, book-binders, varnishers, all ply their handiwork from morning till night, the apprentices learning, and those who have acquired the requisite amount of proficiency being regarded as journeymen or masters, and receiving their pay accordingly. They may leave when they like, and there are now some two hundred tradesmen working in Shanghai, who learnt their craft at this establishment. The progress made by these youths in art, too, is really marvellous. It would be difficult to describe the admirable productions we have seen in the various studios, and the great talent which is there displayed, without seeming to trench upon the borders of exaggeration. But all who have admired the exquisite delicacy of what is generally known as Ningpo carving, will have no difficulty in imagining the same niceness and finish of detail and beauty of effect, transferred to a painting on canvas. The principal line of art, however, in which the pupils of the Fathers have distinguished themselves, is undoubtedly that of sculpture; and the Spanish lay-brother who once presided over this charming study, produced himself the figure of a dead Christ, so beautiful in its proportions, and so pathetic in the expression of the lifeless features, distinctly traceable under the veil which covers them, as to leave a deep impression on the minds of all beholders. The pupils of the College (children of Catholic families) are educated in every branch of learning likely to promote their interests and welfare among their own people. The study of the Chinese classics is so well enforced that a large number of former pupils have been successful in the competition for literary degrees, while the study of foreign literature and the sciences of history, geography and arithmetic is not neglected; for, as Dr. Martin of Peking ably observed some years ago at the Synod held at Chefoo, no one who had read Confucius would ever revile him, and his writings would be incorporated into the future Christianity of the country. He believed that the works of Confucius and Mencius would as certainly be integral parts of the future Christian civilisation of China as the *De Officiis* of Cicero had been in the civilisation of the West. Wisely, therefore, do the Catholic missionaries build their educational structure upon the foundations already laid, instead of incontinently tearing them up and seeking to lay fresh ones. To sum up our observations in two words: the inmates of the Jesuits' College at Sikawei are taught everything likely to be of service to themselves, and to make them of service to the cause of those who teach them.

Now we have not indulged in this short recapitulation of the work which is being done in the neighbourhood of Shanghai for the mere sake of crying up this or any other institution in particular. It is because we think a very deep principle is here involved, and that two most important lessons may be learnt; one referring more especially to the ethics of missionary enterprise, and the other bearing with almost equal power upon the future political prospects of the Empire. The wisdom shown by the Jesuits in all their dealings with the Chinese has lain chiefly in retaining and using what their Protestant *confrères* appear to have rooted up. The Protestants have yet to learn that the man who commences his propagandist labours by vilifying Confucius is preparing but a cold reception for Christ. The Romanists on the other hand have recognised the truth of Mahomet's aphorism that to every country Allah has given a prophet in its own tongue; so that by respecting and treating with tenderness the cherished books, creeds, and superstitions of the Chinese they have conciliated where others have shocked, have availed themselves of the very weapons brought against them, and have sown the seeds of future strength by the education and training of the young. We regard this matter from a purely impartial point of view. It is a question of expediency and administration. Imagine a number of colleges such as we have described scattered here and there over the length and breadth of China. Eliminate the idea of religion altogether for the nonce—regard them simply as centres of education and enlightenment. What results would not be accomplished in a hundred years? There is now a considerable village at Sikawei, inhabited almost exclusively by men and women who have been brought up under the care of these foreign preceptors: for there is a neighbouring establishment of Sisters, where girls are cared for too. Supposing the influence of Western knowledge to emanate from many such seats of learning, and communities to be thereby formed in various portions of the Empire consisting of men and women conversant with the ethics and sciences of the West, what results might we not consistently expect? Not political results: none of those mighty upheavings of an oppressed and struggling mass against the tyranny of their oppressors, or even a bloodless revolution in which the superior enlightenment of the educated people would bring into glaring relief the blindness of the rulers of the land. But to feel that an elevating, enlightening, and purifying influence is at work among the millions of Cathay; to feel that the leaven of Western knowledge and Western truth is at work, however slowly, in the great lump of Chinese humanity; to feel that something is being done to eradicate the old-world rubbish which chokes up the path of true intellectual progress;—to this we may, and we do, look forward. Facts—proofs—logical reasonings, and the clear, cold light of common everyday science, such as is taught in every village school in England, would do more to clear away all the clinging mists and fogs which now obscure the mental vision of the Chinese than all the ridicule and vilification in the world. What student of Mangnall's Questions could believe in Fêng-shui, or the meaningless jargon that we find in Han Wen-kung and similar writers, expressive of the universal faith which is cherished in demonology and fetichism? It is for this that we should work. Preparation must come before fruition. We very much doubt whether the

Chinese would be benefited by a sudden and violent political shock. Let the people first be educated; let some of the more poisonous and deep-rooted weeds first be pulled up, and the good seed sown instead; and then, whatever changes may occur in the government of the country, however great may be the political disorganisations which are written in the book of fate, the true conquest of China will already have been commenced.

And now, to conclude an unconscionably long chapter, one word to Catholics and Protestants alike. Whether China is to come into the comity of nations in a true sense depends upon whether China is to cast her idols to the moles and to the bats, and to accept the faith of Western lands. We make this assertion in the face of the fact that much uncertainty prevails in the West on the subject of Christianity. We know that many thinking men in Europe have "renounced as illegitimate the conception of Cause" —and treat the dogmas of Christianity with undisguised contempt. Still there can be no doubt that until the spirit of Christ's religion gets abroad in China we shall not approach the Chinese upon the highest grounds, and there will be misunderstandings and difficulties without end. This being the case it is the primary duty of the missionary to exhibit the spirit of the religion he preaches everywhere and always in his communications with the natives. He must of course preach zealous sermons against superstition and idolatry. He must attack Fêng-shui, and—hardest task of all— wean the people from their cherished Ancestral Worship; but beyond all this he must show that the doctrines of the Cross require and enforce a higher standard of morality than is demanded by Confucianism, Buddhism, Taoism, Mohammedanism or any of the faiths which appear to compete with it. When the Duke remits the punishment of death that hung over the head of Shylock he does it "that thou shalt see the difference of our spirit," and this is the idea which should be prominently present in the mind of the missionary from first to last. It has always appeared to us that one great opportunity was lost by the Roman Catholic missionaries after the Tientsin Massacre. They should have allowed the civil

authorities to take the most vigorous steps which lay in their power
to secure the murderers of the Sisters. The course of justice and
law should have been allowed to go on unchecked up to the last
moment. But at the last moment the Christian should have
shown the difference of his spirit. On the very execution ground
where the wretched men were bound and awaiting the headsman's
sword, the Priests should have appeared headed by their Bishop
with all the pomp and dignity which the Romish Church knows
so well how to lend to her processions—and demanded the pardon
of the sentenced men. Had this been done, the hands of all the
missionaries from Manchuria to the Bay of Yulin would have been
strengthened, and the national heart would have been reached.
It may be objected that this policy would partake of the nature of
a theatrical display; but the criticism, though plausible, is superficial. We fail to see what *moral* end is gained by the apparent
participation of missionaries in an act of retributive justice. The
end and aim of missionary teaching is not the enforcement of
Treaty rights, nor yet, as has been unfairly said, "the forcible dif-
"fusion of Christianity." The utter misapprehension of Christian
ethics on the part of the Chinese demands a public refutation; and
what more striking proof of their true nature could be offered than
a public act of intercession, on the part of the sufferers, for the
lives of their persecutors ? We have censured the Catholic missionaries for their assumption of official rank, and their insistance
on the right of protecting all their converts. But as they do claim
this right, and occupy so influential a position among the mandarins, let them put their power to a noble use. As it is, the
Christians allowed a few miserable and probably innocent men to
be sacrificed, and the feeling of irritation against missionaries was
increased and not diminished. We have reverted to this subject
because we believe that the policy here advocated if acted on in
future disturbances between the missionary and the native will
be productive of the best results. Granted that a disturbance arises
between a preacher of the Gospel and a mob of villagers in a remote
city or village. Let the Consul take the most active measures he

can to bring the guilty parties to justice; but let him at the last moment explain to the wrong-doors that *at the intercession of the injured missionary* the punishment has been remitted. If in the general interests he thinks its needful to take strong measures—which he may sometimes do—let him take pains to explain that he does it as a civilian, and not at the instigation of the minister of Christ. It is impossible that conduct of this sort should fail to produce a desirable effect upon the Chinese. They may be stolid, they may be prejudiced, they may be full of bigotry; but gradually they would be won by conduct like this. Dogmas must have their place in every theological system and the special doctrines of the religion we profess must never be timidly hidden, or presented in accommodated forms to suit the ignorance of the heathen; but the first thing Chinamen should be made to feel is "the difference of "our spirit." This will be found to prevail and to exercise perceptible influence if only foreigners are consistent in presenting it to the people. Foreign officials in China have many opportunities of good, and if they will act on the principles we have laid down, firmly and quietly, they will help on the cause of progress far more than by embroiling themselves with the authorities at Peking.

CHAPTER XIV.

Chinese Views of Foreign Culture.

THERE is probably nothing upon which more stress has been laid by English writers as calculated to promote the advancement of the Chinese in intellectual accomplishments and to inspire them with respect for the foreigner, than the translation of scientific works into the language of China. The significance of this proceeding is undeniable, and has been fully and practically recognised in many ways. We need only point to such an institution as the Chinese Polytechnic, the nucleus, we trust, of a future school of science: to such a publication as the *Chinese Scientific Magazine*, recently started under auspices the most favourable, by Mr. Fryer, of the Kiangnan Arsenal: to the many works of a purely technical nature which that gentleman is engaged from day to day in translating for the benefit of the Chinese Government and the guidance of native engineers:—we have only to point such phenomena as these, we say, to illustrate the importance attached to instructing the Chinese people in the sciences of the West, by those best fitted by their position and acquirements to be their educators and guides. Nay, more: the practical response made by the Chinese is an additional proof of the success attendant upon the efforts so ably put forward. The gunboat, purchased from a foreign firm or constructed upon the very latest principles of foreign ingenuity: the newest invention in the way of fire-arms: the most approved appliances for the engineering operations which are now being commenced in Formosa, Tsi-ngan Fu and elsewhere, are sufficient witnesses of the perfect appreciation by the Chinese of foreign skill, and their willing acknowledgment of their own inferiority in this respect.

So far, so good. And yet what does it all amount to? How far have we advanced in the estimation of the Chinese by our recognised proficiency in engineering? Just this much, and no more: the foreigner is now looked upon as an uncommonly clever mechanic. He understands all about building a ship and casting artillery—they cannot deny that. He is a really excellent workman: a superior sort of blacksmith, in fact, with a very useful and practical knowledge of the fundamentals of his trade. But we doubt whether a single step has been gained towards instilling into the Chinese any respect for Western intellect or intellectual systems, as such. The native simplicity of the official mind upon this point is striking in the highest degree, and we believe that without indulging in any rhetorical flourishes we are safe in affirming the contempt of the Chinese for Western ethics to be perfectly honest and sincere. Their conceit is of the most natural and artless character, founded upon ignorance almost sublime in its ingenuousness. An amusing example of this took place not long ago, illustrating in a cogent manner the theory that we advance. An English gentleman, having received an act of courtesy from the Chinese authorities of a native Arsenal during a trip in the interior, wrote a letter to the manager, in English, expressive of his high appreciation of the kindness he had received. The note was couched in the terms of well-bred courtesy usual among educated people, and was duly translated to the officer in question —a mandarin of high rank, and brother of the Governor-General of Chihli. His astonishment was unbounded; he had no idea, he said, that a foreigner could possibly express himself with such grace and polish. But after all, the reason was not difficult to find. Ever since foreigners had taken to learning Chinese and studying, in the original, the principles of the Superior Person, there could be no doubt whatever that their manners had wonderfully improved. The old maxim about *Ingenuas didicisse*, etc., etc., received additional exemplification of its significance;

and the worthy man was profoundly impressed with this unexpected proof of the humanising influences of the classics !

We submit therefore that it would be in the highest degree advisable for our translators to turn their attention to works of a more purely intellectual and ethical nature. Whether from a political or a religious stand-point it is necessary that the Chinese should be led to have that respect for the literary culture of the West which they are so willing to accord to its superiority in purely mechanical achievements. We have often wondered, for instance, why missionaries have never yet succeeded, as far as is known, at any rate, in converting a single mandarin to Christianity. The reason now is, if not clear, at least less obscure. Knowing nothing of foreign philosophical systems, the Chinese literate has a hearty contempt for every canon of morality but that which he has been taught to look upon as the highest wisdom within human reach, and of course Christianity is placed upon the same inferior footing. The religion of a barbarian race, to whom the Divine utterances of the Master are utterly unknown, is, must be, a tissue of illogical and superstitious folly, on a level in fact with every other so-called formula or system of belief in general acceptance in the West. His contempt for it is inevitable, because of the low estimation in which he holds all foreign ethics of whatsoever scope or tendency : his rejection of it a foregone conclusion, based upon his profound belief in the infallibility of the Confucian philosophy or the systems of Chu Fu-tsze and Tsze-sze. Is it not imperative, therefore, that these misconceptions should be made an end of ? We should like to see some of our standard English works translated into the vernacular. We need not particularise ; it is enough to put forward the suggestion and leave the details of its execution to those best fitted to undertake it. Works on political economy, profane and religious history, philosophy in its strictest sense, and even those by our greatest masters of life-picturing, are all worthy of being thus employed. It may seem curious to recommend such authors as Herbert Spencer and John Stuart Mill as aids to the missionary in his propagandist labours, but we believe that the effect upon the Chinese mind would be thus far desirable,—that they would arrest attention and command respect.

So much for this view. Further considerations, in connection with Chinese moral and religious ethics, we reserve for treatment in another chapter.

CHAPTER XV.

A Superficial View of Buddhism.

A GREAT ruler once travelled some distance to see a celebrated Buddhist priest, and to receive instructions from him. On entering his cell, the priest made no salutation, nor did he rise from his seat; the ruler was angry, and asked why this rudeness to a stranger, an officer of state and a guest? The priest replied, "The world is unreal; a delusion, in which everything is illusive; "so to salute or not to salute a guest, there is no difference." The ruler was still more displeased, and drawing his sword began beating the priest over the shoulders, saying, "Take this quietly, "if there is no reality in the world!"

It would almost appear as though Molière had had this old Buddhist story in his mind when he drew the exquisitely comic portraiture of Marphurius, the doubting philosopher. "Il n'y a "rien de certain," says he, "et nous devons douter de tout . . . . "Ainsi il ne faut pas dire *Je vous parle;* mais, *il me semble* que je "vous parle." The climax of this capital skit was absolutely identical with that of the one we have detailed above; for when his interlocutor, enraged at the wise man's jargon, laid a lusty stick about his shoulders, thereby eliciting very unmistakeable howls of pain from the sufferer, he assured him, that, on his own showing, there was no reality in it. "Corrigez, monsieur le philosophe," said he, "cette manière de parler. Il faut douter de toutes choses; "et vous ne devez pas dire que je vous ai battu, mais *qu'il vous* "*semble* que je vous ai battu." The analogy between the two stories is singular enough, and, as we have already remarked, would seem to imply that Chinese ethics were not altogether unknown to the witty Frenchman; but the assumption is, after all, unnecessary. There are many points of resemblance between the early speculations of Chinese philosophy and the later developments of Western thought. Bishop Berkeley's theories are no inapt illustration of this as regards many of the ethics of Buddhism, and in another direction there are probably to be found, in the more advanced phases of materialism, several proofs of the saying of the Wise Man that there is nothing new under the Sun: that the thing that hath been, it is that which shall be; and that if there is anything whereof it may be said, See, this is new—it hath been already of old time which was before us. To follow up this subject would require far more time and space than can be devoted to it in the present chapter; we wish now only to draw attention to a few features of Buddhism which strike us as being often overlooked by people generally, much to the prejudice of what may be termed the most powerful religious system in China. Buddhism has we believe a firmer hold upon the Chinese—that is, upon their minds and hearts—than any other moral influence to which they exposed; for irreligious as they may be, and, we fancy, comparatively speaking are, they have, in common with every human family, religious instincts and yearnings not to be satisfied by the cold precepts of Confucius. It is a singular fact that in spite of the alleged scepticism of the Chinese in matters relating to faith, there are few people so completely under the guidance, and indeed mastery, of the Unseen. The next world and the existence of invisible and intelligent agencies are to them realities, and realities which have a very strong influence upon their public, their private, and their inner life. It is not to be wondered at, therefore, that their most potent spiritual system should contain in itself not beliefs and speculations merely, but precepts: and that those precepts should be of a sufficiently practical nature to appeal to the common sense of those brought under their sway. Decision of character and force of will are strongly advocated in Buddhist works of instruction, as necessary to the accomplishment of any task

worth undertaking: the vacillating man is likened to a piece of
iron without temper, the undecided woman resembles dry grass,
which has neither root nor stem.   Under the entire Heaven, says
a philosophic poet of this school, there is nothing difficult; the
difficulty is only to be found in the mind of man.   The search of
wisdom is inculcated with an amount of earnestness and vigour
which reminds us of the Proverbs of the preacher-king. "By it one
" penetrates the subtleties of all knowledge and arrives at full per-
" fection.   The man who prosecutes this search must awaken all
" the energies of his spirit, and concentrate all the powers of his
" mind as a warrior on the day of battle, or as a judge sitting in the
" Hall of Judgment, who gathers up all the evidence, converging
" the powers of his soul to one point, and admitting no shadow of
" a doubt."   Nor do the teachings of Buddhism permit the cultivation of that dreamy state of mind, that foretaste of Nirvana, the
jewelled realm of happiness, to so great a degree as may be generally supposed.   "Rest not too long in lonely places and alone,"
writes an old Buddhist literate, in not unmusical cadences.   " A
" man who rests too much alone is, to other men, as dry wood to a
" flourishing tree covered with blossoms and fruit: places of rest
" are loved by all, as the world is full of turmoil and confusion, but
" pleasant retirement weakens the spirit, and men always covet the
" Unknown,—often the Impossible.   One must not remain too long
" in pleasant places, nor desire too ardently the Unknown.   Intel-
" ligence is the food of wisdom, and wisdom is the proper use of
" decision."   But the most remarkable precept of all is one which,
perhaps, was borrowed from Confucius.   "Know thyself," says the
Buddhist: " this serious duty no one, not your nearest friend, the
" best of fathers and the tenderest of mothers, the most affectionate
" of daughters and most dutiful of sons, can ever perform in your
" stead.   Examine yourself: seek to know your own instincts and
" passions."

The singular analogies which have been found to exist between
the ethics and observances of Buddhism, and those of Christianity,
have been, and still are, a source of bewilderment to many.   The

perplexed annoyance of the early Catholic Fathers who on their
first arrival in the East were confronted with what appeared to
them a travestie of both their ceremonial and their faith, was tempered by a hope that, after all, the similarity might prove of use
to them, and smoothe the way to a readier acceptance of revealed
religion.   But still the problem remained unsolved, and remains
so until this day; even Abel Rémusat, a great authority upon
such subjects, having done little more than parrying the thrusts of
sceptical writers, who drew from the phenomenon conclusions unfavourable to Christianity.   We do not believe that Catholicism
deliberately borrowed any specific rules of discipline and ceremonies from Buddhism, nor can we agree with those who find in
Buddhism the origin of Christianity; still there is no doubt that
a vast deal has yet to be cleared up, and a solution offered of the
mystery, acceptable to men of thought.   No existing differences
between Buddhism and the Roman form of Christianity affect in
the slightest degree the fact that a certain influence, common to
both, must have produced, in other directions, resemblances so
striking; and while we differ from those who look upon the two
systems as simply varied modifications of the same radical idea, it
is difficult to deny that there are distinct traces of consanguinity,
however distant the relationship may be.

Such, we take it, is the conclusion at which any impartial observer is bound to arrive, from a superficial point of view.   We
say an ' observer '—not a student: for the analogies which to us
appear so undeniable, in no way touch the essentials of either
faith.   The resemblance lies mainly, indeed we may almost say
entirely, upon the surface.   The moral precepts of Buddhism are
quite distinct from the fundamental theories of the system, and
may therefore be considered superficial without any violence to
language.   Many of the precepts of the Gospel are to be found in
the Buddhist writings, but in every case they are purely moral
and nothing more.   The Buddhist is forbidden to indulge the passions, to steal, to murder, to grasp at wealth, to lie, to take a higher place than that to which he is entitled, to eat in the afternoon,

and to paint the face; to several of which there exists an analogue in the Sermon on the Mount. But they [may be found with fluctuations in most other religions; the common verdict of humanity has been delivered against the gross and open sins, and there is nothing strange in their condemnation by the Buddhist sect. And a deeper resemblance than this, between Buddhism and Christianity, we fail to find. In all radical and fundamental doctrines the two systems are simply antipodal. Nay, more than this; Buddhism, when analysed, will be found to be a most extraordinary mixture of materialism and mysticism: a creed of nothingness, wrapped in an ascetic's robes: a ceremonial system, the secret of whose symbolism is illusory. And why? Because in the Buddhistic heaven there is no God. It is a religion of Atheism. Its teachings are those of the extreme school of advanced thought in the West at the present day. Matter is looked upon as eternal. The existence of the world, says Buddhism, as quoted by Bishop Bigandet, sometime Vicar-Apostolic of Burmah, its destruction and reproduction, all the different combinations and modifications to which matter is subject, are the immediate results of the action of eternal laws, and exist of themselves. The entire universe is under the sway of eternal and immutable laws, which, like those of many modern thinkers, are without a law-giver. So far, at any rate, there is not much in common between Buddhism and orthodox Christianity. We are not now saying that such ideas are immoral or the reverse. We wish simply to show that, like more modern speculations, the religion of Buddha dispenses with a Deity, and therefore, for that reason if for no other, cannot have a very close relationship with Christianity; while the tendency to envelop its negative theology—of course the term is absurd—in ceremonial observances, is almost suggestive of the recent developments of Comtist ritualism. One fact, at any rate, may be gleaned therefrom: and that is, that the theories now gaining such ground in intellectual circles are by no means new, but were spun out of the brains of old Chinese philosophers two thousand years before the birth of Christ. It only strikes us as a little strange that people should assume so hostile an attitude to the grand theory which has been recently placed upon the basis of scientific truth, and, with evolution staring them in the face from every line, almost, of the first chapter of Genesis, should have jumped to the conclusion that, if the theory be true, there is no room in the Universe for God. It is however curious to find these ancient sages arriving at some dim apprehension of truths which were destined to be hidden from Western searchers for so many ages: but they fell into the same error as the one we have just referred to, and, tracing every phenomenon to a special cause, denied the First Great Cause of all. Nor is there any resemblance between the two religions under discussion in what may be termed the third essential article of the Buddhistic creed. There exists, we are told, an Eternal Law, which, when it is effaced from the memory of man, may be again renewed and recovered, solely and entirely by the incomparable genius and matchless wisdom of certain extraordinary personages called Buddhas, who appear successively and at certain intervals during the different series or succession of worlds. "These Buddhas announced this law to all reasonable beings then "existing. The principal object of this doctrine is to show to "these beings the means of setting themselves free from the in-"fluence of the passions, and of becoming isolated from everything "that exists; so that men, being emancipated from the action of "all good and evil influences, which forces mortals to turn in a "vortex of existence without end, may attain to the state called "Nirvan, or complete repose." The clear induction of which we take to be that every great reformer who has appeared in the world of mysticism or metaphysics, is an incarnation of Buddha; from which conclusion to the next is but a single step, and Christ himself must be, by the Buddhistic theory, a prominent figure on the list.

We think that the above hurried sentences contain sufficient to prove that there is no real analogy between Christianity and Buddhism, and that the resemblance which exists is superficial, though, as we believe, not accidental. Asceticism exists in all religious systems and may be found in every part of the habitable globe, in one form or another; it is in fact more the result of temperament than creed, and is as natural, if not so universal, as the religious instinct itself. The monastic system is an important element in Buddhism, and of this we think we cannot adduce a better instance than is found in a certain Sect or Order of Buddhists known as Phongies or Talapoins. These devotees represent, and, as far as appears, not unworthily, the extreme ascetic form of their religion; for their professed object is to carry out the laws of Buddha in an austerer and more perfect manner than their brethren in the faith. It is Gautama, the last incarnation of Buddha, whom the Phongie sets up before him as his special pattern, and it is probably in the life led by a conscientious eremite of this school that we see the great religion of the East in its most interesting, if not most favourable, aspect. The dirty, low-browed, yellow-robed creature so familiar to us in our daily walks, with his ludicrous expression of sanctimoniousness, is not a fair representative of his creed; he is a debased and carnal being, immoral and uncultured; and it would be a great injustice to condemn the system to which he belongs without enquiring more deeply into the subject, and pursuing our researches somewhat further. There are few travellers in China, doubtless, who have not visited some Buddhist monastery of fame, and been present at a religious service by no means unimpressive. It is not easy to forget the strange beauty of the scene at Ku-shan on the river Min, as, winding upwards through the luxuriant undergrowth and rich foliage of the mountain, the path leads the traveller to where the first faint strokes of the water-bell fall musically on his ears. The marvellous quiet and loveliness which surround the monastery, hung, as it were, midway between earth and sky,—the towering peak above—the silent corridors—the monotonous chant of the three hundred priests, as they gather in their yellow robes in the 'sanctuary' of the building twice in each four and twenty hours— all combine to produce an impression on the mind of a European visitor, not easily shaken off. Some of the monks are, it is true, heavy-looking, fat, and stupid : one or two have a decidedly bad expression, lending colour to the report that a few have previously led an infamous career, and only escaped punishment by embracing a monastic life ; but there are others upon whose upturned faces are the marks of intellect, culture, and devotion. The abbot of the monastery we remember well : a aged, spare man with finely-cut and almost handsome features, courtly in his manner, and generally prepossessing. Such a life is favourable to reflection, and, as the nearest foretaste of Nirvana, is well adapted to the mystics who, under the name of Phongies, embrace it with such eagerness.

The Phongie proper is hardly a priest. He is more strictly a recluse, giving himself up wholly to religious meditation and, during the three months of Lent, practising self-denial in its austerest form. The Order does not seem to flourish very extensively in China, if it exists at all. Its principal home is Thibet, where it luxuriates under the protection of the Grand Lama, the Supreme and semi-royal Pontiff. There is an elaborate hierarchy, the grades of which are regularly acknowledged and strictly observed. The entrance of a boy into the Order is an imposing ceremony ; in many respects it bears a strong resemblance to the admission of novices in the Catholic Church, and is thus described by Monseigneur Bigandet. The lad is mounted upon a horse richly caparisoned, or seated in a magnificent palanquin, carried upon the shoulders of four men ; sometimes, of a greater number. During the triumphal march, he is preceded by a long line of men and women dressed in their richest robes, and bearing a great quantity of presents for the religious houses. The procession, gorgeously appointed, moves slowly through the streets to solemn music, until it reaches the monastery ; whereupon the young candidate is delivered into the hands of the Superior. His head is then immediately shaven ; he is deprived of his rich attire, and clothed in simple yellow ; and from that moment his identity is lost. He is then a novice, and his sole idea is to rise to the rank of a Talapoin or professed member. To this end he must study the prescribed rituals and receive instruc-

tions as to his course of conduct. The rules and ceremonies are
all written in Pali, the sacred language of the Buddhists, and the
book containing them is regarded with unbounded awe. Some
copies of it have leaves of ivory, and are magnificently carved.
The exaltation-ceremony is too long to be introduced, unfortunately : but a few salient features may be mentioned. The candidate
has to listen to a solemn harangue, accompanied by many inclina-
tions of the body : he then avows himself free from leprosy, asth-
ma, cough, corruption of the blood, and witchery of giants and
sorcerers : swears that he is a man, a legitimate son, freeborn, etc.,
etc. ; and in reply to the question " What is your name ?"—responds
" My name is Wago "—(a vile and unworthy being). Prayers and
exhortations follow, of a strangely impressive character, and the
first part of the ceremony concludes with the words : " Let the
" candidate pass from the state of sin and imperfection to the per-
" fect state of Rahan." The four capital sins—licentiousness, theft,
murder, and spiritual pride—are then denounced in almost elo-
quent terms ; the last-named being particularly condemned. " No
" member of the company must ever arrogate to himself extra-
" ordinary gifts or supernatural perfections, or, for vain glory, cause
" himself to be regarded as a holy man. . . . . Sooner may
" the lofty palm-tree which has been felled by the axe become
" green, than a chosen one, guilty of such pride, be re-established
" in the holy state."

Ethics such as these can hardly fail to be of the deepest interest
to every man of thought : the Christian, the philosopher and the
theorist. There is a dignity and a pathos about many of the precepts, articles, and observances of this Buddhistic sect which we
are not wont to associate with Buddhism as it appears to a careless observer, and it is well that our views should be enlarged
upon a subject of such importance. We believe there is more in
the religion than a mere tissue of dreamy, brain-perplexing, unpractical speculations ; there are indications of high morality, deep
convictions, and honest efforts at a nobler life, however much the
fine gold may be dimmed.

CHAPTER XVI.

Astrology.

A VERY valuable treatise might be written, comparing the astronomical system of the Chinese with the observations taken by the ancient inhabitants of Chaldœa. We imagine there is no doubt that the knowledge possessed by those old mystics was much more advanced than that which has been attained.by the sons of Han at any period of their history; but at the same time it would be deeply interesting to trace the connection between the discoveries and conclusions arrived at by two of the most wonderful nations in the world, and compare the various points on which they differ or agree. It is very strange, however, that the Chinese should not have made greater progress in the Queen of Sciences. They stand very much where they did two thousand years ago, and the golden characters which bespangle the dark volume of the sky are no clearer to the dwellers on these vast plains than they were to their ancestors in the remotest era of their existence. But this fact—for we may safely treat it as such—may be accounted for in two different ways. In the first place, the Chinese have never been celebrated for what is generally called inventive genius. Now this sounds like a fallacy when we remember that they enjoy the credit of having invented gunpowder and printing, and were in possession (according to some calculators) of the mariner's compass when the world, judged by the vulgar reckoning, was not quite two thousand years old. But while we may award them the praise that is due for having, in the course of forty centuries, achieved the triumph of making say four valuable discoveries, we must not forget to consider what, after all, is the more important point, *viz.*, how far these discoveries have been improved upon, and have so led to any lasting benefit; and we think we are not far wrong in applying the same test to their observations of the heavenly worlds. Their knowledge is at present of the haziest, and mixed up with superstitions of the most puerile nature, though it is difficult to conceive how such superstitions can coëxist with even the meagre amount of knowledge which they actually do possess. There seems nothing graceful, nothing poetical about the Chinese astronomical superstitions; nothing which can compare in point of moral or æsthetic beauty with either the nature-myths of the Vedas or the pantheistic legends of the old Greek mythology. The devouring of the Sun by a Dragon, and its subsequent ejection from the stomach of the monster by an emetic of hideous noises— which may well turn anybody sick—can hardly be called a poetical metaphor descriptive of a solar eclipse. The second and perhaps more cogent reason, however, why the sciences of mathematics and astronomy are not more studied than they are, is, that proficiency in ethical literature forms the principal if not the only stepping-stone to Governmental preferment. The aristocracy of China is the literary class; and the literary acquirements of a highly-educated Chinese, though enormously extensive in one sense, are absolutely restricted when viewed in the light of modern research. The emoluments of the State are, with few and trifling exceptions, reserved for the benefit of those most deeply versed in the writings Confucius and his peers. The practical advantages to be derived from a study of mathematics are consequently very limited, and we may affirm that, however great the respect paid to astronomy in olden days, it is the *astrological* tendencies of the Chinese which at present preserve the study of the grander science from falling into complete desuetude and neglect. This is all the more to be regretted when we consider the pitch of astronomical knowledge that there is every reason to believe was attained by the Chinese at so early a period of their existence. It is estimated that the Chinese had advanced so far in this science as to construct a calendar two thousand six hundred years B.C.—while the Athenians had only reached the same stage six hundred years before that era; and yet it is an astounding fact that they were not acquainted with the apparent motion of the heavens (we do not speak of the planets) until three thousand years later than the date above-mentioned, or nearly six hundred years after Hipparchus. Long before that, however, they had been able to calculate eclipses; although the amount of knowledge which they must clearly have possessed in order to enable them to do this has failed to disabuse the public mind, though all these centuries, of the firm belief that a Dragon is eating the Sun. Indeed so great was the importance attached to eclipses, that if a predicted eclipse failed to occur, the reigning prince allowed himself to be persuaded by the blundering stargazers that it had been warded off by his transcendant virtues, which had called forth the special approval of Heaven; while the mortification of an Emperor at the unexpected occurrence of one of these phenomena was exemplified in the case of Chung-kang, 2156 B. C., who ordered the execution of two celebrated astronomers of the day, for not having given him proper warning of the approach of the dreaded sign.

We have now before us a semi-astrological publication but little known to foreigners generally, and which we think is of sufficient interest to warrant an extended notice. Its title is the 大淸國光緖二年時憲書 *Ta-Ts'ing Kuang-sü jeh nien shih hien shu, i. e.* the Imperial Almanac for the Second Year of the Reign of Kuang-sü of the Great Pure Dynasty, and we procured it through that all-powerful medium *cash,* for as yet China is ignorant of the courtesies due to the fourth estate. This little book is published by a special bureau attached to the Board of Rites at Peking, and contains many things which seem rather strange for this year of grace 1876; a slight review of the contents therefore may perhaps interest some of our readers. The first page contains a table of good and bad days for starting on a journey, and the Chinaman who should fail to avail himself of the valuable information therein contained under such circumstances must be very foolhardy. A list of the lucky days for entering on that most hazardous of all speculations, marriage, fills the second page, and on the third are all the unlucky days for this risky business. Imagine a man so stupid as to get married on an unlucky day! Next comes a table of the feasts,—there are usually only twenty-four, but owing to the spring festival again occurring in the twelfth moon (which will cause great prosperity) there are twenty-five distributed through the 384 days which go to make up the present year. Then comes a list of days on which to commence house-building, careful attention to which table, by the mechanic, will most assuredly prevent the structures he erects from coming to grief through fire. It also preserves the inmates from sickness, and other ills that flesh is heir to. How simple, and how much more economical, too, than our troublesome plan of opening annual insurance-policies! Following this comes a table which gives the beginning and length of the twenty-four solar terms, together with the rising and setting of the Sun for each day throughout the year, according to the latitude of different places, etc., calculated by the Astronomical Board at Peking. Up to this it is printed in red, the lucky colour; and the cover is also red. Then come the months from the first to the twelfth, (there are really thirteen, as there is a second sixth, or intercalary month this year) with the ceremonies to be observed for each day, printed in black; while over each, in red, is information useful to diviners, soothsayers, etc. As a specimen of these ceremonies, we will give the directions under the first day of the first moon:— Rise early, and after bathing and dressing in your best clothes, proceed to the temple and there burn incense. On leaving your house to be careful to go first towards the south. Even should the temple lie in a northerly direction, first proceed south, and then gradually turn the other way. In cases where it is found impossible to do this, remain in doors till some lucky day, when you may go out without any risk!—The next and last is a table of two cycles, with the twelve branches and the symbolical animals arranged for the use of diviners, from which the present writer derives the interesting information that he was born under the auspices of the Dragon.

This Almanac has probably the largest circulation of any in the world, the number being estimated at several millions. The Calendar is an Imperial monopoly, and no other than that prepared by the Board of Rites is allowed to be published, the law on this point being so strict that a violation of it would be punished by death. Two or three editions are printed for the convenience of the people, the prices of which vary from three to ten cents a copy. Dr. Williams tells us that " no one ventures to be without an almanac " lest he be liable to the greatest misfortunes, and run the imminent " hazard of undertaking important events on black-balled days ;" adding, " and it is to the discredit of the Chinese Government to " aid thus in perpetuating folly and ignorance among the people, " when they know that the whole system is absurd and false."

The Roman Catholic missionaries inform us that formerly, and it is possible now, the almanacs were distributed through the Empire in the following manner :—" On a certain day appointed for " the ceremonial in the capital the principal officials repair early " in the morning to the Palace, while the members of the Board " of Rites, arrayed in their state dresses, proceed to their hall to " escort the books, which are carried in procession to the Imperial " residence. Those which are intended for the Emperor, the Em- " press, and the Queens, are bound in yellow satin, and enclosed in " bags of cloth of gold, which are placed on a large gilded litter " borne by forty footmen, clothed in yellow. Then follow ten or " twelve smaller litters, enclosed with red silk curtains, and con- " taining the books to be given to the Princes, which are bound in " red satin, and enclosed in bags of silver cloth. These are follow- " ed by men bearing on their shoulders other conveyances, on which " are piled the calendars intended for the grandees of the Court and " the generals of the army ; the cavalcade is completed by the Pre- " sident and members of the Bureau in sedans, followed by their " usual attendants. On arriving at the Palace, the golden bags are " laid on ten tables covered with yellow damask, when the mem- " bers of the Bureau, having first prostrated themselves, deliver " them to the proper officers, who receive them kneeling, and carry

" them with great ceremony to the foot of the Throne. The silver
" bags are sent in a similar manner to all the Princes of the royal
" family, after which the Ministers and other great officers of state
" present themselves in turn and kneel with reverence to receive
" their Almanacs, which are regarded as gifts from the Emperor.
" The ceremonies of distribution at the Court being concluded, the
" books intended for the use of the people are sent by the Bureau
" into every province of the Empire, where the forms observed at
" Imperial Palace are repeated at the offices of the chief-officers;
" after which, the people are allowed to purchase their Almanacs."

The author of the *Middle Kingdom* tells us that the Government
looks upon a present of this important publication as one of the
highest favours which it can confer on tributary vassals or friendly
nations; and we are naturally curious to know whether any of our
representatives have ever received so overwhelming a mark of the
Imperial condescension.

CHAPTER XVII.

A Chinese Munchausen.

BETWEEN twenty and thirty years ago, a gentleman, who appears modestly to have concealed his name, took the trouble to translate the observations of a travelled Chinaman, who once went so far from home as Java, Batavia, and Singapore. Mr. Wang Ta-hai, the adventurous person referred to, was evidently looked upon by his compatriots as a marvel of learning and experience, for the pamphlet in which he detailed his impressions was honoured by no fewer than five prefaces; one by the translator, one by Chow Heo-kung of the Huan-luy College, (an institution we have been utterly unable to identify) another by a literary gentleman named Li-wei, of Peking, a fourth by Liu He-ching, wife's uncle to the author, and a fifth by the gifted traveller himself. From the words of Mr. Liu, we gather that his niece's husband was in many respects a rather eminent man; that in the year 1750 he crossed the seas, and, having acquired high literary honours, published a work on Batavia upon which the Prime Minister, Tsai Wan-kung, passed a very high compliment. The Peking gentleman regrets that his fellow-townsman should have wasted so much talent upon a strange and distant region which had not yet come under the influences of the civilising doctrines of China; but the collegian's preface is the most characteristic. It is written gracefully and well, and evinces many evidences of culture. The writer deplores the lack of geographical knowledge which existed in his country, and congratulates himself upon the novel information here afforded. "In the time of the Emperor Seuen-tih," he says, "of

" the Ming Dynasty, (1430) the order for Wang San-pao to proceed
" towards the Western ocean for the purpose of collecting pearls
" and precious things, is recorded in the national history : his road
" lay through An-nan westward, but the chart of that country was
" concealed by the Superintendent Liu Ta-hea, who had no desire
" to pass over the sea, by which means the track of the Western
" ocean remained unknown. Our Government, extensively over-
" spreading all things as the heavens do the earth, has caused its
" unfathomable favour overwhelmingly to reach the Islands of the
" Sea ; so that all who have blood and breath without exception
" honour their parents, and even the people of the Great West
" (meaning Europeans) have thought of bringing their cunning
" accomplishments to scheme after rewards. Latterly, however, the
" readiness of the Imperial astronomers to estimate the acquire-
" ments of our countrymen in order to promote and employ them
" is daily more manifest, and people from all parts of the Empire
" come pressing forwards, soliciting a thorough examination, by
" which a vast amount of native talent is obtained, without depend-
" ing on foreign aid. Thus it is that those distant countries have
" now but few persons to visit and inspect them, and there is not
" so much as a fairy seated on the leaf of a red lotus to bring us a
" book from thence." He then goes on to praise the author for his
perspicacious and useful work ; which, he says, serves to testify
that the instructions of their august Dynasty are gracefully wafted
over the sea, like the influence of Draco among the stars. .

We are sadly afraid, however, that the courtly expressions of
these gentlemen were utterly misplaced. It is very likely that
Wang may have been, as it is said, an excellent son, and a man of
many parts : but he seems to have been either strangely credulous,
or to have had very little regard for truth. The impression he
received from intercourse with the Dutch settlers, too, was most
unfavourable ; he compares them to " the man who stopped his
" ears while stealing a bell "—a proverbial expression intimating
that they try to hide their vices from themselves and think that
they are as much concealed from others. This stern critic of bar-

barian morals informs us that the Dutch possess neither benevolence, righteousness, propriety, wisdom, nor truth; that they are over-bearing and covetous; that widows marry a month after the decease of their husbands; that they never leave anything behind them to tranquillise their descendants, and that the only virtue they have the shadow of a claim to, is sincerity. Nor did the outward forms of colonial Christianity appear at all impressive to our traveller; indeed the account he gives of a Sunday's service is ludicrous in the extreme. "Every seven days," he writes, "there is a ceremony-"day, or sabbath, when from nine to eleven in the morning they "go to the place of worship to recite prayers and mumble charms. "The hearers hang down their heads and weep, as though there "were something very affecting in it all; but after half-an-hour's "jabber they are allowed to disperse, and away they go to feast in "their garden-houses and spend the whole day in delight, without "attending to any business." After this we are not surprised to find our friend giving utterance to the wildest conceivable stories, all calculated to pander most fully to his readers' natural love of the incredible. His simplicity is marvellous. He is so struck by the appearance of bluish-tinted sheet-lightning, that he can only exclaim, "Truly does the poet say, If you want to see wonders you "must just go to sea." Then he calls Mecca the residence of Buddha, and gives a rare description of the place, which he says is paved with yellow gold and beautiful gems, and protected by a hundred genii. Nor are natural curiosities wanting; and the pundits of Peking are treated to some most terrifying accounts of the Sea-Man, the Sea-Priest, the Flying Head, and Savages with Tails. The clerical monster referred to is said to be rather an unusual phenomenon; its appearance indicates a storm, it has a mouth from ear to ear, and laughs aloud, horribly, at the sight of sailors. The Flying Head is simply a Malay superstition, still existing, which the wonder-loving Wang doubtless swallowed, as he did everything else. A tooth-extracting tribe also commands his attention. These extraordinary folk, he tells us, are addicted to praying every night, towards the setting sun; and derive their name from a singular practice of pulling out the hair, extracting the teeth, and stripping off the clothes, of their dead friends. " This is one of the cruelties " of false religions," is the traveller's pious and intelligent remark. He then mentions a Secret Society, existing among the Javanese, Malays and Dyaks, which reminds him of White Lotus sect of his own country; the members of which, by virtue of incantations, become invulnerable, their bodies turning to brass and their bones to iron. The only things able to harm them, says the author, are pigs' fat and the blood of dogs. In other matters however his observations are more interesting, utterly babyish though they be. He speaks of the balloon, or Celestial Boat; the telescope, or Thousand-li Mirror; the mariners' compass, or *South*-pointing Carriage; and other appliances, which filled him with amazement and perplexity.

Such is a brief sketch of what appears to have been regarded as a standard work of travel during the eighteenth century in China. One can read such things now with amusement, unqualified by remorse; for the schoolmaster is abroad in the country. The absurd book before us was hailed as a miracle of wisdom and erudition when it was first published; now, we may almost say that, at least by a very considerable portion of his readers, the author would be laughed to scorn. China has grown wiser during the last hundred years, and is beginning to grasp the fact that beyond the Four Seas which include her vast domains there is a world—not, indeed, the world of savages and monsters in which she once believed,—but a world of wisdom, progress and enlightenment, with which it will soon be her lot to march.

CHAPTER XVIII.

Chinese Domestic Romance.

THE social life of the Chinese is a subject about which the general run of foreign residents in China know next to nothing. Many excellent books have been written upon the laws, religions, literature, and politics of the country; but how few have any real insight into the domestic character of these strange people! A man may wander through the labyrinthine paths of Chinese ethics for weary years, may become saturated with the speculations of Chinese sages, may even dally with the lighter forms of literature, such as plays and novels, and yet be very far from familiar with the living, working, suffering, and withal joyous folk themselves. The aims and interests of every-day domestic life in China are a sealed book to numbers whose intimacy with the more salient features of Chinese society from the standpoint of foreign observation is undeniable, and perhaps profound; the exclusiveness of China as a nation is reflected in the reserve of the individual Chinaman, and the man himself continues, probably till the end of the chapter, a stranger to his European friend. We believe that some glimpse, however slight, into the privacy of Chinese life is the only means whereby we can acquire a just appreciation of the Chinese character; and although the writer has had comparatively few opportunities of cultivating this acquaintance, the experience of ten years' residence in China has not been without its interesting results. From time to time, as occasion has presented itself, we have collected incidents, here and there, which are valuable inasmuch as they represent the Chinese in a novel and attractive, because natural and vivid, light; the people are here seen as they are, and not as they appear to a superficial passer-by; and we therefore select from the mass of anecdotes before us a few of those most calculated to entertain and instruct our readers. Some are illustrative of the eccentric superstitions so universally received; others derive their point from the curious marriage-customs that are observed; a third class exemplifies the marvellous ingenuity of the 'heathen Chinee' in ways that are dark as well as in tricks that are plain; while there are not a few which prove beyond a doubt the susceptibility of the black-haired race to the tender passion of love. We need only add that we have every reason to believe in the strict veracity of all the stories that we now propose to recount; trusting that any of our readers who are of an unduly sceptical turn of mind, and find some of the yarns too tough, may be amused, even if not convinced.

We will begin, then, with a romance in real life which is said to have occurred not long ago in the neighbourhood of Hankow. A travelling merchant—not a pedler, if you please—took unto himself a wife, of whom he seems to have been very proud; for the lady was fair to look upon, and realised all those eccentric · graces so dear to Chinese poets of the erotic school. Shortly after this Fortunate Union, however, the bridegroom's duties called him away from her side, and he was compelled to take a fond farewell, with the dreary prospect of an absence extending over no less than two years. He accordingly consigned his bride to the care of his mother, and left; but proved himself, even while away, an excellent husband, furnishing the ladies with as much money as they needed, and writing with commendable regularity. At the expiration of the two years he came back; and as he turned down the street in which he lived, he entered into conversation with a fishmonger, whom he had previously known. It struck him that this tradesman put on a peculiar expression of face when he recognised him, and used an equally peculiar expression of speech when he enquired after his mother. Curious, but still unsuspicious, Huang (for such was the good man's name) approached his house with due caution, and, unperceived, stole round to the back, where he could just peep into his wife's apartment. There was my lady his wife, her lips thickly vermilioned, and her cheeks as white as flour could make them, tricked out in as much tinsel as she could stick about her person, and ogling herself affectedly in a mirror. While engaged in the contemplation of these artificial charms, the returned husband saw an old coolie-woman come into the room, to whom the lady spoke in a squeaking voice of unusual arrogance; and another moment convinced him that it was no other than his unfortunate old mother. Affecting, however, to ignore the change that had come over both ladies, he stepped with simulated joyfulness into the apartment, and embraced them with true conjugal and filial warmth; then, when the first greetings were over, informed his wife that their final re-union must be postponed still for a few days, as he had a little more business to transact before he could settle down comfortably with her again. Mrs. Huang seemed to think it rather strange, but of course submitted; and when it was nearly dark, the husband took a short leave of her, and set off on his pretended journey. Then, under cover of the night, he watched the house; and subsequent events showed him that he had not watched in vain. Taking up the position he had assumed before, like a celestial 'Enoch Arden,' he had the pleasure of beholding the 'Philip' who was in the habit of consoling his wife during his absence. There sat the gay creature, in her gewgaws, and gimcracks, and paint, with her ridiculous head on one side, howling, in true Chinese fashion, some love-ditty to her paramour across the table. Both were indulging somewhat freely in the bottle, and the feast went merrily on. The poor old mother-in-law, of course, was somewhere in the kitchen. Later in the night the husband stole into the room, his wife being just then elsewhere. The gentleman was sleeping off the effects of his debauch; and Huang looked curiously at him for a few seconds. Then, producing a sharp knife, he skilfully and noiselessly stabbed him in the throat, dividing his windpipe and killing him on the spot; then, as quietly withdrew. The lady returning shortly afterwards, went to the settee and tried to arouse her lover; "Get up," she cried; "why "sleep you thus heavily? fie! have you upset the wine? What is "all this wet?" Then she struck a light, and found that it was not wine, but blood; and her paramour lay dead before her. However, she was a strong-minded person, and did not waste any time in lamentations. Seeing or guessing the position of affairs, she proceeded to chop up the dead gentleman and to joint him carefully; after which she put the pieces into a large cooking-pot, filled it with water, and boiled him to a good rich broth. Next day she announced her intention of visiting her parents, and taking with her, as a birthday present for her mother,—so she told her mother-in-law—a large cauldron of soup. On her way she took the opportunity of accidentally tipping the whole thing into the river, and thus, she flattered herself, all possibility of discovery was at an end. While at her parents' house she was rejoined by her husband and his mother, and there was a very merry dinner-party in honour of this happy reunion of man and wife after such a long separation. After dinner the old folks called on Huang for a story or a song. Huang agreed; and, fixing his eyes upon the guilty woman, he recited, in verse, the entire history—just as we have told it here—of her faithlessness. His allusions grew more pointed as he proceeded, until the lady, unable to bear it any longer, pleaded a sudden headache, and fled to her apartment. In her absence, Huang told her parents all the truth; and the poor old couple, though heartbroken at the discovery of their daughter's wickedness, commended his moderation and prudence above measure. On going upstairs, it was found that the wicked wife had hung herself; and her parents gave Huang their youngest daughter to console him under his disappointment. Now this is a true story, and its moral is not far to find.

So much for the fate of a wicked wife. Now for a story about a good one; a far more agreeable subject. It has often been affirmed that, owing to some defect (or otherwise) in their mental constitution, the Chinese are incapable of falling in love. We should be sorry to hazard a verdict upon a question so delicate; but it is

undeniable that the great esteem in which *post-mortem* conjugal
fidelity is held, and the great lengths to which it is carried, are
hardly in favour of so cynical a view. Here however is a genuine
love-story, the details of which are romantic in the extreme, and
which we have never heard equalled by anything of the sort in
Europe. A young Chinese gentleman, some few years back, betrothed himself to the daughter of a neighbouring friend, and the
marriage-day was fixed. Very shortly however before the day
arrived, the Chang-mao rebels made an incursion into the city, and
some severe fighting ensued, in which the bridegroom-elect was
taken prisoner. He was carried off a distance of some leagues,
and became eventually the adopted son of a wealthy old rebel who
had no child of his own to cheer his declining years. The months
rolled by, and no tidings of her lost lover reached the maiden ; and
in course of time her parents proposed to her another match. The
girl however replied that although her wedding had not actually
taken place, she still looked upon herself as the betrothed wife of
her first *prétendu*, and she was content to wait until fortune
restored him to her arms. The parents insisted, but at length,
finding it was no use, they were on the point of giving it up ;
when the old gentleman was surprised by a visit from the father
of the youth that had been taken prisoner, who came with tidings
of his son. Not only had he been adopted by somebody else, but
he had accepted another lady as his wife. Armed with this proof
of his unfaithfulness, the parents of the girl renewed their entreaties, informing her that now indeed she was absolved from all
allegiance to her old suitor, as he had married some one else. " It
" matters not," replied this paragon of constancy ; " he can probably
" support a couple of wives, and I am quite ready to be his number-
" two wife, if I cannot be his number-one ! " This extraordinary
assertion struck both the fathers so forcibly that they immediately
sent an expedition in search of the object of her devotion, and acquainted him with the fact ; and it says wonders for the generosity
of Chinese women towards their rivals that the lady whom he had already married urged her husband to reward his old love by again of-

fering her his hand. Nor was her plea in vain. A few days afterwards, the expectant damsel espied, coming along the road, a poor, broken-down man in the garb of a beggar, who very humbly sought admission. It was her former lover come back; bereft of home, and money, and wife. The very night that this excellent creature had urged her plea, a terrible flood broke over the district, which made a clean sweep of everything in its way; amongst other catastrophes, destroying the house in which he lived, and drowning his faithful wife, while he himself escaped with the skin of his teeth. He was received by the woman he had well nigh forgotten, with open arms, and married her forthwith; and our readers may form their own opinion as to whether he deserved his luck. At any rate, we don't remember many Western heroines who have carried either generosity or faithfulness to such unheard-of lengths. The constant couple are now living within a hundred miles of Shanghai.

Strong-minded ladies are by no means confined to Western countries, and we begin to think that even the women of China are far from being the mindless puppets they are generally represented. Some time ago a wealthy tobacco-grower from Shanse arrived in Shanghai on business, bringing his son with him. Now the young lad had plenty of money at his disposal, and while his father was engaged in the transaction of business he, fresh from the country, and quite dazzled with the magnificence of the model settlement, found no trouble whatever in enjoying himself amazingly. When his father's visit was over, it was with great reluctance that he accompanied him back to his native place; and highly delighted was he when, a year or two afterwards, the old gentleman determined to let him pay a second visit to the agreeable spot. He arrived there with his pockets full, and sadly neglected the business on which he had been sent. He gambled madly night after night, and rapidly lost all his money. At length he was reduced to such a pitch of destitution that, not daring to show his face at home, and indeed without the means of getting there, he was fain to accept the post of door-keeper in an establishment which had been the scene of some of his most discreditable orgies. Meantime his father waited and waited, and the prodigal did not return; till one day, his daughter-in-law—for the hopeful youth was married —asked him whether he did not intend to take any steps to recover his lost son. " What steps can I take ?" said the old man, brokenly : " he has been away nearly three years now, and there is no know- " ing what may have happened to him. He may be dead!" " Yes, " and he may *not* be dead, too," retorted the damsel. " I shall go " and look for my husband myself." " You ?" replied the old man, astonished, " why, what good will you be ? What do you know of " the world ? How can you, an unprotected woman, go about all " alone ?"—" Give me thirty thousand taels and leave me to act," rejoined this cool young lady, who was not much over twenty. The papa-in-law said he would give her three hundred thousand if she would only get him back his son; and the arrangement was made forthwith. The girl then proceeded to shave her forehead and disguise herself in male clothes, and, accompanied by a single old servant, set out for Shanghai. On her arrival she seems to have known by instinct what sort of places to look for her husband in, and her experiences must have had the charm of novelty to the fullest degree. The handsome, richly-dressed youth, with pockets lined with money, was well received at all the restaurants, gambling-houses and other places of entertainment, and the dollars circulated freely. All this time, however, her search was fruitless. At length, outside a house, ragged, dirty, and half-starved, she saw a being who rather reminded her of her lost husband. Casting a careless glance at him as she passed, she turned in at the door, and, calling for some refreshment, began to chat with the inmates. The place was doing well, they told her; they were growing rich; lots of people from the country came there. Shanse ? Oh yes, a good many customers hailed from Shanse; why, that poor devil crouch-ing at the door was a Shanse-man, and once as rich and gay as the young gentleman himself. The ' young gentleman ' laughed care-lessly, paid for his refreshment and sauntered away. The next day he—she, rather—returned, and offered to purchase the poor Shanse-man of the proprietor. The bargain was soon struck, and then she

entered into conversation with her miserable husband. He told
her he was the most wretched of men : that his father was a wealthy
gentleman in the North : that he had a wife at home : but that he
had irretrievably disgraced himself and did not dare return. But
if the honoured one were a Shanse-man, would he take a letter for
him to his family ? "It would probably be better to take you in
"person," rejoined his wife. Then, beckoning him to follow her,
she led him to the hotel where she was staying : took off her cap,
and asked if he indeed did not recognise her ? The unfortunate
fellow saw that it was his wife ; and utterly ashamed, he fell at her
feet crying, and knocked his head to her upon the floor. No time
was lost in paying his old debts and getting him some decent
clothes, and then the reunited couple went home again together.

But enough, for the present, of married life ; now for courtship.
Our readers are of course aware that all marriages are arranged between the parents of the couple, with the aid of a regular middle-
man or broker ; and excellent as this plan may be, it very often
leads to sad results. Nobody has as yet started the theory—as
far as we know—that the Chinese have any hereditary connection
with the lost ten tribes of Israel. There are some points of resemblance, however, between the sons of Han and the sons of Abraham, both races being considerable adepts in spoiling the Egyp-
tians. Of course we all remember the cruel hoax by which Laban
succeeded in palming off his unattractive, sore-eyed daughter Leah,
who probably wore green spectacles, upon that very innocent
young man, his nephew Jacob ? Well, a somewhat similar case occurred not long ago, not very far from Shanghai. A well-
to-do middle-aged Chinaman was very anxious for a son ; but he
and his wife had lived for many years in married harmony without being blessed with any family whatever. He therefore decided that the only thing to be done was to take a second wife, and
looked about him, accordingly, for a suitable young person. But
he was a very fastidious gentleman, and hesitated to introduce into his domestic circle any lady of doubtful manners or ordinary
appearance. At last, when he was almost giving up the search in

despair, a friend said to him, " What is the use of looking about
" you in Shanghai ? Soochow is the place ; it is famed for the
" beauty of its women: why not go and try your fortune there ?"
The idea recommended itself to the childless gentleman, and he
lost no time in putting it into execution. Off he went in a pass-
enger-boat, and arrived at the ' Paris of China' in something under
a week. Shortly afterwards he happened to be tiffining in a res-
taurant, when another visitor entered into conversation with him ;
to whom, his tongue being somewhat loosened by wine, he con-
fided the reason of his journey. The stranger, who had quietly
taken the measure of his man—which was quite in keeping with
his profession, as he happened to be a tailor—cautioned him in a
friendly way against the sharpers, of whom he said there were
many in the neighbourhood; at the same time proffering his own
assistance. " I think," said he, " I can introduce you to a charm-
" ing girl, a customer of mine ; the daughter of one of our richest
" and most respectable families. But it will be a difficult task.
" To-morrow, however, I am going to take her some clothes I have
" been embroidering for her; you can come with me in the cha-
" racter of my journeyman." The merchant agreed with delight,
and next day the two set out together. They soon arrived at the
house, which was large and handsome, and after some chaffering
with the servants were admitted into the presence of the ladies.
The mother lay upon a couch ; her daughter, a really very pretty
and delicate-looking girl, stood by her side. The room was taste-
fully decorated, and everything bespoke the wealth and respectability of the inmates. The tailor and his supposed assistant delivered
their parcel of silk embroidery, and took orders for another suit ;
and departed, the merchant in a perfect ecstacy with the beauty and
accomplishments of the maiden. Well, to make a long story short,
he soon began operations and laid formal proposals before the parents ; always, however, through the medium of the tailor, whom he
enjoined to conceal the fact of his being already a Benedict. His
courtship prospered, and he spent about a thousand taels in wedding
presents of the most costly and beautiful description ; while his

friend the tailor, who, before the introduction, had expatiated upon
the smallness of the lady's feet with all the unctuousness of Sir
Anthony Absolute in describing the charms of Lydia Languish,
manufactured a ravishing little pair of slippers, a perfect triumph
of his art, for the bridegroom to give his bride. At last, the happy
day arrived, and the ceremony was performed in a hired house
with great rejoicings. The bride was dressed in all the colours of
the rainbow, and her face was hidden from the profane light of day
by a blushing scarlet veil. Overflowing with satisfaction, the
happy husband carried her off when all the festivities were over,
and, in the retirement of the nuptial chamber, uncovered the lovely
face. Horror! was he dreaming? An old woman, wrinkled and
bent, stone blind and hideous to behold, stood in unveiled ugliness
before him; while under the couch, in mockery of his rage, were the
dainty little slippers she was to wear. The unfortunate man turned
livid with wrath and disappointment, and not unnaturally vented
his passion upon the old crone beside him. "Wretched hag," he
cried, dragging her to the door, "making a clean breast of this in-
"famous conspiracy, or it will be worse for you." But the old
woman, so far from replying, turned out to be not only blind, but
dumb, and groped helplessly about the room to make her escape,
emitting piteous but inarticulate sounds of terror. In fact, the
merchant had been duped. The villain-tailor had mysteriously disappeared with all the booty, the family to whom he had been introduced knew nothing whatever of the plot, and the merchant
was too cruelly humiliated to wish his shame published by going
to the mandarins for justice. No, he came back to Shanghai only
the other day, a sadder and a poorer man.

The love, or loyalty, or whatever else the passion may be called,
which Chinese girls appear so unaccountably to cherish towards
the future husbands whom they have never seen, is curiously
exemplified by a case which occurred some years ago at Putung.
A girl of good family was betrothed to a youth of the name of
Chao, who unhappily died shortly before the day appointed for the
espousals. The bereaved bride was inconsolable, and entreated her

parents to allow her to visit the coffin of her lost love. This request was refused, on grounds of propriety ; but the girl, breaking all bounds, ran away to the house of mourning, and, throwing herself on the floor beside the corpse, howled in a most determined manner. All attempts to pacify her were useless ; and she insisted, moreover, on taking up her abode with the dead lad's parents from that time forward, and devoting herself to them until their death. This was very heroic, of course, but it seems that the old people would rather have been without her. However, she would take no denial, and absolutely did stay and earn enough to pay for her own keep, and to contribute towards the other expenses, for about five years. Then the old couple died ; and this virtuous maiden, having honoured them with burial, prepared for her own doom. About this time political matters were in a very unsettled state, and it was rumoured in the neighbourhood that the T'ai-p'ing rebels were approaching fast. The excesses of the insurgents were of course well known and dreaded, and the girl was fully aware that if they reached the place while she was alive, her unprotected situation would expose her to the loss of liberty and everything else that she possessed. She accordingly dressed herself in all her richest clothes, as though for a festivity ; and then—so goes the story— took a needle, threaded it with silk, and *sewed her garments securely on to her own flesh.* This done, she drank poison, and died. The very next day the rebels came ; and discovering this lovely corpse, and seeing at a glance the proof of the girl's purity and honour, they treated her with the profoundest reverence. So far, indeed, from robbing her of a single jewel, they gave her honourable interment, and, it is further said—though this is probably apocryphal—the body preserved all the freshness and beauty of life for ten days after its decease.

In the following stories, however, constancy and true love win the day. The widow Wang resided in the vicinity of one of the great cities of China, her family consisting of a young son and daughter, the only relics of her dear departed old man. In the next village there lived a gentleman and his wife of the name of

Liu, who also had a daughter and a son. Now as the families were on terms of much friendly intimacy, it seemed only natural that their *entente cordiale* should be cemented by a marriage between the young people; and so an engagement was arranged, by a professional middle-man, between the son of Mr. Liu and the daughter of the buxom widow. During the period of betrothal, however, and while preparations for the ceremony were going on, it so fell out that the bridegroom-elect was taken sick; he had the misfortune to break a bloodvessel in his lungs, and for days lay helpless in bed, hardly expected to recover. The widow thereupon suggested that the match should be broken off; it would be simple folly, she said, for a young girl to bind herself to a confirmed invalid who might die at any moment and leave his wife disconsolate for life. The Liu family, however, thought differently, and urged the widow to allow her daughter to come and visit the sick youth, in order if possible to arouse him from the state of apathy into which he had fallen. Mrs. Wang was scandalised, and refused; but as the Lius appeared to make such a point of it she was quite at a loss how to act. Now it so happened that in the service of this discreet matron was a servant-girl, who seems to have been admirably adapted to play the part of a *soubrette* in one of Molière's comedies. This girl accordingly proposed to her mistress that they should have recourse to stratagem; the young people had never seen each other,—why not dress up the son to represent the daughter? Then he could go and 'do the civil,' and come back again without fear of detection. No sooner said than done. Mrs. Wang wrote to say that her daughter would come and see her betrothed, though she would not be able to stay long; and meantime the artful servant dressed young Wang, a lad of sixteen, in girl's clothes, and initiated him into the mysteries of feminine deportment with much ability. The only real difficulty lay in his large feet. The two then set out together,—the false bride and her maid. They arrived at the bridegroom's house, and were received without suspicion; then paid a visit of sympathy to the sick youth's bedroom. But the Liu family would not hear of the two guests leaving under at

least three days, and Miss Liu took such a fancy to the supposed
Miss Wang that they found it simply impossible to get away at all.
The servant girl argued and chattered most energetically, for detection was imminent; what was the use of their staying? she
said; the young man was far too sick to be married; why not let
them go, and then come back when he was well?—"Oh, as far as
"that goes," said Miss Liu, "the marriage had better take place at
"once; I will represent my brother at the ceremony, and they can
"be married by proxy!" So this enterprising damsel dressed herself in boy's clothes, and the girl-bridegroom was married in due
form to the boy-bride; much to the satisfaction of everybody concerned. The secret was not discovered by the parents until some
months afterwards, when of course there was nothing for it but to
confirm the marriage. The invalid having recovered in the meantime, the originally-intended wedding took place between him and
the bashful lady to whom he had been really betrothed, and the
two curiously-matched couples lived happily together ever afterwards.

This was a romantic match enough, but here is one still more
remarkable. Some years ago, there lived a wealthy mandarin who
had two wives. The lady who held the superior rank was blessed
with a singularly unattractive daughter; she was short, deeply
pitted with the small-pox, and her features outrageously distorted.
Everything that money could buy, however, was hers; and she did
her best to counteract her deformity with the costliest silks and
jewels obtainable. The daughter of the number-two wife was pro-
portionately pretty; and the two girls occupied different pavilions
in a large and handsome garden. Now it fell out one day, when
they both about sixteen years of age, that a young student was
amusing himself with the manly recreation of kite-flying, just outside the garden wall; when, as luck would have it, the string broke,
and the kite fell fluttering over, quite close to the rooms occupied
by the prettier of the two girls. This adventurous young person
hopped timidly out into the garden, picked it up, and found that
upon it was pourtrayed the face of a handsome youth, who, to her

imagination, must needs be the owner of the kite ; and inspired by
the romance of the situation, she took up a pencil, wrote hastily
some love-verses upon it, and flung it over the wall again. But
the entire scene had been watched by the ugly sister, and, burning
with jealousy, she determined to turn it to her own advantage.
Accordingly she sent her Abigail to find out the owner of the kite,
to represent her as having written the verses, and to arrange an
interview in the garden—a most improper proceeding, of course,
and one which was only excusable from the extreme youth of the
plain though sportive lady herself. The maid soon put the plan
into execution, and the deluded *siu-tsai** found himself at the appointed time outside his charmer's window. When, however, he
found that he was expected to walk up, he heartily. wished himself
out of the scrape ; but there was no help for it. He was shown
into the lady's boudoir, and found the lady herself hiding behind the
curtains. A pretty pair of lovers, truly ! and the lamp was burning so low he could hardly see where he was. The coy creature
confessed that she had written the *billet-doux ;* but it was impossible for a long time to coax her out of her concealment, until
the lover threatened all sorts of desperate measures if she did not
satisfy his curiosity. At last, with great reluctance, she showed her
blushing features. The *siu-tsai* stared in blank amazement at the
grotesque object which he saw before him ; and then, with a cry of
rage and disgust at having been so grievously taken in, he bolted
down stairs and made the best of his way over the garden wall.
Shortly afterwards, the father of this gay Lothario announced that
he had arranged a marriage for him with one of this very mandarin's
daughters : and upon enquiry he concluded that he was doomed to
be bound for life to the ugly creature who had made love to him
on that memorable night. "Very well," he replied, "if I must, I
"must ; but I tell you frankly I'll never either look at her or speak
"to her, and I shall marry somebody else immediately afterwards."
But there was no help for it, the marriage-day arrived, and this
graceless youth behaved as badly as ever he could. Both sisters

* *i. e.,* graduate.

were given in wedlock the same day, and both of course were strictly
veiled. Everybody was scandalised with the indecent behaviour
of the young bridegroom; the other was an elderly, respectable sort
of man who had been chosen on account of his position. After the
wedded couples had retired, however, the comedy began in earnest.
The *siu-tsai* (who, by the way, had grown in the meantime to be a
chü-jin)* simply refused so much as to look at his bride, but took
his mattrass and flung it down in another room. To all her prayers
and enquiries he turned a deaf ear, or retorted by some cutting
remark upon her moral and physical deformities. At last she
rushed to her mother, who immediately took up her cause and let
that young man know what it was to have a mother-in-law. Then
she took her daughter by the hand and led her into the young
man's room; who, lifting his eyes, beheld before him one of the
most charming maidens he had ever seen. Mutual explanations
followed, and the night which had begun so tempestuously ended
in happiness and repose. But meanwhile a far worse scene was
being enacted in the other bridal chamber. The plain sister was
under the impression that her old flame was to fall to her share, and
mightily disgusted was she when her real husband stood revealed.
"Good gracious me!" she exclaimed—or whatever may be the
equivalent for that in Chinese—Ai-yah! perhaps—"Why, how old
"you have grown since last we met! and pray where did you get
"those nasty moustaches from?"—"Oh indeed, madam," replied
the husband; "so you have already had a lover, have you? Though
"you're mistaken in thinking I was the favoured man." The lady
uttered a shriek of despair at this terrible revelation, and was
altogether so disgusted by the turn affairs had taken, that she resorted to the not very uncommon expedient of hanging herself
upon the spot.

There is at present a young lady in Shanghai city who has had
four husbands in about as many weeks; having been forsaken by
every suitor immediately after marriage. Indeed, her history is a
curious one. She is described as being fair to look upon,—accord-

---

* *i. e.*, licentiate.

ing to Chinese taste—and in every way calculated to attract ad-
mirers; her feet are of the tiniest, her eyes of the narrowest,—and
yet somehow or other there has always seemed some obstacle in the
way of her getting a husband.   At length a marriage-brokeress
took compassion upon her—or rather, saw her way to turn the
despised lady to good account.   She took her home with her;
painted her face, and arrayed her in the most attractive jackets
she could muster.   Thus dressed, the girl really looked very well;
and very shortly a suitor appeared in the person of a gentleman of
some means, who had been left a widower and childless.   The
brokeress—'white ants,' they call these ladies in China—asked him
ninety dollars; which he, enraptured with the beauty of his new
bride, willingly paid upon the spot.   The marriage rejoicings passed
off quietly enough, and the husband took the fair one home in
much satisfaction.   But alas! favour is deceitful and beauty vain.
A vacant stare was all the reply vouchsafed to him by his wife
when he addressed her; then she broke into a cackling, senseless
laugh, and he found that she was *mad*.   Disgusted at being so
imposed upon, he packed her back again to the person from whom
he had purchased her, with a verbal message that he made her a
present of the idiot and the dollars too.   Nothing could have suited
the lady's views more admirably; and next day the mad lady was
again at the disposal of the highest bidder.   This time the applicant was a man occupying some small post in a yamên, and he
paid bargain-money to the extent of twenty dollars; in the meantime, however, a married but childless barber appeared upon the
scene, and he bought her for a hundred, which he paid, money
down, and carried off the prize before the other.   The jilted one
thereupon abused the 'white-ant' roundly, and refused to listen to
her attempts at a compromise; a wife he had bought and a wife
he would have, and the one in question happened to be particularly
to his taste.   The old crone's eyes twinkled.   "Bide a wee," she
said—or words to that effect; "wait a day or two longer, and you
"shall have her back."   The event justified the prediction; the
very next day the disgusted barber bundled back the unfortunate

idiot, preferring to lose his dollars than his face.* The business
so far had prospered; two hundred and ten dollars had come rolling
in, and another man was hooked already. This man—the yamên-
runner—had meanwhile taken a trip up the river in order to
present his devotions at some shrine at Mow-shan near Nanking,
with a view to securing success in his matrimonial schemes;
and during his absence, his number-one wife, fearful lest he
should bring back a still more formidable rival, clinched the bargain,
and brought the lady home. But she might just as well have purchased a wild cat. No sooner had the new wife arrived, than her
malady took a more serious form than ever, and the house was
turned into a perfect beargarden. The afflicted and much-despised
lady was summarily packed off home again; and married next day
to a traveller from the country, who paid a similarly heavy price,
and did not find out that he had married a maniac until he had got
her as far as his residence at Hoochow. Back she came again,
poor thing, like a bad penny; she probably found another husband
the next week; and meantime the lady who had got possession of
her reaped a golden harvest.

But it is not only in matters matrimonial that the Chinese are
such accomplished swindlers. Knavery in China is just as much
a fine art as it is in Europe, and woe-betide a greenhorn if ever
he gets into the meshes of a moral agriculturist. When Moses
sold his horse for a gross of green spectacles with brass rims, he
certainly made an unfortunate bargain; but he got off far more
easily than an ingenuous youth of the Middle Kingdom, connected
with the silk-trade, whose recent most extraordinary adventures
we have lately heard about. A gentleman of the family of Ch'ên
—no relation, we believe, to a certain eminent magistrate of that
name—some time ago sent his son from Hoochow with a cargo of
Tsatlee for the benefit of the eager silk-inspectors of Shanghai,
with directions as to its realisation. On the way, he fell in with
two most agreeable fellow-travellers, who hailed his boat and en-

* To "lose face" is a Chinese idiom meaning to suffer in reputation, to have the
laugh against one.

tered into friendly conversation with him. What was his noble
name? What was his honourable birth-place? Hoochow? Delightful! Their despicable residence was Hoochow also. They must
be permitted to bear him company. So they journed on together
until they came to Chia-ho, where they all three rested at an inn
for a day or two, and where, be it remarked, there happened to be
a very attractive lady. The day after their arrival, the two strangers received a visit from a youth of unusual personal beauty, dressed in rich silks and riding a handsome horse. A long and mysterious colloquy then ensued, which greatly excited the curiosity of
both Ch'ên and the attractive lady, who seem to have watched the
interview by peeping furtively through opposite windows; but of
course they were too far off to hear what passed. At length the
tsi-tsi ku-ku* came to an end, and the young gentleman rode away.
During the afternoon a messenger arrived with an invitation for
the two strangers to a wine-party. They replied they would be
delighted to come; but there was a young friend travelling with
them, a fellow-countryman, and they felt a kind of reluctance at
leaving him all by himself. The messenger scouted any such idea,
and very warmly included young Ch'ên in the invitation; which
Ch'ên, thanking his new friends for their thoughtfulness, accepted.
That night they set out to go to the party as arranged, and a long
way they had to travel. Down this street and up that one—on
and on they went, and Ch'ên wondered when they were ever going to arrive at their destination. At length they turned down a
long, deserted lane in an out-of-the-way quarter of the town, and
halted in front of a strange house. Inside, however, everything
looked bright and promising. The charming young gentleman was
there, and capital company he proved; the dinner was excellent,
and the wine—well, the wine was more potent than it ought to
have been. Poor Ch'ên! it was his first champagne; and he got
awfully drunk. What happened to him then, he doesn't know;
but he had a sensation of being carried about somewhere, round
and round, and then lumped down in a dark place and thrashed

---

* Whispered colloquy.

within an inch of his life. Then he became unconscious; and when
he awoke next morning, he felt very penitent, because very sore
and very sick. Rolling his hot-coppery head from side to side,
at last he opened his eyes. It was a singular scene. He was in a
strange boat, surrounded by well-dressed servants, while, lounging
on the principal seat, was the handsome youth of the previous night.
Struggling into a sitting attitude, he began, not unnaturally, to up-
braid this *roué* with being the cause of all his misfortunes, and demanded of him why he was detained, and by whose authority he
had been beaten. "Beaten, by my servants?" was the reply.
"Well I am sorry for it, if it hurt you; but frankly, I hardly won-
"der at it," added the young man, with a half-rueful, half-comical
glance at his companion. "And why not, pray?" demanded Ch'ên.
"Why not?" shouted the other—"why, look at yourself!" Ch'ên
looked at himself, accordingly—poor victim! and like the old woman in the song began to doubt his own identity. His hair was
covered with an elaborate *coiffure* and stuck full of glittering pins;
his fingers were adorned with gilded nails; he had got on a girl's
chün-tsze, or embroidered petticoat; and his face was painted a
bewitching pink. His friendly fellow-travellers had drugged his
wine, and then palmed him off in the darkness upon the young
gentleman, instead of the girl at the inn for whom he had paid
them six hundred taels of silver; the servants had thrashed him
for an impostor when they discovered what he was; and the
thieves had made off with his cargo of Tsatlee silk. So the com-
panions in tribulation journeyed sadly on together, and laid their
joint complaint before the Tao-t'ai of the nearest town.

If thieves are cunning, however, there are many mandarins who
are more than a match for them, by a very long way. For example, there is a Che-hsien, or district magistrate, at Shê-mên, near
Hang-chow, who enjoys a most extraordinary and deserved reputation for honesty and shrewdness, to judge by a specimen of his
judicial powers which has just reached us, and which certainly
eclipses the judgment of Sancho Panza. A country bumpkin was
travelling from Shê-mên to Kan-chow to spend his New-Year ho-

lidays with his friends at home; carrying with him, in a bundle, his savings for the past twelve months. Now his little store of money amounted to no less than twenty ounces of silver; and his friends cautioned him to be very careful of it, and, above all things, to conceal the fact of his possessing such enormous wealth. When therefore he arrived at a certain inn where he was going to spend the night, he gave his precious bundle into the hands of the inn-keeper, as is usual in China, for safety; in answer to all enquiries assuring him that there was very little money in it, and that he was quite unable to specify the sum. The surprise of the host, therefore, when he found the real amount of the silver, was un-bounded; and, what was worse, the temptation was too great for him. The consequence was that when the man's bundle was re-turned to him next morning it was considerably lighter than it had been before; and the guest complained that he must have been robbed. The host, however, reminded him that he had said there was very little in the bundle, the previous night; how then could he talk about there having been twenty ounces of silver? It was an attempt to extort money, and the host was virtuously indignant. So there was nothing for it but for the unlucky pea-sant to appeal to the mandarin, who, fortunately for him, was this very man Liu. The complainant and the accused were soon before him, pleading their respective causes, and the latter continued to protest his entire innocence. At last the Che-hsien told him ab-ruptly to hold out his hand. "Oh, don't be frightened," he conti-nued; "I am not going to hurt you." Then taking a pen he dip-ped it in the ink, and wrote upon the palm of the man's hand the characters 銀子 *ying-tsze* (silver). "Now," said he, "you go and "kneel down in that corner with your face to the wall, and take "care you *don't lose those characters;* if you do, I shall conclude "you are guilty of stealing the money; so squeeze your hand up "tight." The man did so, wonderingly, and then the Che-hsien sent for his wife. "Where is the money you and your husband "stole?" asked the mandarin. The woman protested that she knew nothing about it; that no robbery had ever taken place in their

house, and so on. "Here, you," cried Liu, addressing the man in
the corner, "how about that 'silver'—have you still got it safe ?"
"Yes, yes," replied the prisoner, opening his hand to assure himself that the characters had not disappeared. "Do you hear that ?"
said the mandarin, turning again to the woman ; "your husband
"confesses, you see ; so you had better make a clean breast of it,
"too." The unlucky woman then acknowledged the crime and
prayed for mercy ; the mandarin slapped her face as a mild correc-
tion ; and told the inn-keeper that as it was his first offence after
keeping an inn for fifteen years he would let him off with a fine
of five thousand *cash*, to be paid to the man he had robbed. The
silver was then restored intact, and the countryman went on his
way rejoicing.

Another mandarin of the same name, residing at Nanking, seems
also to have distinguished himself by his success in extorting a
confession from a criminal of peculiar truculence ; more by good
luck, however, than good management. For a long time the robber, a man named Mêng-'rh, had been the terror of the neighbourhood. His courage was only equal to his crimes ; and daring
though he was, no single word of confession had ever being wrung
from his lips. At last the head of the police department got him
into his hands, and having secured his person set about making preparations for the necessary torture. These consisted simply in
melting a small quantity of copper, which was to be poured over
the criminal's flesh in case of obduracy. The responsibility of
dealing with so noted a pest to society was not lost upon the officer, and he felt his reputation was at stake. So he commenced by
asking him, in a pleasantly conversational style, whether he felt at
all cold. "Rather," was the cool reply. "Have some wine ?"
asked Liu. The robber though the doubt implied quite superfluous, but hinted that he preferred *ho-tsew*. [This is a white or co-
lourless spirit of excessive strength which is much drunk in the
country : not the yellow wine commonly known to foreigners as
samshu]. The refreshment was served, but the robber pulled a
face and complained that it wasn't warm enough. "Pooh !" he

said, contemptuously, "you fellows don't know to heat wine."
Then,.with a significant glance at the pot of boiling metal on the
stove, he deliberately took out two lumps of burning charcoal and
placed them on his knees; thus holding the wine-cup over them
till the wine was hot and the flesh of his legs all burnt. "You
"see," said he, "I don't mind pain. I know all about your molten
"copper. Not the slightest use, I assure you!" and then went on
to talk of other matters. Poor Liu was simply nonplussed. "Look
"here," he said, to the extraordinary being in front of him,—"I
"have pledged my honour to wring a confession out of you; you
"hold my rank and button in your hands. Torture, I see, will
"have no effect; I throw myself upon your charity!" This very
novel appeal had the desired result. "Liu," said the robber, "you
"are not a bad fellow, though you are not a success as a manda-
"rin." He then confessed to having committed thirteen murders,
and said he did it to support his aged parents. The crime which
was charged against him that day, however, he said he did not do;
and if he confessed to that, somebody else would be confessing to
it afterwards, and then Liu would get into trouble. The two thereupon become bosom friends; and Liu is now looked upon as a
perfect Solomon, while the robber was amicably decapitated the
other day.

The following incident, tragic and terrible though it be, is nevertheless vouched for as true in every particular. Nor is there
any inherent improbability in it. The crime on which it hinges
—that of matricide—is so dreadful in Chinese eyes that neither
names nor places are given, and the city where it occurred is mer-
cifully protected from (very undeserved but) everlasting infamy,
by its non-identification. We are told simply that in a certain
town 'north of the river,' there was a widow, who had a rebellious
son. The son was married, and his wife, who seems to have been
a pattern daughter-in-law, had borne him two children. One day
when the young man was absent from home, the grandmother took
one of the little boys out for a walk, upon some errand to a tea-
house; but while she was there, the poor little chap, who seems to

have been crowing and laughing in her arms, made a sudden spring
—as children will, sometimes,—and fell clean into a large *kong* of
boiling water. The screams of the poor old woman attracted
everybody in the neighbourhood, and the child was fished out immediately; but its injuries were so frightfully severe that it died
there and then. The mother, alarmed by the report, hastened to
the scene, and, true to the instincts of a Chinawoman, seeing that
her child was lost past all hope of recovery, turned her attention
to comforting the elder woman. The grief of the poor old body
was intense, and, mingled with it, was a dreadful apprehension of
her son's wrath on his return. A day or two afterwards his wife
informed her mother-in-law that she must visit her parents for a
short time; she wouldn't be long; "but," she added, "if your son
"comes back in my absence, tell him I have taken both the child-
"ren with me." Very soon the husband returned, and gruffly asked his mother where his wife and children were. The old woman
answered according to instructions, and tremblingly saw him de-
part. Arrived at where his wife was staying, she told him that
one of the boys had fallen sick and died; but unfortunately the
occurrence had made too great an impression in the neighbourhood
for the secret to be kept long, and he soon heard the true version
of the story. He then went home, followed by his wife and sur-
viving child, and taxed his mother with it. Both women, however,
stuck to their story, although the frightened and despairing looks
of the old grandmother confirmed the rumour he had heard. He
turned away with a sinister look and said no more: but that night
he left his bed, crept noiselessly into his mother's room, and with
his own hands strangled her in her sleep. Next morning, of course,
it was discovered, and there was a tremendous excitement in the
street. The neighbours came pouring in, caught the murderer,
and were for haling him to the Che-hsien there and then; but a
respectable old man restrained them. "Do nothing of the kind,"
said he. "Don't you know that if this is reported officially to the
"authorities the city will be branded with infamy, the mandarins
"will be dismissed, and the whole lot of us sent packing? I am

" the brother of this poor woman ; leave me to deal with her son."
The neighbours saw that he was right, and gave way at once.
" Now go, some of you," said he, " and bring me here two coffins."
Off rushed some of them, and meanwhile he went to the Hsien,
who of course had heard the report, and was in a pretty state of
mind. According to Chinese custom the unfortunate mandarin
would be irretrievably disgraced, and the corners of the city walls
cut away and rounded off, as a sign of the horrible crime which
had been perpetrated there. " Don't you interfere," said the old
man. " You know nothing about it officially. You will only be
" disgraced, and it will do you no good for the wretched fellow to
" be publicly sliced. Leave it to me; I will be responsible."
The mandarin made him an obeisance of unqualified gratitude and
respect.   " May you become an official," said he, " you will be in-
" deed a blessing to the people." So the old gentleman walked
quietly back, put his dead sister into one coffin, his living nephew
into another, buried them both in due form, and went home to
breakfast.

Such facts as this are sufficiently horrible, but they are of value
as affording correlative illustration of the extraordinary pitch to
which filial piety is carried in China. Here is a more agreeable
story, comic even in its most harrowing parts, and highly romantic throughout. At Nanking there lived an old man and his wife,
to whom had been born, late in their married life, a son. This
child was betrothed soon after its birth to the baby daughter of a
neighbouring friend, with whom the old gentleman—Kia, we will
call him—was on very intimate terms. When however the little
bridegroom-elect had reached the age of twelve, the Chang-maos
took possession of the city, and general confusion was the result.
Some people went in this direction, others in that, many families
were ruined and households broken up, and among other disasters
the unfortunate child was stolen. After the fall of Nanking and
the re-establishment of Imperial rule, by Colonel Gordon, the father returned to the city, disconsolate at the loss of his son, and
tried to retrieve his fortunes. While there he one day saw a lit-

tle rebel-boy just the age of his lost child, and not unlike him in the face; and as there appeared no chance of his ever becoming a father again, he purchased the lad and adopted him as his own. By degrees things quieted down, years passed by, and his old friend—whom we will call Yih—wrote him a letter, reminding him of the old bond between them and suggesting that the time was about ripe for the conclusion of the marriage; not having heard, in his enforced exile, of the change in the identity of his proposed son-in-law. The wily Kia, carefully concealing that trifling circumstance, replied in warm terms, the sooner the better; and an early day was fixed upon for the ceremony. Meanwhile, however, the son of Kia had grown up a fine youth, and on escaping from the hands of his captors found his way back to Nanking, where he arrived in a sorry plight indeed, to find the old house burnt down, and no trace of his parents anywhere. Thereupon he bethought himself that he would try and ferret out his father-in-law elect; and by great good fortune he was successful. Yih was astounded at a new claimant turning up for his daughter's hand; and, glancing at the youth's travel-stained dress and haggard looks, thought he must be some impostor; but he soon found that there was probably more in his story than he at first imagined. So they went off together to the house of Kia; and Kia recognised his son, although the wicked old fellow was too much afraid of being found out in his deceit to acknowledge him. "My son, indeed! my "son?" he said, contemptuously; "nothing of the sort, Sir, I as-"sure you. He's my nephew, if you like; but my son? Pooh! "What does he know about it?" But the old mother recognised him, and proclaimed with tears of joy that it was indeed her long-lost son, who had been stolen from her six years before. The neighbours all came flocking in, and many of them knew him again too; so there was great rejoicing. But of course this was not particularly agreeable for the adopted one, and he soon began to assert his claims in a manner that would take no denial. Finding, however, that it was no use, now that the rightful heir had turned up, and that he had lost his position and his bride as well, dark thoughts of vengeance came across his soul; revenge, ha! ha!—and all that sort of thing. Now for the tragic part. Armed with a knife of great size, and very sharp, he crept out under cover of darkness, and in the middle of the night rapped imperiously at the door of Yih's house. The wretched Yih, who was fast asleep in bed, struggled down stairs in his night-clothes, opened the door and asked his untimely visitor what he wanted. The ousted one coolly replied that he wanted to be married; adding, that unless that ceremony took place immediately, he would be under the painful necessity of killing Mr., Mrs., and Miss Yih with a knife he had brought for the purpose—and afterwards himself. Poor Yih broke out into a cold perspiration, and politely asked the murderous gentleman to sit down and wait while he went to see what could be done. Then he rushed trembling into his wife's bedroom and told her what this dreadful man had said. "Let us "go and call the neighbours," he panted; "let us get a lot of peo- "ple round the house, and then tie his legs and take him to a " mandarin."—"Let us do nothing so stupid," retorted his spouse. " Go back directly, and tell him he shall be married in two days " if he only behaves properly now. We'll *marry him to the ser- "vant girl!* False bridegroom, false bride; oh, how thick you men " are!" So the gentleman stayed with them for two days, and then the marriage ceremony took place, to the great delight of old Kia, who had been let into the secret. Kia's son was married to Miss Yih at the same time; and then everybody swore eternal friend- ship all round. What occurred after the bridal veils were lifted, and the fiery young gentleman discovered the hoax that had been played upon him, we leave to the fancy of our readers; but they may be sure that there was a great row in the house. The false bride turned out an awful vixen, and when last we heard of them she was leading her husband, now entirely subjugated, an uneasy life in the neighbourhood of Nanking.

Who says the Chinese are not a romantic nation? We have al- ready given instances of their conjugal and filial devotion, all more or less curious to our Western ideas, but the story that we are now about to recount simply transcends everything we have heard, for extravagance. Living in a village in the province of Kwangtung are two brothers, types apparently of the poor but honest Chinese rustic. "Brother," said the younger, one day, "you are forty years "of age; why don't you marry? At this rate we shall never be "able to perpetuate our father's family, nor to raise for ourselves "any sons against our declining years." "The reason I do not "marry," responded the other, "is that I cannot afford it,—other-"wise I would;" whereupon the younger of the two implored his brother to sell him, and buy a wife with the proceeds! The propo-posal, however, was indignantly scouted by the elder; "What," said he, "exchange a brother for a wife? Never! a wife I may at "any time be able to procure, but I can never get another bro-"ther." But a wealthy neighbour, overhearing the conversation, called upon the two, entered into an insinuating colloquy with the elder man, and finished by offering him thirty taels of silver for his *hiung-ti*.* The temptation was too strong; the young man was sold, and went into voluntary captivity to his new master, receiv-ing board and lodging in return for his services, while the elder went and bought a wife with the money. On the arrival of this lady at home, however, she began to question with her lord, as to the whereabouts of his brother. "I always heard," she said, "that there were two of you; what has become of him?" "My "dear," replied her spouse,—"the fact is, I have sold him; and "what is more, if I had not done so, I should never have been "able to get you." Whereupon his wife was greatly shocked; and going back to her father's she told him the whole story, beseech-ing him to furnish her with the means of buying back her brother-in-law. Two days afterwards she returned joyfully with the neces-sary amount, which she deposited for safety under her bed; but alas! a short time only elapsed before the box containing it most strangely disappeared. This so affected her mind that she tried to hang herself; and was so far successful that she was put into a coffin and taken out to be buried. Present at the funeral was a

---

* Younger brother.

sister of the widower; swathed up to the eyes in white bandages, and howling as only jackals and bereaved Celestials can howl. Suddenly there came on a fearful thunderstorm; the rain poured down in torrents; crash succeeded crash, and flash followed flash, until one riband of flame passed through the body of the disconsolate sister-in-law, stretching her a corpse upon the ground. As she fell, her jacket opened, and out tumbled the missing coin! The same flash that killed her, shattered the coffin and aroused the apparently dead wife; and so the judgment of Heaven was fulfilled. The false sister was speedily packed away in the coffin, and buried; the husband and wife trudged piously home with their recovered treasure; the younger brother was redeemed from slavery, and the family are now living happily together, as anybody who cares to go and visit them may see for himself.—Now this story is vouched for by no less respectable an authority than a licentiate of Canton; but whether it redounds most to the credit of Chinese morality or the licentiate's inventive powers, we leave to our readers to decide.

The practice of selling one's relations, referred to in the above story, is a very singular phase of Chinese domestic life; and for the benefit of any fair reader who may honour this book with her perusal, we will give another instance of it, kindly furnished by a lady friend of our own. The experiences of ladies in England who live at home at ease and are lucky enough in these demoralised days of universal education to get hold of a servant who is really 'a treasure,' must often be of a somewhat entertaining kind: but we fancy that those who have left their 'ain fireside' for the gorgeous East could recount many anecdotes of their amahs and other personal attendants which would beat any of Dean Ramsay's tales. The lady in question, then on the point of leaving Shanghai for a southern port, had an amah, or Chinese maid, who happened to suit her very well, and whom she was naturally very anxious to take with her. The amah was perfectly willing to go, but the amah's mother wouldn't hear of it. The prospect of losing her only child was far too serious to be entertained for a moment, and the old woman was most pathetically obdurate. The lady sent her amah again and again to try to win her over; the amah invariably returned, assuring her mistress that she had 'bobberied' her mother and done all she could, but without avail. At last, when the case seemed hopeless, the maternal heart relented, and the lady was informed by the aged one that she could have her daughter, body and soul, for the sum of three hundred dollars!—We believe that the bargain fell through.

Among the high military officers of Tso Tsung-tang's army, now engaged in the North-western campaign against the Mahommedans of Kansuh, there is said to be a very remarkable man. Many years ago he was a robber, and during a long series of feats of ingenuity and daring, annexed a large chest belonging to a petty military mandarin, which contained his official hat and button. At the same time he conveyed no less a sum than a hundred thousand taels from the same unfortunate personage: a large amount, and very possibly exaggerated, but the exact figure is after all a minor point. Suffice it to say that he took away the bulk of the officer's fortune, and all his insignia of rank. Thus provided, he travelled in a North-westerly direction, and began to sigh for an honester and more honourable career; and finally, being a man of enterprise and courage, determined upon entering the army. This he did; and in a comparatively short time—partly from sterling merit, and partly, perhaps, from sterling coin,—rose surely and rapidly to a very much higher position than the one which he had assumed. No clue, meanwhile, had been discovered as to the robbery, and the luckless victim—a man of the name of Tang—of course had to 'eat' his loss. But not long ago, as fate would have it, he succeeded in tracing the robber; and reaching the contingent of Tso's army where he was in command, demanded an interview. The old rascal, having heard the visitor's name and guessing his business, consented in a dignified and gracious manner; arrayed himself in all his robes of office; commanded that the man should be admitted, and received him with great ceremony, rigorously insisting upon the regular *ko-t'ow*. Charged with the crime, he admitted it with a winning frankness that staggered his accuser not a little : " And now," said he, "what do you propose to do ?" Tang replied, of course, that he intended to expose his villany, and memorialise the Emperor, and take whatever revenge he could. " Pooh, pooh," said the ex-robber; " who would believe you ? " Look, I am now a high mandarin, far higher than ever you were, "and far richer too. Let us settle this small business amicably. " I will give you half my fortune, which is more than what I stole, "and you shall have your button ; and, if you like, a good com- "mand in my regiment." Tang thought a minute, and then consented ; and the strangely-assorted couple are now serving under the same banner, the firmest and best of friends !

It is said that Spiritualism has many adherents among the Chinese, and there is no doubt that there are few nations fonder of stories relating to ghosts, and matters generally connected with the unseen world. A good deal is often adduced setting forth the demoralising influences of these researches in Western lands, but we have just heard such a good story showing the other side of the question, in the experience of an inquisitive Chinaman, that in common fairness we think we must let our readers have the benefit of it. There was once a man named Wang, who professed a high admiration for the accidents of wealth and honour. To him a mandarin was worthy of all reverence ; the richer a man was, the more he stuck to him. Like many Western sycophants who dearly love a lord, this gentleman made it the business of his life to pander to the wealthy and influential in order to reap the reward of their patronage ; but on one occasion he rather overreached himself. It so happened that he lodged one night in a temple ; and waking up in the small hours of the morning, he thought he heard voices in the vestibule. As it grew light, he got out of bed to see who was there ; but what was his amazement, when, instead of living men, he found only two corpses, ready coffined for burial. Approaching stealthily, he read the names of the deceased, which were emblazoned upon the coffins ; one of which was that of a wealthy and powerful mandarin, the other, that of a poor

scholar who had died in obscurity. With an eye ever to the main
chance, Mr. Wang began to offer extraordinary honours to the
manes of the mandarin; burning joss-sticks, rapping his empty
old head upon the ground in front of the coffin, and doing his best
with prayers and offerings to secure the good offices of the ghost,
imploring him to bless him and sometimes to visit him in his
sleep. Then, turning to the poor dead student, " Phew, phew ! "
he said, with an elevated nose; " and pray what business have
" you here, lying in this impertinent manner so close to this great
" man ? Aren't you ashamed to meet him in the prison of the
" earth (hell) ? " So he contemptuously went away, tenderly dust-
ing all the impurities off the mandarin's coffin, but leaving the
scholar as he was. Some nights afterwards, this good man had a
dream. A venerable personage in rich and flowing robes came to
his bedside; and Mr. Wang, overjoyed at the vision, believing it
to be no more than the realisation of his prayer, began chinchin-
ing and knocking his head to the mysterious visitor with tremendous energy. But the ghost replied, in a slow and measured voice;
" Why all this respect and worship ? It was only the other day
" that you reviled me and contemned me, as I lay dead on the
" temple floor ! " " What," gasped Wang, feeling fearfully small,
" are you the scholar ? I made sure you must be the mandarin."
" Ah, that was just your mistake," replied the spectre, drily. " You
" should never jump to conclusions. Your rich mandarin is now
" a poor devil of a ghost without a rap to bless himself with, or
" anybody else. But I don't mind doing you a good turn, if you
" will transfer your reverence to me. You want to be rich ? Good.
" Now in such-and-such a village, just outside such-and-such a
" cottage, there is a weeping willow; go and dig under it; you
" will find a treasure of unmeasured wealth." So saying the shade
vanished; and Mr. Wang lost no time in securing the fulfilment of
his dream. As soon as it was light he shouldered his pickaxe and
his spade, marched off to the village in question, found the willow-
tree, and commenced operations. But no sooner had he worked
himself into a profuse perspiration without coming to anything of

value, than the door of the neighbouring cottage opened, and the
tenant, seeing a man digging in his grounds, asked him what on
earth he meant by his impudence.   Wang stood speechless; and
being unable to give a proper account of himself, he got the soundest thrashing from the angry villager that he had ever endured in
his life.   He gave up all belief in Spiritualism from that day !

The belief of the Chinese, generally, in diabolical influence, is
however universal.   No story is too wild for acceptance, even
with the cultured classes ; and there are perhaps few races, if any,
who live in greater bondage to the supernatural.   Indeed the more
one lends an ear to Chinese stories of the marvellous, the more
phases of superstition are found to flourish among every portion of
the populace.   Vampirism, incubism and metempsychosis form
the basis of a very large number of the tales that continually pass
current from mouth to mouth, while, as is well-known, the Chinese live in perpetual fear of the influence of the dead.   Here is
a case in point.   During the T'ai-p'ing troubles there lived at Nanking a most virtuous peasant who, in addition to tilling his ancestral plot of ground, eked out an honest livelihood by selling tea
and wine.   One day in the summer months there happened along
a priest of the Buddhist sect, who, tired and thirsty from the
weight of a heavy bag, sat down and ordered some refreshment.
This was quickly served, and the ecclesiastic, growing happy under the influence of rest and liquor, entered into a conversation
with the worthy host.   He told him how he was attached to the
sacred Island of Poo-too, and how he had wandered all over Chekiang and Kiangsu collecting money for a grand monastery that
he intended to build in the neighbourhood of Nanking.   The peasant lifted the bag, and was much impressed with the priest's further assurance that it contained considerably over a thousand
ounces of silver.   "And now," said the Buddhist, "I am going to
"repose a great trust in you.   I can see you're an honest man:
"and I want you to take charge of this treasure for me while I go
"and finish collecting the necessary balance in the country round.
"To prove my confidence still further, I give you free permission

"to make use of five hundred ounces while I am away; and I "hope you will turn it to good account." The farmer was half-afraid of his good luck; but he gave the cleric house-room for that night, and next morning the two friends parted. The money was soon invested in various enterprises, and Liu—that was his name —grew rapidly a rich man; in fact he laid out his five hundred taels with great judiciousness, and trebled the sum in no time. But month after month went by, and the priest was never heard of. At last one day, after two years had passed, during which his conscience had pricked him not a little, the worthy peasant had a dream. He was sitting at the door of his cottage on just such another hot afternoon as when he had first seen the priest, when he nodded, and was soon snoring. And as he slept he thought that, sitting where he was, he saw the figure of the priest approach-ing. He sprang up to welcome him; but making no sign of re-cognition the priest passed by his chair, and went behind him into the house. Up started Liu, rubbing his eyes, in pursuit. No sign of any one, however, could be found: but a servant met him and announced that her mistress, old Liu's daughter-in-law, had just given birth to a son. Liu instantly recognised the coincidence as supernatural; and, looking upon the new-born child *as an incarna-tion of the dead Buddhist*, named him 'Ho-shang' (priest). He grew up, however, a dreadful scapegrace: he was extravagant, he gambled, he did everything that was improper and was never chidden, because his parents regarded him as a supernatural being. Nor did they dare to refuse him any money; for, believing him to be the priest, they fancied that this was the only way in which they could pay off the grandfather's mysterious debt!

Necromancy is a great trade in China, and the writer must con-fess to having been much staggered by sundry revelations con-cerning his past life contained in a mysterious document compiled from certain calculations based upon the hour and date of his birth, etc., by a celebrated astrologer of Hangchow. We need not enter into details; but may assure our readers that the lucky-hit theory is quite inadequate to account for the singularly accurate particulars given by this professional quack, who had never seen us in his life, and was under the impression that he was being consulted by a Chinese. Sometimes, however, magicians get horribly sold. A youth, eager to pry into his future life, visited a Buddhist priest in Peking, and requested to know his fortune. The priest examined his face with much care, and after a respectable amount of mummery, assumed an expression of extreme horror, assuring the unfortunate lad that he had better drown himself at once. Somewhat startled by this recommendation, the applicant not unnaturally wished to know why. " Because," replied the old villain, " terrible trouble is coming upon your family and " yourself, within the next three days ; a catastrophe will befal you " infinitely worse than death, unless you choose death yourself " first. Now just you go and jump into the Shih-li river, outside " the Yung-ting Mên; or if you can't drown, why you'd better " hang yourself; or if you can't manage that, why, cut your throat;" and we can fancy him adding, like the Duke of Venice, Get thee gone—but do it. The wretched fellow went meekly away, and bent his steps to the fatal spot. On the way, however, he met a friend, who asked him what he was crying about. He told his piteous tale. " Is that all?" was the reply; "we can soon ar- " range this little matter." So he told him that if the extreme poverty of his family and clamouring of his creditors had anything to do with the disgrace predicted by the priest, he (the friend) would satisfy all claims; and in the meantime he would stick by him and never lose sight of him until the fatal three days were over. And so he did; and three more peaceful and quiet days they neither of them ever passed. Then came the sweet moment of revenge; and going to the temple where the old priest lodged, they both set to and slapped his face till he could hardly see. The priest cleared out in double-quick time, and is now pursuing his nefarious trade in an adjoining parish.

There is a mandarin of the name of Huang, in Kiang-si, given over entirely to the hobby of casting horoscopes. It is an amiable or at least harmless form of insanity, but on a recent occasion the

good man's folly caused a very serious disaster. Be it known that
he has five sons, all of whose fortunes were foretold immediately
they were born. The eldest was to develop into a great Minister of
State ; the second was to become a member of the Han-lin College,
and acquire great fame for learning ; the remainder were one and all
to become earls. The old man's heart swelled with paternal pride
as his calculations turned out so brilliantly in every case, and he
already looked upon himself as the father of the most distinguished
family\ *in futuro*, in China. A time approached, however, when
the birth of yet another scion of this remarkable stock became imminent ; an expectation which made the old man more elated than
ever, for on this occasion he would be a grandfather. So he put on
his spectacles, reckoned to a nicety according to the day, week,
month and year of the infant's birth, and then waited anxiously for
the most important datum of all—the hour at which the auspicious
event should take place. He saw by the signs that if only the child
were born at a certain moment, then fast approaching, the planetary
conjunction would be most favourable ; riches, honours, and fame
loomed brilliantly in the vista of futurity ; and the excitement of
the expectant progenitor of all this greatness knew no bounds.
Message after message did he sent into his daughter-in-law's room,
but all to no purpose. At length the opportunity passed, and
clouds gathered over the astrological horizon. It was but too plain
that if the child were born then, the direst calamities would result.
Disgrace, crime, poverty, misfortunes innumerable waited upon
the fatal hour. Up sprang the amateur magician, and, trembling
in every limb, sent word to the nurse in attendance that the child
wasn't to be born on any account until he announced that the omens
were more favourable. The prohibition was unnecessary, and
another anxious but more hopeful day was spent. At last the
prospect cleared. Riches, honours and the rest of Heaven's blessings again appeared in the magic mirror. But again the vision
dimmed ; and just as the last ray of prosperity was fading hopelessly away, news arrived that the little stranger had appeared,—
but, alas ! stillborn. The poor old mandarin burst out into a pas-

sion of lamentation: "Oh, unlucky fate!" he cried; "had the "child been born only a quarter of an hour ago, he would have "become a marquis at the very least!"

Several capital stories come from Soochow, a place which plumes itself upon being one of the most fashionable and elegant cities of the Middle Kingdom. In bygone days it was doubtless a charming residence enough, as is proved by the popular proverb, Above is Heaven; below are Hang and Soo.* At present, however, it is more than half in ruins, and presents a truly pitiable appearance in many parts. Still it is a very favourite resort, being beautifully situated near the T'ai-hu, a lovely lake studded with romantic islets. At Soochow, then, there lived some years ago a mandarin's son, named Chên, who was one of the ugliest, as well as one of the richest, men in the town. His legs were of very unequal length; his right arm was withered; his face was drawn grievously to one side, and there was something unpleasant the matter with his head. A gentleman so peculiarly afflicted of course found it a difficult matter to get a wife; none of the marriage-brokers would undertake his case; his ugliness outweighed his shekels; no respectable father would give his daughter to so eccentric-looking a being. Now it so happened that on the romantic little island of Tung-tung-ting-shan there lived a country gentleman of much repute, whose daughter was said to be of unusual fairness; and upon this maiden did the deformed one, in imagination, fix his somewhat uncertain eye. The project was a wild one, and he had much difficulty in persuading a middleman to act for him; indeed, a promised brokerage of five hundred taels was only just sufficient to induce one of this fraternity to undergo the risk of practising the necessary deceit. The bargain once struck, however, the broker went to work in a most businesslike manner. He called upon Mr. Ung, the lady's father, and laid the proposals before him in due form; expatiating upon the rank of Chên's papa, the wealth of the entire family, and the elegant accomplishments of Chên himself. He unfolded sheets of exquisitely written manuscript in proof of his client's scholarship—the

* Hangchow and Soochow.

poor creature was unable so much as to hold a pen—and nevor referred to his blind-eye or his halting leg. Three visits served to bring
the negociations to an end, and the broker returned triumphant. A
few weeks afterwards, however, Mr. Ung remarked that it would
be only civil if his future son-in-law were to call and have family
worship with them,—*i. e.*, pay his respects to the ancestors, and so
on; and this very natural request put both the broker and his
principal into a desperate fright. Chên then bethought of him of
a certain poor relation, a student, whom he had often snubbed; him
he sent for, and spoke to him with unusual condescension. " I
" know I have behaved coldly towards you," said he ; " but let by-
" gones be bygones. I mean to be a perfect brother to you for the
" future ; and meantime there is just a foolish trifling little matter
" in which I fancy you can be of service to me." The student
listened gravely, and waited to hear what followed. Bit by bit
Chên told him all the story, and finished up by saying that he
wanted his cousin to go and personate him at the preliminary festivities. " You shall have the pick of my wardrobe," said he, " and
" I'll not ask you for a thing again ; and I'll pay you five hundred
" taels into the bargain." The student thought a while, and then
said that he would do it. A procession of gaily decorated boats
two days afterwards crossed the lake, one containing the fictitious
bridegroom ; arrived at the island, the whole village turned out to do
them honour, old Ung made a grand feast, and there was altogether
a great excitement in the neighbourhood. In a few hours, however, in the midst of the merry-making, a most terrible wind sprang
up ; the waves of the lake were lashed into fury, and there was a
tremendous storm. Then it turned bitterly cold, and the snow fell
thick and fast. It was perfectly clear that to attempt to return
across the lake would be madness ; and the old gentleman, who
was enchanted with his son-in-law, proposed that the wedding
should take place there and then. Chên's cousin stared aghast ; the
broker turned pale ; here was a contingency they had neither of
them contemplated. But it was no use. Their protestations were
drowned in the unanimous voices of all the guests; and there was

nothing for it but to submit. The marriage ceremony was performed; and three days had even then to elapse before they could return. At length, however, they crossed the lake, Ung accompanying his daughter to her new home; when, on the opposite shore, whom should they see but Chên, stamping about and tearing his face with rage at the long absence of his cousin. Then, when the wedding party landed, and the truth came out, his passion was fearful. He half-murdered the bridegroom in five seconds, and it was with great difficulty the combatants were separated. Old Ung's astonishment at beholding his son-in-law in the clutches of such a misshapen monster was comical in the extreme, and the substitute bridegroom then told the old gentleman exactly the state of affairs. "You forced me to marry your daughter," said he, " but I have still been loyal to my cousin; I have protected his be-" trothed for three days and nights; I am still wearing my wedding " clothes, and I am now perfectly willing to give her up." But the old man wouldn't hear of this, and adopted him upon the spot; the broker got five hundred blows to match the amount of his brokerage, and Chên has had a horror of matrimony ever since.

In the same neighbourhood there is a Buddhist monastery of considerable fame, where the inmates preserve with much zeal the character attributed by tradition to the monks of old. They quaff ha-ha! and they laugh, ha-ha! according to the song which still celebrates the virtues of their predecessors, and lead a life in which the epicurean takes decidedly the precedence of the ascetic. For many years they kept open house and entertained freely, the Abbot himself being Symposiarch of the revels; gambling was a great feature of the general attractions, and the monks and lay brethren seem to have been a gay set, and more renowned for punch than piety, for as the Spanish proverb says, If the Abbot plays cards, what can you expect of the friars? But, one day, this holy man was seized with sore pains, and died. Then all the people gathered together about the house, as people always do gather about a place where anything dreadful has happened, and began to talk scandal about the deceased. They wondered how an assemblage of friars, who of course had taken a vow of poverty and were supposed to live on boiled grass, or straw, or whatever may be the diet most congenial to sanctity in China, could have afforded to give such expensive entertainments; when, in the midst of their gossip, they heard a plaintive howl wafted faintly towards them from behind a curtain. The strains were most musical, most melancholy; in fact, they emanated from a lovely woman in distress, who was mourning the loss of her spiritual lord and master. Somewhat startled by this revelation, they asked the monks what they had to say in explanation of so strange a discovery; " Oh," replied a burly friar, " that afflicted lady is—a—our Lady " Abbess." And in a way she was; for she was the true and lawful spouse of the deceased, who in his earlier days had been a leader of much eminence among the T'ai-p'ings, and an intimate friend of the Chung-wang. When Colonel Gordon and Li Hung-chang captured Soochow, he fled for his life, taking with him his wife and household goods (he was a wealthy man), and found refuge in this monastery, which was unusually large and consisted of a sufficient number of separate buildings for him to hide himself from the Imperialists, and the lady from his too curious guests. The corpse was enthroned and worshipped with incense in accordance with Buddhist rites; and then given to the widow, who buried it in a handsome tomb as that of a good Confucianist. This event happened a few months ago.

One more Soochow story, and we will wing our flight to the Capital itself. It is a dreadful affair, and the circumstances are almost unprecedented for atrocity and shame. Two men, named respectively Shên Chao-hsia and Ku Juh-tai, had a quarrel with a third party named Ku Juh-shang; the particulars of which we do not know, but which resulted in the murder of Ku Juh-shang by the other two. Of these, Shên was arrested, but speedily came to an understanding with the Inspector of Police, a rascal of the name of Wang-tien, whom he bribed largely to conceal his guilt. Ku Juh-tai, less fortunate, was seized by the police, bound, gagged, and carried helpless into the presence of Wang-tien. He was then coolly informed by that guardian of the public peace that, on his life, he was to say nothing to implicate his former confederate Shên. He was to inform the Che-hsien, a man named Li, that he, Ku Juh-tai, had been guilty of a conspiracy with the wife of Ku Juh-shang against her husband's life; that the latter's suspicions were aroused, and a deadly scuffle ensued, in which the injured man was killed by his wife's accomplice. Ku stared aghast, and at first flatly refused to tell any such egregious lie; whereupon Wang-tien strung him up by the heels, with his head within a few inches of the floor, by way of bringing him to his senses. Meantime the widow of the murdered man was arrested, and threatened that if she did not confirm the story she would have copper-wires run into her breast; and she, poor thing, not knowing that the admission of such a crime would entail her decapitation, gave a bewildered consent. When the two unfortunates were brought before the Che-hsien, therefore, such was the version they both gave; but on their second appearance at his tribunal they retracted the story, and implored him to believe that it was only under the barbarous threats of Wang-tien that they had been induced to make the statement. This new view of the question seems to have had such an effect upon the judicial mind that the enlightened Che-hsien ordered them to be taken back to prison and beaten with many stripes; a command which Wang-tien obeyed by burning the woman's flesh with heated irons. Some time afterwards they were brought up before the Nëeh-t'ai, or Provincial Judge, the former Tao-t'ai of Shanghai; and this official, to his credit be it spoken, expressed the utmost horror of the barbarity that had been practised. He immediately referred the matter to the Fu-t'ai, Wu, who regarded it in the same light; and we believe that the settlement of it was as satisfactory as could be expected. But it is a shocking proof of the inherent cruelty of the Chinese, and while such things are possible among them it is difficult to form a very favourable judgment of their moral sense.

And now a quaint though pleasant scene presents itself. The wondrous walls of Peking rise to view, with their limitless extent

of smooth brick and their green, tent-shaped turrets stretching as
far as the eye can reach, in a splendid semi-circle. Wide, sunny
thoroughfares lie within those old walls, lined with richly-decorat-
ed, odorous and umbrageous shops, resounding with the monotonous but musical chant of the itinerant vendor, and picturesque with
long strings of savage-looking Mongolian camels, gorgeous wed-
ding-processions, and scarcely less imposing funeral cortèges.
Further on, we find ourselves amid the quieter beauty of the Imperial city, just outside the Palace gates, with its ornamental waters, its beautiful Marble Bridge, and the romantic-looking pavilions of the mandarins and princes, peeping out of the shady
groves and gardens, whose foliage is reflected in the broad lake;
while, in the centre of the whole, rise the yellow roofs of the Winter Palace itself, tier above tier, in the midst of the Imperial
grounds, an enclosure which, known as the Sacred or Forbidden
City, is surrounded by a huge, towering wall encircled by a moat.
Many are the disagreeables of Peking; villanous are the stenches,
blinding is the dust, and execrable are the municipal arrangements,—indeed, such is the state of many of the streets that men
have been known to get drowned in the gutter; and yet, for perfect repose, for complete Orientalism, for a sort of sleepy fascina-
tion, eminently conducive, however, to study and reflection, the
capital of China is unrivalled. Its open sites, too, are numerous
and magnificent; in every conceivable respect it is a city of most
splendid capabilities. But to describe Peking, it would be necessary to devote an entire work to that one subject; and as we are
far too unfamiliar with it to make any such presumptuous attempt, our readers must be satisfied with the slight sketch that
we have limned above. Besides, it is with domestic life in this
strange city that we are now concerned; and we think that the
few stories which have reached us thence will not be found entirely without zest. Here, for instance, is a tale no less remarkable
than true.

The other day, an old gentleman hired a mule-cart to go from
the Tê-shên Gate to the southern part of the capital; and on the

way he dropped down dead. The carter was very much alarmed; and laying the corpse down by the side of the road in the charge of two watchmen, he set off in his cart, post-haste, to report the occurrence to the nearest magistrate. But it was then somewhat late in the day, and the mandarin was unable to go and inspect the corpse till next morning; the unfortunate men in charge, therefore, were compelled to sit and keep guard over it all night long. The clouds rolled up, threatening and black, entirely hiding the moon; the wind blew cold, the road was wild and lonely, and the watchers sat silently beside the corpse. At length they could bear it no longer. Their teeth chattered, partly with cold and partly with the horror of their situation, and they agreed at any rate to light a fire. Accordingly they went together into a neighbouring copse to gather fuel; and when they had found sufficient to make a jovial blaze, they groped their way back to the spot where they had left the old man. Judge, then, of their amazement at finding he was *gone !* Either the corpse had come to life, or somebody had carried it off; but that it had disappeared there certainly could be no doubt. For a while they stood in sore perplexity: then one of them suggested that, as there was a cemetery not far off, with some unburied coffins, they should go and get another corpse to take the old one's place. No sooner said than done; they went with most indecent haste and broke open the first coffin they could lay their hands on, pulled the corpse out neck-and-crop, and laid it by the roadside. Next morning, before it was well light, the mandarin appeared. "Where is the corpse of this old man?" he demanded of the two watchmen. They replied by uncovering the recumbent figure at their side, when lo! it was discovered to be a young and prepossessing girl, who had apparently met with foul play, for the dark-blue line around her throat showed that she had died from strangulation. The unhappy watchmen saw the danger they were in and told the mandarin the entire truth; which he seems so far to have believed as to institute enquiries. A sad story of crime was then brought to light. The poor girl was the daughter of a merchant named Tung, and her mother was dead.

Her father had then purchased a second wife of a man who professed to be her elder brother ; but who concealed the fact that, by contracting a second marriage, she would commit bigamy. But the worthy merchant took her in perfectly good faith, and was always very hospitable towards his brother-in-law, whose fraternal assiduity in visiting his ' sister' was quite affecting. The merchant's young daughter, however, seems to have distrusted her stepmother from the first, although she probably never suspected the deception that had been practised on the family. On one occasion, however, during Mr. Tung's absence, the villain showed himself in his true colours; he charged the unprotected girl with having slandered him to her father, and then, enraged by her spirited rejoinder, strangled her on the spot. On the return of old Tung, his false wife told him his daughter had died suddenly of a virulent disease; and he, suspecting nothing, gave orders for the body to be interred. Such was the story brought to light by the enquiries of the mandarin ; and no time was lost in bringing the two guilty creatures to justice, who were strangled as their crimes deserved. The next question of course was, where was the corpse the watchmen had left in the road; and in two days more the problem was solved by the old gentleman in person. He informed the many anxious enquirers that he was subject to fits of a cataleptic nature, and that he had been seized with one of these while on his journey; that on awaking he had found himself lying in a very uncomfortable place, and feeling uncommonly cold he had got up and walked home. He expressed much sorrow at having been the cause of so much trouble; but our informant considers it was all very providential, as the old gentlemen's indisposition was indirectly the means of punishing two monsters of iniquity who were no longer fit to live.

A sadly comic tragedy occurred at Peking shortly afterwards. There were two brothers, the younger of whom, being comparatively wealthy, lived inside the city; the elder, who was in more straitened circumstances, residing without the walls. The poorer of the two had contracted an unfortunate habit of perpetually

borrowing money, which long threatened to bring about his total
ruin; and very soon the smash came. His principal creditor was
a terrible fellow, who threatened to take his life if he failed to get
his money; and poor Chao was in a sad quandary. At last he
was brought to such a pass that there was nothing left for him to
pawn except his wife, and from this there seemed no escape. The
creditor was willing to compromise the debt, and an arrangement
was proposed; but Mrs. Chao not unnaturally objected. She said
she would far prefer to strangle herself; but her husband thought
that that would be a most unprofitable transaction for all parties,
and tried to persuade her to be patient. The lady, however, was
not to be so easily disposed of, and went to hold a consultation
with the wife of her husband's wealthy brother in the city. " I
" think the best plan would be for me to come and stay with *you*
" a little while," said Mrs. Chao senior; "don't you?" "Certainly
" not!" replied the other, hastily—" why, the man would find you
" in no time "—which was perfectly true, and a most cogent argument, only the lady had other reasons for not desiring her sister-
in-law's presence. "The best way will be for you to go and stay
" with your husband's mother," she resumed; and the pawned
lady adopted the advice forthwith. But when the creditor came
for her the next afternoon there was a slight disturbance; for the
bird had flown, and so had the bird's mate. Of course he stormed
for a long while, and then enquired of the neighbours where his
prey was most likely to be. They answered, in perfect good faith,
at her sister-in-law's; and off he started to find her. Now Mrs.
Chao junior was of a serious turn of mind, and much given to seeking spiritual guidance at the hands of a certain priest who frequently
dropped in to tea with the family during the husband's absence; indeed, so interesting were their conversations that it was frequently
near morning before this ghostly person retired again to his monastery. It was quite a similar case to that of Mrs. Weller and the
red-nosed man; and the ecclesiastic fattened famously at the expense of the unlucky husband, as many other holy men have done
elsewhere. Thus, it so fell out that when the creditor came thundering

at the door, both priest and penitent were terribly alarmed ; the lady
fled precipitately, while her companion made one bound through an
open door, sprang upon an unoccupied table, and pretended to be
fast asleep.   In two minutes in burst the creditor with three or
four strong coolies, who, concluding that the occupant of the guest-
room must needs be the lady they were seeking, pounced upon the
priest (it was pitch dark) and carried him away all swathed up in
his wrappers, in a chair.   When they arrived at home, however,
and discovered the mistake, the priest had to pay for his part of
the adventure with the soundest thrashing he had ever had in his
life.   Then his disgrace was such, he thought, that he could never
go back among his saintlier brethren ; so he became a beggar and
eventually died of starvation.   Nor could his penitent survive the
shock ; and she hanged herself forthwith.   The obdurate creditor,
seeing that he had caused the death of two innocent persons, also
died, of fright ; and the impecunious gentleman is borrowing away
as merrily as ever, though he says he will never try to pawn his
wife again !

Chinese doctors, as has been frequently remarked, are for many
reasons a very unenviable race of men.   If they happen to fail in
their endeavours to cure a patient with perhaps an incurable disease, they run a risk of incurring serious punishment, which varies in severity according to the rank of the sick person ; and they
are continually being made, not only the victims, but the instru-
ments, of some untoward hoax.   For instance.   In the neighbourhood of Peking, just outside the walls, there lived some time ago a
worthy follower of—whoever may be the Chinese counterpart of
Esculapius ; and he enjoyed a widespread reputation for ability.
Indeed so great was his fame that he found it advisable to move
into the City itself, where he established himself in a large
house and speedily secured a handsome practice.   One day two
individuals, who appeared to have followed the ancient calling of
shoplifters, went to a large silk-mercer's, and asked to be shown
some patterns of silk and satin.   There was to be a grand wedding, they said, at the house of a wealthy mandarin ; the ladies

were anxious to have the most splendid dresses procurable; would the shop-keeper oblige them by bringing out some samples of his most costly fabrics, and accompanying them to the bride's house? The unfortunate mercer was delighted, and speedily got together some rolls of satin worth in all a couple of hundred taels. They then mounted their carts, and proceeded to the house of the physician, the *hu-t'ung* or lane in which he lived being quite crowded with the various conveyances of his wealthy patients. "Look," said one of the rascals, "how many rich folk are paying "visits of congratulation! These people will give you a handsome "price for your goods, you may be sure." Now it was the custom of the worthy doctor to see the general body of his patients in an outer room; but those who wished for a more private and confidential interview could, by paying an extra fee, be received in the inner apartments. So these two scamps told their victim to sit down in the porchway while they went in and took the satins for the approval of the ladies; and, leaving him amid a crowd of the poorer patients, paid their fee and passed into the private consultation-rooms. The doctor listened to their imaginary symptoms, and gave them a prescription; whereupon they gravely thanked him, and took their leave by a side door especially reserved for the convenience of the 'swells.' Meanwhile the luckless mercer thought the young lady was a long time making up her mind, and at length requested the porter to go and see if she wasn't nearly ready. That individual stared, and evidently thought the visitor's disease was mental rather than physical; but when the *dénouement* came, and the victim found that he was in a doctor's house, that there were no ladies in the case, and nobody was in pressing need of any silk, he rushed madly to look after his cart. Of course it had disappeared; so, curiously enough, had his two friends; and he has never yet had the satisfaction of asking them what became of his two hundred taels'-worth of precious silk.

Indeed it is probably in Peking that swindling reaches its highest pitch of ingenuity. Here is a good example, though the details of the occurrence are comparatively trifling. In the Sz-t'iao

Hu-t'ung there lives a widow-woman of a certain age and slender fortunes. So slender, indeed, are her resources that during last New-Year time she was compelled to pawn nearly everything she had in the house, and was looked upon quite in the light of 'one 'of our best customers' by the pawnbroker. Now it so happened that this widow was next-door neighbour to a wily old fox of a fellow, upon whom these constant visits to the *mont-de-piété* had been by no means thrown away. So, looking in one morning, in a friendly sort of way—"How is it with you, neighbour ? " says he : " why, what a handsome bracelet ! " for it so happened that the poor old woman had come so low as to be reduced to pawn a real gold trinket, which was probably some heirloom in her family. The sly old fellow examined it well and then proposed that he should save her the trouble of a walk and take it to the pawnshop for her. To this the widow consented, and in due time her friend reappeared with the pawn-ticket and a handsome sum of money. But when the day of reckoning came, she found that old Mr. Hsü (for such was the good man's name) had pawned *two* bracelets— one a facsimile of the other ; that he had received a liberal sum for each ; and that the second bracelet, though apparently like the first, was really made of brass. The pawnbroker was enraged, and threatened Hsü with all the pains and penalties of the law if he did not at once redeem his pledge. "Don't make a disturbance," replied he ; " you shall be paid in three days. Meanwhile let your "assistant come and live with me to see that I don't run away." The broker consented ; the youth moved to old Hsü's house, and was treated like a prince. That night they went to the theatre, and while the lad's attention was engaged with the performance, old Hsü slily dropped the pawn-ticket, as though by accident. With great satisfaction he watched another guest, as great a scamp as himself, pick it up. The finder looked at it : found it was for a real gold ornament worth twenty times as much as the value of the ticket ; and promptly hid it in his sleeve. Two days after- wards the old fellow had the satisfaction of hearing that his debt ot the pawnbroker had been paid by the thief at the theatre, and the latter genius became the proud possessor of a piece of a worthless metal and the victim of a cleverer rascal than himself.

We have already doubtless trespassed upon the patience of our readers. One more story, however, and then we will conclude. It is probably known that the Chinese exercise much solicitude with regard to the comfort and well-being of their deceased relatives in the unseen world, and are in the habit of supplying them with such necessaries, in the shape of eatables, paper money, and so on, as they are able to convey to them without personal loss to their own pockets. On the Ling-fêng Shan, near Ningpo, there stands the temple of a most amiable divinity named Koh Sëay-ûng, whose priests present to every worshipper, on behalf of the P'u-sa himself, a cheque for one thousand taels. In certain cases, this cheque is redeemed in the present life—*i. e.*, the devotee acquires wealth; if not, it still holds good after death, and the ghost of the dead man will be able to get it cashed in the other world. Lately, however, a poor man got dreadfully sold—all through his own fault, though, in consequence of getting tipsy on the strength of his prospective riches. After paying his devotions and receiving the coveted cheque, he seems to have gone to a tavern where he got very merry in his cups, and reached home in a state in which the physical had obtained decidedly the upper hand of the intellectual. In fact no sooner was he within his own doors than he tumbled flat down, with his face as purple as any peony. His wife thought he was dying: "No, no," he hiccuped, "I am only drunk: see, I "have the thousand taels—good in this world, good in the next— "it's all right." So saying he fell over on the bed and appeared to have no more life in him; whereupon his wife burst out into lamentations at his supposed decease, and the whole family joined in lugubrious howlings for some time. Then the bereaved lady remembered the thousand tael note; "Ah," she sobbed, "my poor "husband will want it where he has gone; I will lose no time in "sending it after his spirit;" a laudable design which she forthwith put into execution in the usual manner, by burning the cheque, in order to transmit it to the other world. Unfortunately, however, she was a little premature; about an hour afterwards the man woke up from his drunken stupor, and when he found his wife had burnt the cheque, so far from appreciating her kind intentions, he laid about him and gave her a sound thrashing for her pains!

CHAPTER XIX.

Chinese Jews.

THREE hundred years before Christ, Israel had already learned to put up with an unsettled and wandering existence upon the Earth. It is remarkable, says Ewald, in his *Geschichte Israels*, to observe how the wide diffusion of the Greeks was now followed by a similar dispersion of the Judeans and Samaritans. It may even be said, he continues, that the earlier shocks were now suddenly succeeded by one of far greater violence, which tended to scatter Israel continually over a wider area, so that fresh masses of Israelitish posterity were driven out into the wide world, which was then becoming almost wholly Greek. "It is somewhat difficult "to survey all the foreign countries to which the Judeans, with "the Samaritans often close at their side, spread during these cen-"turies, and where they made themselves settled homes. Even "before Alexander, many were already living dispersed among the "heathen in all quarters. From the countries beyond the Eu-"phrates and Tigris, where large numbers had continued to reside "ever since the Assyrian and Babylonian days, and had long been "naturalised, they spread one by one, very soon after the victori-"ous expeditions of Alexander, Seleucus, and Antiochus the Great, "into the remoter regions of the East, as far as India and China." How perfectly this is supported, as far as China is concerned, by the observations of travellers and students, we shall now undertake to show.

We learn from Chinese sources, that, towards the close of the earlier Chow Dynasty, about 255 to 200 B.C., an immigration took place of strangers from the West. They were a peaceful, commercial, and religious folk, strongly attached to their peculiar faith, and always ready to drive a bargain with the natives of the country. They became settlers, and were known among their pagan neighbours as the T'iao-kin Këaou, or the Sect which removed the Sinew. The period of Chinese history marked by their arrival was a troublous one, full of political complications and of civil war; a state of things which had produced great social disorder, obscuring the light of the classics and undermining the moral tone of the people to an alarming extent. The Jew, who looks upon his dispersion among the Gentiles as a means employed by Jehovah for the leavening of that corrupt mass, sees in this immigration at this special time a direct dispensation of Providence, and hails it as a fresh fulfilment of the prophecy that in the seed of Abraham should all the families of the Earth be blessed. It is to be regretted that the details which have come down to us of the history of the Jews in China should be of so very meagre a description. So scanty, indeed, is the stock of information, that many persons have hesitated to accept the facts of the immigration and subsequent sojourn of the Jews as in any way historical; one argument employed being the apparently cogent one, that no mention whatever is made of the affair in any of the Chinese annals. This, however, may be easily explained. There are several interesting phenomena in the history of China, now in existence, which are rigorously ignored in all contemporary records; from motives of prejudice, expediency, or pride. The Jewish colonies now extant are not mentioned in the annals of the day; it is therefore not surprising that those which existed two thousand years ago should be similarly overlooked. Again, the bulk of the ancient local records was lost during the reign of the Huang-ti Tsin-shih, who flourished 246 to 200 B. C. Be this as it may, however, the existence of Chinese Jews is as much a matter of fact as that of Polish, English, or German Jews, and even in this intensely individualistic country they have preserved for many centuries their own peculiar idiosyncrasies. The principal Jewish colony seems to have been founded at K'ai-fung Fu, the capital of Honan; where a large and handsome synagogue was erected, and profusely adorned with sentences from the Hebrew Law. But the immigrants appear to have been unfortunate in their selection of a home, although they were probably influenced by their old love of the leeks and the onions, the vineyards and oliveyards, the well-watered valley and richly cultivated plain, in making this their choice. K'ai-fung Fu doubtless appeared like a field that the Lord had blessed. It was a splendid city in the olden days, and famed for its gardens and its palaces; but if the Jews had pitched upon a Chinese Tyre or Chorazin they could hardly have undergone greater trials. Seldom perhaps has a place been subject to such reverses as K'ai-fung, and yet survived. Fourteen times was this devoted city ruined by inundations; six times was it destroyed by fire; nine times overthrown by earthquakes, and eleven times besieged and taken by assault. But there are records still extant, in the form of memorial tablets, erected with the sanction of the authorities; though whether those in existence are the original tablets, which have been preserved, or copies, merely, appears to be uncertain. The point, however, is unimportant. From one of these it is gathered that the Jews, the foreign Sect which did not eat the Sinew, came to China under the earlier Chows; and that the mythical Chinese hero, P'an Ku-shih, is identical with the Jewish Adam. The Jews are spoken of in the highest terms, their classics and religion being praised as comfortable to those of the native literati. An account of the building of a synagogue appears in another record, and, from all that we can gather, the children of Israel appear at one time to have occupied a position of influence and consideration. However it may be explained, too, Jewish legend appears to have tinctured much of the ancient literature of the Chinese; for, in addition to the analogy we have already alluded to, we find in some old books the story of a woman who was turned into a statue while fleeing with her family, because she looked back: of the descent of manna; of the Sun being stopped in its course by a General to complete a victory, and of a rock producing water upon being smitten with a stick. It is the opinion of those who have studied the subject that these and similar traditions were brought to China by Jews in the first instance, and became subsequently incorporated into the ancient literature of the country.

Of the present condition of Chinese Jews it now remains for something to be said. There are colonies of Jews at Hangchow, Soochow, and elsewhere, possessing, or having possessed, many precious relics of their ancient ritual. The Soochow Jews have, we are informed, received much generosity from their wealthy coreligionists, the Sassoons ; but we are not aware whether any specific measures have been taken to excite an interest in the Israelites of China in more extended circles. Does not the venerable Sir Moses Montefiore, the nearest living representative, perhaps, of Israelitish royalty, take the deepest concern in the welfare of his scattered brethren ? That they are still in existence is undeniable ; but we fear that they are rapidly becoming indistinguishable from the heathen among whom they live. They have scrolls of the law, but are unable to read them ; they have synagogues, which, however, are generally deserted ; they possess a faint, though not wholly indistinct, remembrance of the grand national belief in the One True God ; and they deal principally in money-changing and old clothes. But here we will drop the pen, and invite our readers' attention to the graphic account we reprint below, of the visit of a missionary gentleman to what may once have been the centre of Jewish influences and Jewish life in the " Land of Sinim " :—

Arriving [in K'ai-fung Fu] on the 17th February, I enquired for the Jewish Synagogue, but getting no satisfactory answer from the pagan inn-keeper, I went for information to one of the Mahommedan Mosques, of which there are six within the walls. I was well received by the Mufti, and the advent of a stranger from the west, who was reported to be a worshipper of the true Lord, drew together a large concourse of the faithful. At the request of the Mufti, holding a New Testament in my hand I addressed them in relation to the Holy Book of Jesus Christ, whose name he pronounced with reverence, as that of one of the most illustrious of their prophets. The Jews he denounced as Kafirs, and evinced no very poignant sorrow when he informed me that their synagogue had come to desolation. It was, he assured me, utterly demolished, and the people who had worshipped there impoverished and scattered abroad. "Then," said I, "I will go and see the spot on which it stood ;" and directing my bearer to proceed to the place indicated by the Mufti, I passed through streets crowded with curious spectators to an open square, in the centre of which there stood a solitary stone. On one side was an inscription commemorating the erection of the Synagogue in the period Lunghing of the Sung dynasty about A.D. 1183, and on the other a record of its rebuilding in the reign of Hung-che of the Ming dynasty : but to my eye, it uttered a sadder tale—not of building or rebuilding, but of decay and ruin. It was inscribed with *Ichabod ;* 'the glory is departed.' Standing on the pedestal and resting my right hand on the head of that stone, which was to be a silent witness of the truths I was about to utter, I explained to the expectant multitude my reasons for "taking.pleasure in the stones of Israel, and favouring the dust thereof."

"Are there among you any of the family of Israel ?" I enquired. "I am one," responded a young man whose face corroborated his assertion : and then another and another stepped forth, until I saw before me representatives of six out of the seven families into which the colony is divided. There, on that melancholy spot on which the very foundation of the Synagogue had been torn from the ground and there no longer remained one stone upon another, they confessed with shame and grief that their holy and beautiful house had been demolished by their own hands. It had, they said, for a long time been in a ruinous condition. They had no money to make repairs ; they had lost all knowledge of the sacred tongue ; the traditions of the fathers were no longer handed down, and their ritual worship had ceased to be observed. In this state of things they had yielded to the pressure of necessity, and disposed of the timbers and stones of that venerable edifice to obtain relief for their bodily wants.

In the evening some of them came to my lodgings, bringing for my inspection a copy of the Law inscribed on a roll of parchment, without the points, and in the style of manuscript which I was unable to make out, though I had told them rather imprudently that I was acquainted with the language of their sacred books. The next day, the Christian Sabbath, they repeated their visit, listening respectfully to what I had to say concerning the Law and the Gospel, and answering, as far as they were able, my enquiries as to their past history and present state.

Two of them appeared in official costume, one wearing a gilt and the other a crystal button ; but far from sustaining the character of this people for thrift and worldly prosperity, they number among them none that are rich and but few who are honorable. Some indeed, true to their hereditary instincts, are employed in a small way in banking establishments, (the first man I met was a money-changer); others keep fruit-stores and cake-shops, drive a business in old clothes or pursue various handicrafts, while a few find employment in military service. The prevalence of rebellion in the central provinces for the last thirteen years, has told sadly on the prosperity of K'aifung Fu, and the Jews have not unlikely, owing to the nature of their occupations, been the greatest sufferers. Their number, they estimated, though not very exactly, at from three to four hundred. They are unable to trace their tribal pedigree ; keep no register, and never on any occasion assemble together as one congregation. Until recently they had a common centre in their venerable synagogue, though their liturgical service had long been discontinued. But the congregation seems to be following the fate of its building. No bond of union remains, and they are in danger of being speedily absorbed by Mahommedanism or heathenism. One of them has lately become a priest of Buddha, taking for his title *pen-tau* (本 道) which signifies ' One who is rooted in the Knowledge of the Truth.' The large tablet that once adorned the entrance of the synagogue, bearing in gilt characters the name of Israel (一 賜 樂 業 E-sz-lo-yeh,) has been appropriated by one of the Mahommedan Mosques, and some efforts have been made to draw over the people, who differ from the Moslems so little, that their heathen neighbours have never been able to distinguish them by any other circumstance than that of their picking the sinews out of the flesh they eat, a custom commemorative of Jacob's conflict with the angel.

One of my visitors was a son of the last of their rabbis, who, some thirty or forty years ago, died in the province of Kan-suh. With him perished the last vestige of their acquaintance with the sacred tongue. Though they still preserve several copies of the Law and Prophets, there is not a man among them who can read a word of Hebrew, and not long ago it was seriously proposed to expose their parchments in the market place, in hopes they might attract the attention of some wandering Jew, who would be able to restore to them the language of their fathers. Since the cessation of their ritual worship, their children all grow up without the seal of the covenant. The young generation are uncircumcised, and, as might be expected, they no longer take pains to keep their blood pure from intermixture with Gentiles. One of them confessed to me that his wife was a heathen. They remember the names of the Feast of Tabernacles, the Feast of Unleavened Bread, and a few other ceremonial rites that were still practised by a former generation ; but all such usages are now neglected, and the next half century is not unlikely to put a period to their existence as a distinct people.

Near the margin of the Poyang Lake there stands a lofty rock, so peculiar and solitary that it is known by the name of the ' Little Orphan.' The adjacent shore is low and level, and its kindred rocks are all on the opposite shore of the Lake, whence it seems to have been torn away by some violent convulsion and planted immoveably in the bosom of the water. Such to me appeared that fragment of the Israelitish nation. A rock rent from the sides of Mount Zion by some great national catastrophe and projected in the central plain of China, it has stood there, while the centuries rolled by, sublime in its antiquity and solitude. It is now on the verge of being swallowed by the flood of paganism, and the spectacle is a mournful one. The Jews themselves are deeply conscious of their sad situation, and the shadow of an inevitable destiny seems to be resting upon them.

Poor unhappy people ! as they inquired about the destruction of the Holy City and the dispersion of their tribes, and referred to their own decaying condition, I endeavoured to comfort them by pointing to Him who is the consolation of Israel. I told them the straw had not been trodden underfoot until the ripe grain had been gathered to disseminate in other fields. The dykes had not been broken down until the time came for pouring their fertilising waters over the face of the earth. Christian civilization with all its grand results had sprung from a Jewish root, and the promise to Abraham was already fulfilled that "in his seed should all the nations of the earth be blessed."

CHAPTER XX.

The Chinese Theory of Creation.

CHINESE philosophy,—in the usually-accepted meaning of the phrase, which refers not to morals, but to cosmogony,—is rightly regarded as the most abstruse and intricate system ever conceived by the mind of man. It may be doubted whether the entire mass of all that has been written in elucidation of its mysteries, by the most learned Western scholars, has succeeded to any great degree in rendering it at all familiar to their readers, if, indeed, its exponents have themselves arrived at any satisfactory solution; it is acknowledged on all hands to be yet almost a sealed book, and so essentially cast in the mould of Chinese mental processes as to present a well-nigh inexplicable problem to the keenest or most subtle intellect. It is even now a moot point among sinologues whether the speculations of Chinese sages admit the idea of a Personal and Omnipresent Deity, identical with or higher than the Ultimate Extreme which, as far as has been discovered, appears to bound their vision; while there are not wanting those who trace, in the all-pervading principle of Duality which lies at the root of Chinese cosmical hypotheses, the germ of the obscenest rites of heathendom. The charge involved in this view of Chinese philosophy has, to our mind, no more weight than one which we may suppose to be brought against Christianity, founded upon the evil practices of the church of the Nicolaitanes. On the contrary, we hope to show, in however superficial and perfunctory a manner, that the theories which are identified with such names as Confucius, Chu Fu-tsze, and even the prehistorical Fuh-hi himself, are

far from being either so visionary or so esoteric as they are generally supposed; that they present not a few elements in common
with the cosmogony called Mosaic; that foreshadowings of an even
fuller revelation are, dimly and tentatively notwithstanding, still
unmistakeably to be discerned; and that, in other respects, the
most audacious speculations advanced by the bold thinkers of the
nineteenth century, starting, as professed, from a standpoint where
all is dark as the primeval Chaos, have not yet reached a much
higher plane than that so early occupied by the sages of the East.
In the days of long-ago, when the civilisation of the Middle Kingdom was yet unborn, the mystery of mysteries lay heavy on the
minds of men naturally prone to thought, and it lay and lay until
by virtue of its own inherent vitality it struck root in the rich
though uncultivated soil. Its growth was spontaneous, and resembled that of the primeval forest, where the trees are huge and
gnarled, though their tops may reach almost to heaven. Then, as
idea brought forth idea, and conviction followed conviction, forming a chain of postulates, the half-inspired sage evolved a system
of emblems whereby to express, more clearly than by words, the
progressive development of all he saw around him; and this resulted in the Diagrams called after Fuh-hi. The theory we are
endeavouring to limn has been ably amplified by Mr. Alabaster in
his *Occasional Papers on Chinese Philosophy*,* which, for a fresh,
lucid, and novel handling of the Doctrine of the Ch'i, deserve the
studious perusal of all sinologues. According to him, it is to the
cogitations of some ancient Emperor or sage, as he sat watching
the eddying currents of a running stream, that the later philosophers owe the more elaborate cosmogony now attracting the attention of European scholars;† for in the tiny whirlpool and gurgling
sluice he saw, or thought, at least, he saw, the action of the same
forces as those which produced the world. He gazed long in fancy
upon this miniature of the Universe, and after years, may-be, of

---

* *The Doctrine of the Ch'i*, by Chaloner Alabaster, H. M. Consul at Ningpo. Published in the *Celestial Empire*, Shanghai.

† See articles on the Chinese philosophers by the Very Rev. Dean Butcher, D. D.,
in the *Edinburgh Review*.

contemplation, laid the foundations of the system subsequently formulated by Confucius, and ratified by the name of the great philosopher. The Confucian Cosmogony, as it is now generally called, was subsequently formulated in its turn by the eminent commentator who flourished in the Sung Dynasty, the Augustan era of Chinese history, Chu Fu-tsze; and it is to his works that we turn as the highest authority upon the subject. Like many other philosophers, Chu Fu-tsze was a statesman of great ability, and held in high honour at Court. He shared, to the fullest extent, all those personal peculiarities which in England would be called pedantry, but which in China are extolled as propriety and love of order. The old prehistoric sage, dreaming his life away in the contemplation of a bubbling rivulet, weaving strange fancies destined hereafter to form a well-knit fabric for others to embroider, is to our mind a far more venerable figure than the precise, sententious pedagogue of the twelfth century, with his square-toed shoes and formal way of living. When fatigued by study, we are told, he would rest himself by closing his eyes and sitting bolt upright; and when refreshed, he would rise, and with measured steps walk about for relaxation. Yet it is to the plodding and studious mind of Chu that we are indebted for the most elaborate treatise upon the system accepted by the entire Chinese people in explanation of creative processes; and it is the fundamental principles of this system to which we now appeal in support of the theory that we have before us.

The Chinese philosophy is, in its inception, essentially Pythagorean; or, to speak more correctly, the Pythagorean philosophy is essentially Chinese. The first symbol with which we are confronted is the 太一, the Great One, or Monad, of Pythagoras. This is the primeval Essence, self-existing and alone, from which proceeded, subsequently, the world. This Monad then divides, and two parts become the Ying and the Yang, or the Male and the Female Principles of Nature. The Ying is Heaven, the Father: the Yang is Earth, the Mother: and from these two springs all else. The analogy between this scheme and that of the Greek philosophers has been conclusively traced by Canon McClatchie in his well-known translation of Chu Fu-tsze,* and it is unnecessary for us to reproduce the intricate reasonings by which he advocates his cause; besides, we have a different end in view. We only pause for a moment to point out what strikes us as being an equally remarkable resemblance, and totally distinct from that noted by the Canon. Is the great disruption of the Primeval Chaos, and its division into two great sections, Heaven or Light on the one hand, Darkness or Earth on the other, in no way suggestive of a cosmical system for which far greater age and authenticity have been claimed than for the teachings of the Chinese sage? The Genesis of Moses is not so diametrically opposed to the Genesis of Chu Fu-tsze as may be imagined; the Mosaic writer speaks with equal distinctness of the Primeval Chaos, which was subsequently divided into Firmament and Earth, the former of which "God called Heaven." Of course the theistic principle is not clearly defined in the Chinese philosophy; but we shall see as we go on how far we are entitled to demand for this system a higher place in the opinion of the orthodox than they have hitherto accorded to it.

We will now proceed to glean what facts we can from the writings of Chu Fu-tsze himself. It is well, we think, to abstain from any preliminary explanation of the *terms* employed, for the simple reason that, by offering such, we should forestall our own argument; but it will become apparent that upon the correct rendering of the Chinese text depends, exclusively, the accuracy of our conclusions. Without further preamble, therefore, we turn to the Forty-ninth Chapter or Section of the works of Chu Fu-tsze, in which he treats of the generation of the animated Cosmos; and the first sentence runs as follows :—

In the entire Universe, where there is no *li* there is no *ch'i*, and where there is no *ch'i* there is no *li*.

Now this passage has been translated by Canon McClatchie

---

* *Confucian Cosmogony*, by the Rev. Thos. McClatchie, Canon of S. John's Cathedral, Hongkong, and Trinity, Shanghai.

somewhat peculiarly. The mere inversion of words is of comparatively trifling importance; what we object to most earnestly, and unhesitatingly repudiate, is the rendering of *li* by Fate, and *ch'i* by Air. In the first place, Air is seldom a proper rendering of *ch'i*, and Fate is never an equivalent for *li*. To say that in the entire universe there is no Fate without Air, nor Air without Fate, conveys neither sense nor meaning; and we may boldly affirm that Chu Fu-tsze never wrote such nonsense. Of course, the key to the whole system of philosophy is to be found in the proper translation of these two words; and we are convinced that, by reason of the inadequate and erroneous readings adopted hitherto, great injustice has been done to the philosopher. It is unnecessary to spend more time in pointing out the utter irrelevancy of the Canon's version; it forms a cogent example of the darkening of counsel by words without—meaning. Before, therefore, we continue our quotations, we shall venture to suggest a rather different translation, which will, we think, throw some light upon the Confucian theory; postponing our defence until we have tested its trustworthiness. The rendering we suggest is simply as follows: *Ch'i* is Matter, *Li* is Mind; and we submit that, studied with this in view, the mystic sentences are plain. Our first quotation will, therefore, read as nearly as possible thus :—

In the entire Universe, where there is no Mind there is no Matter, and where there is no Matter there is no Mind.

To be perfectly just, however, we must premise that although Chu Fu-tsze ascribes to *li* the attributes of Mind, its prevailing idea— perhaps a rather hazy one—is that of supreme, self-acting Law. Of course a physical law implies force; but to translate the word *li* by force or motion, would be to violate the proprieties of language. To express this idea another character is called into play, viz., *Tao*. The primary signification of this is road, course, or direction,—secondarily, process; while *li*, therefore, may be translated the all-pervading Mind or Law, *Tao-li* is necessarily the *operation* of that Law. But to proceed. The next paragraph we wish to quote is the third in order, and runs as follows :—

This Heavenly Mind *(li)* first existing, then most certainly Matter *(ch'i)* exists. The *ch'i* when accumulated forms *chih*, and Nature is then complete.

We have purposely abstained from translating the Chinese terms in the last sentence, for the simple reason that they are incapable of being rendered by any one known English word. Canon Mc-Clatchie, however, finds no difficulty. He simply translates them, "the Air when accumulated forms Substance;" which we submit is not only as unintelligible as if we were, in adopting our own view, to write "Matter when accumulated forms Substance," but is scientifically inaccurate. That *chih* means tangible, visible substance, there is no doubt. No other rendering can possibly be applied to it, as used in the works of Chu Fu-tsze. What, then, is *ch'i?* For it is algebraïcally obvious that, here, this is the unknown quantity. The solution we take to be simply this: that *ch'i*, commonly translated Air, is Matter in its primordial and subtlest form; Matter, to use the modern phrase, in the embryonic stage, invisible, as Dr. Tyndall says, of itself, but possessing the inherent power of becoming visible. The Professor of the nineteenth century simply repeats the Chinese sage who wrote seven hundred years ago. Mark the exquisite ellipticism of the original: *Ch'i tsi, wei Chih.* This, done into the faithfullest and concisest English at our command, runs simply thus: The accumulation of Matter in its primordial or ethereal stage, produces Matter in its substantial form. The fact is one of the simplest in physical science, and it possesses at least the merit of being true, if not self-evident; whereas to say that the accumulation of Air produces Matter, is—entirely to misrepresent Chu Fu-tsze. *Ch'i* is the ether that pervades all space, the embryo from which all material bodies *(Chih)* are produced. *Li* is that Eternal Mind which dwells in and is commensurate with this ubiquitous ether, transforming it, as Tyndall would seem to imply, into the atoms which compose the invisible bodies in their varied forms, and manifesting itself through the active properties of substance, or, as we commonly say, through the works of Nature. Does not each body in the material world contain more or less of this Mind, beginning from the most subtle gases and going through the whole series of organic and inorganic bodies, plants and animals, up to the brain of the philosopher? And does not every being in the spiritual world, also, contain more or less of this Mind, from the spirit of the rudest savage up to the highest type of created intelligence of which we can conceive? It appears to us that a spirit, whether finite or infinite, can only manifest itself through matter in some form or other, nay, must even be contained in matter as a vehicle. Again, the matter in this case must be commensurate with the spirit; *i. e.*, an infinite spirit could only be contained in the ether which, as we suppose, fills space, while a finite spirit, wholly dependent upon the Eternal Mind for its creation and the maintenance of its existence, would be contained in a vehicle of matter of the most ethereal kind. Is not a spiritual body matter in a state of transformation, not appreciable by our corporeal senses? In a word, is not the entire Universe, seen and unseen, a series of transformations of the original ether, the subtlest conceivable form in which matter can exist, the all-embracing *ch'i?*

It must be remembered that with the Chinaman all is theory and speculation. He has not even the most rudimentary knowledge of chemistry, and still talks of wood, air, fire, earth, and water, as the Five Elements. And yet in his gropings he seems to have hit upon the grand idea long cherished by modern physicists, and which, may-be, will be placed upon a scientific basis some day, —the resolvability of all the so-called elementary substances into one prime Element. This seems to have come intuitively to the Chinese mind, and the name by which the element is known is *ch'i.* From *ch'i* all things were evolved, and back to it may they all be traced. And how much further have our own philosophers brought us—those eagles of investigation, who profess to gaze undazzled upon the splendour of Life's Mystery? They, too, see in Matter the promise and potency of all terrestrial life, the universal mother from whose capacious womb all things are produced; while the force or power which thus acts upon it, is, by them, only guessed at, and, while its existence cannot be denied, it is to them, confessedly, a quantity unknown.

One more quotation will suffice. It is to the following effect:—

Being asked whether *li* positively existed before Heaven and Earth, he replied that before the existence of Heaven and Earth there was most certainly this *li*. *Li* existing, then Heaven and Earth existed. If *li* had no existence, then also there could be neither Heaven, nor Earth, nor Man, nor Things ; none of these would have had any containing receptacle. *Li* existing, then *ch'i* exists, flows forth, pervades, generates, and nourishes the Myriad Existences—*i.e.*, the material Universe.

It is clear that in this passage Heaven is used in the lowest sense in which the word is applicable. Heaven and Earth, then, mean simply Creation in its widest acceptation,—the Universe at large ; and this Universe is directly attributed to the influence of the *li*, or Creative Mind, upon the *ch'i*, or embryonic Matter. We therefore fail to see how the philosophy which rests upon this principle can fairly be called atheistic, or even, in its strictest sense, savouring of pantheism. Nay, more ; we entirely decline to believe that, by studying the works of Nature, without the aid of Revelation, any clearer or distincter idea of God can be obtained, than this. The stage reached by the philosophers of Professor Tyndall's school in the present day is really very much the same as that reached by Chu Fu-tsze, Confucius, and the other sages of the East. The principle of life, or vital force, as Tyndall says, is an insoluble mystery : the creative process is the manifestation of a Power absolutely inscrutable by the mind of man. The Chinese arrived at the same conclusion centuries upon centuries ago ; but they went a step further, and gave this Power a name. They called it *Li,* and saw in it the intelligent, self-existing, and exhaustless source of Life in all its phases.

Amplifications of this grand belief, the root of all religion, abound in the Chinese classics. As we have before pointed out, the word for Heaven is used not only to express the material firmament, but also for that Supreme and Intelligent Power which overrules humanity at large, and animates the entire world. Thus we have a greater than Chu Fu-tsze, saying, 天 卽 理 也 *T'ien, tsi li yay,*—Heaven is the *li*, or Heaven is the Mind (of Things) ; and again, what is more remarkable still, 性 卽 理 也 *Sing, tsi li yay,*—The Properties (of Things) are the Mind;—that is, are the manifestation of Heaven. Our own Western philosophy has almost led us to ignore this Eternal Mind which rules the Universe, and actually and personally does all that is done therein. We say 'it' blows, 'it' rains, 'it' thunders, but what is this It? We say certain bodies enter into chemical combination or are decomposed; but whose work is it, and whence comes this exhibition of power? Plants and animals multiply and grow, but what is the overruling influence at every step? We can come to no other conclusion than that all these works of Nature, or active properties of matter in its various forms are simply the direct manifestation of the hidden Principle, or *Li*, that dwells in all things, and that this *Li* is no other than that Creator in whom we live, and move, and have our being.

One word more, and we have done. There is yet another system of cosmogony, familiar to us all, between which and the Confucian scheme we think a certain analogy can be traced. We have spoken of *li* as the archaic principle of Life—Creativeness; and of *tao* as the operation of that principle,—according to the teachings of Chinese philosophy. How much difference there is between this theory and the doctrine contained in the following passage, we will ask our readers to decide:—

In the beginning was *Tao*. *Tao* was united with the Divine Spirit; *Tao* was the Divine Spirit. Thus *Tao* in the beginning was united with the Divine Spirit. The ten-thousand things (= everything *) were made by, or originated from, *Tao*. In all creation there is nothing not made by (*Tao*). In *Tao* was life; the life also is the light of men.

This, as may be easily detected, is simply a retranslation into English, from an independent standpoint, of the Chinese version of the First of John, in which *Tao* figures as the equivalent of the original Λογος—the manifestation of God in His Creative power. The idea is already familiar to the Chinese mind, as we have shown above, and the coincidence is striking in the extreme. The early sages were perhaps not quite so wide of the mark after all, and

---

* Everything *exclusive* of Heaven and Earth, however, according to the common acceptation of the original.

their intricate speculations may have covered, not only a *belief* in the First Cause as the origin of all things—a belief shared by the keenest investigators of the present day, between which and belief in a personal Creator is but a single step; but also a *faith* in that Supreme and All-pervading Power as more than a Creator—as a Preserver, fostering and nourishing the Life that He Himself has given. The indoctrination of the Chinese with the Western religion is attended doubtless with enormous difficulty; but although we should be very chary in expressing a definite opinion on so abstruse a subject, is it quite impossible that, in the direction we have indicated, one tract of common ground, one common starting-point, may be discovered? The Chinese have a vast Pantheon, and their 'Shang-ti' may be the Zeus of the Greeks: but it was to the Greeks, with all their array of male and female deities, that Saint Paul said, speaking of their Unknown God,—" Whom, therefore, " ye ignorantly worship, HIM declare I unto you."

CONCLUSION.

The *Far* East is now almost a misnomer. The opening of the Suez Canal and the completion of telegraphic communication have brought both China and Japan very near to England, and a journey from Southampton to Shanghai is to-day attended with far less difficulty than, twenty years ago, surrounded the traveller in going no further than Ceylon. Is it too much to hope that, ere long, the Eastern and Western worlds will be coaxed into yet closer familiarity—that mutual forbearance, ay, and even mutual admiration, based on better knowledge and advancing views, may do something to cement the friendship of the two? It is high time that the people of England should know and care more than they do for the people of China; that they should rid themselves of the idea that a Chinese mandarin is a sort of chimney-ornament whose principal accomplishment consists in perpetually nodding his head, and that a Chinese landscape is like the picture on a willow-pattern plate. We are convinced that the coldness which exists between the two nations is far more the result of *misconception* than is generally supposed. Confucius said, " I will not be afflict- "ed because men know not me; I will be afflicted because I know "not men."* Our own experience of the Chinese has been on the whole a very favourable one, and it is difficult to cherish hard thoughts of a race which evinces so much simple kindliness, generosity, laboriousness and good feeling, as are to be met with in the sons of Han.

---

* Analects: *Heo-urh*, chap. xvi.

APPENDIX.

CHAPTER IV.

Page 27.—It may not be generally known that there is a community of persous in the neighbourhood of Shanghai bearing the ancient Ming surname of Chu, and tracing their descent with remarkable accuracy back to the old Emperors of that line. They are a particularly reserved and disagreeable set, proud and stiff, with manners the reverse of conciliatory. They keep themselves much aloof from their neighbours, and are supposed to be connected with some local branch of the San-ho Hwuy. The woman are chiefly remarkable for extreme ugliness. They have enormously broad faces, with large, heavy jaws, and are greatly given to wearing silver, in the shape of necklets, earrings, and similar bangles.—*Celestial Empire*, April 13, 1876.

CHAPTER V.

Page 42.—The other morning there was a review of Chinese troops at Ningpo, including spearmen, bannermen, the 'tiger' brigade, matchlock and gingal corps, the long Enfield company and a few cavalry. The commanding officer occupied a building at one end of the ground, and on each side of him stood inferior officers, the background being taken up by soldiers bearing weapons which looked very much like pitchforks and choppers stuck on poles. The subordinates never moved the whole time ; they might have been taken for images, they seemed so wholly lifeless. H. E. the Tao-t'ai did not put in an appearance ; it is said he was invited, but replied to the effect that the hot weather (or the expected *douceur* of 300,000 cash to the troops ?) was too much for his constitution, so begged to be excused. At one end of the parade-ground and to the left of the Ti-t'ai's position were two towers, one representing a fortified city, the other being the point from which all the manœuvres were directed. At the further end was a structure of bamboo and cloth, painted to represent the city the troops lived in. From out of the gates of this impromptu city streamed forth about eight hundred horsemen, spear, billhook, matchlock and bannermen, besides a number of 'tiger' men. The commands were given by beat of drum and the sweet and melodious gong, accompanied by (O ! Scotchmen, forgive me) a musical instrument, which when blown sounded like the rapturous strains of the enchanting bagpipes. There was some marching and countermarching, when the gong, etc., gave the signal, matchlocks to the fore. In front of these a number of men with flags were stationed, and when the gong sounded, they waved their flags and the others fired, which they did very well, and there was no straggling. The 'tiger' men were next called upon to exercise their agility. There were about fifty or sixty of these, and they were dressed to imitate tigers. Their weapons included short swords and shields, the latter painted to represent a tiger's head. No doubt it was originally intended that this arm of the service should strike terror into the minds of the uninitiated ; but on this occasion, the reverse was the result.' They went through a good deal of posturing and yelling, and brandishing of swords and shields, and afterwards joined shields, under cover of which the hook, bill, and knife-and-fork men assembled, and then advanced to charge an invisible enemy, which they were supposed to have scattered to the wind. Of course they, too, did a considerable amount of screeching and flying about. Then they retired, and their places were taken by the matchlock men, who again opened fire, while under cover of the smoke the cavalry appeared, and bidding loud defiance, cut the air with their swords, (some had whips instead,) and then scampered off to the rear. Several of the manœuvres having been repeated, the camp was formed, and tents pitched in an incredibly short time. Next the order was given to advance companies, each firing or supporting the other till the whole were close up in front of the Ti-t'ai ; then they retired and advanced again, and held a tournament. Now came the tug of, not exactly war, but agility, and various combats were engaged in between sword and spear, knife and fork, chopper and club, spear and spear, the victor in each case being killed by his next opponent. After many such imaginary deadly passages of arms they all retired within the walls of the city of cloth.

The next part of the programme consisted of the performances of about 230 men who went through the various evolutions to English words of command. These men were not the 'green heads,' (I beg their pardon) I mean the Anglo-Chinese contingent, but city troops commanded and officered by Chinese alone. They did their teachers credit, for all that was required of them was done with remarkable precision. True, the words of command were not always very distinct ; for instance, ' Che-arge,' ' Lead-y,' ' Feyravol-lay !' I noticed, however, that some of the rifles were innocent of ramrods, and I was wondering how the charge was to be rammed home, when the order to load was given. I then saw how it was done. The cartridge was placed loosely inside the muzzle, and then the gun was tapped on the ground, which caused the gunpowder to settle down !

Now came the siege of the tower which represented the fortified city. A number of soldiers with guns and a big ladder were drawn up in front of it, and while some fired their guns, the rest scaled the wall. The scaling party were furnished with some kind of combustible stuff which emitted a great deal of smoke, it being supposed that by this *ruse* the defenders would not be able to see them while climbing. Of course the defenders were defeated, and what purported to be their heads and tails were seen flying gracefully through the air. A shower of rain coming on at the time, the vanquished and victors suddenly retired, and the retreat was brought up by the light brigade—a soldier with a cane clearing the parade ground of the people who were standing between the Ti-t'ai and the troops. He nearly succeeded in capturing a youngster, when the latter jumped a ditch, to the amusement of the onlookers. After a little while the gingal men were ordered out. I think there must have been about 500 of these, including the banner-bearers. Their gingals were about eight feet long, and the ordinary charge of powder I ascertained to be three taels' weight. There is very little recoil with these weapons, as they weigh about twenty pounds, and the charge is not rammed home, but just dropped down the muzzle. Consequently the report from them is not very loud. A few evolutions, such as marching in single file, forming circles, firing and retreating were shown, and afterwards there was another tournament, similar to the others, when deeds of valour were mimicked.—*Correspondent of the Shanghai Courier.*

CHAPTER XIII.

Page 116.—As an illustration of the naïveté and unsophisticated character of certain missionaries to the heathen, we may quote the following legend. A 'reverend' gentleman and his wife, just arrived from their native woods with a view to converting the aborigines, were proceeding to a Northern port in one of the coasting steamers. One day,—so the story goes—a boiled leg-of-mutton and caper sauce was brought to table, and the lady, who sat next the Captain, was served with a plate of it. Long and earnestly did she gaze upon the food ; then, picking up a caper, she gingerly placed it in her mouth and tasted it. The next moment, however, she ejected it with much decision upon the floor : and turning to her entertainer, remarked in a confidential tone,—" Say, Cap'en,' guess them peas is *sour.*"—*Shanghai Courier.*

CHAPTER XV.

Page 137.—A curious remark fell the other day from the lips of an educated Chinaman, *apropos* of the well-known resemblances between certain of the observances of Buddhism and Christianity. Being in the foreign settlement of Shanghai, in company with an English friend, he expressed a wish to visit the Cathedral. Accordingly the doors were opened, and the two gentlemen walked in. At last, after noticing the stained glass windows, the altar, the organ, and the font, the Chinese took up his position in front of the pulpit, from the cushion of which hung a silken fall, inscribed with the sacred monogram IHS arranged in cypher. His attention was immediately aroused, and calling the English gentleman to his side he asked him how it was that a Buddhist symbol was permitted in a Christian church ? His companion was naturally somewhat perplexed, and requested an explanation. " There," said the Chinaman, pointing to the letters—" that is what I mean. That is the " sacred symbol of Buddha, and has been so from immemorial time. In " China it is written thus 卍 !"—*Idem.*

Page 142.—The following aphorisms, quoted by Mr. Alabaster in his papers on the ' Doctrine of the Mean ' in the *Celestial Empire,* offer a striking analogy to certain Christian ethics :—

Tsze-sze (the grandson of Confucius) enquired in what the Perfect Life consisted. The sage answered, The light had broken on him and he too would prophesy ; this is the Perfect Life.

" It lies plain before all, yet still is hidden ; anyone may know something " about it, no one can know all ; the vilest follow in some degree, the best " must fail in following it exactly." All embracing, permeating all, " it is " the greatest by far of all phœnomena, and man alone can find fault in it : " so vastly reaching, that the universe may not contain it ; yet so all pene- " trating there is nought, in Heaven above or Earth below, so delicately fine. " There is nothing to which does not reach ; nothing but is affected by it. " As the hawk is lost to sight in Heaven above us, and the fish dives down to " depths where human eye can never follow ; so the way of life extends from " Earth to Heaven, and while it lies within, and has its source indeed in pure " humanity, and the simplest and commonest of man's relations, yet by it God " and Nature are united."

The great Discovery, remarks the translator, being thus made, that man affords the link between Material Being and Spiritual Existence, the step which lies between Time and Eternity.

The following is a still more remarkable example :—Is this material world all with which we have concern ? Need we, then, have no thought of God, or care for the Spiritual Powers ? Not so.

"The fulness of virtue comes through the spirits :" those Angelic Beings who direct and govern, who personify and give being to the opposing forces through which all things have existence. "You cannot see them, you cannot "even hear them, but there is nothing in which they do not take part. For "them we fast, and put on ceremonial robes, for them religious festivals are "instituted. They are on every side, right, left, above, below. You cannot "measure (as the Ode says) the outgoings or the incomings of the spirit "world, but neither may you disregard them. They are the evidence of "things unseen ; not to be hidden where the truth is known."

*   *   *   *   *   *   *   *

"The faithful and just are not far from the [True] way and this is the rule "whereby to judge.

"What you would not men should do to you, that do not do to them."

"Be to your father as you would your son should be to you ; serve your "prince as you would your servants should serve you : treat your seniors as "you would your juniors should behave to you : deal with your friends as "you would have them deal by you." You may not attain thereto, but it is for that that you should strive.—*Occasional Papers on Chinese Philosophy, by Chaloner Alabaster.*